the
muse of
OCEAN
PARKWAY

the muse of OCEAN PARKWAY

and other stories

jacob lampart

©2011 by Jacob Lampart
First Edition
Library of Congress Control Number: 2010933709
ISBN: 978-0-89823-256-1
MVP Number 124

Author photo credit to Chen Malone
Cover and interior design by Alyssa Nelson and Amber Nelson

The publication of *The Muse of Ocean Parkway* is made possible by the
generous support of the McKnight Foundation and other contributors to
New Rivers Press.

For academic permission or copyright clearance please contact
Frederick T. Courtright at 570-839-7477 or permdude@eclipse.net.

New Rivers Press is a nonprofit literary press associated with
Minnesota State University Moorhead.

Alan Davis, Senior Editor
Suzzanne Kelley, Managing Editor
Wayne Gudmundson, Consultant
Allen Sheets, Art Director
Thom Tammaro, Poetry Editor
Kevin Carollo, MVP Poetry Coordinator
Fran Zimmerman, Business Manager

Publishing Interns:
Ryan Christiansen, Katelin Hansen, Jenny Hilleren, Samantha Jones,
Tarver Mathison, Jenna Miller, Elizabeth Zirbel

The Muse of Ocean Parkway Book Team:
Sarah Bauman, Nicole Davis, Nikkole Martin, Elizabeth Zirbel

Printed in the United States of America

New Rivers Press
c/o MSUMoorhead
1104 7th Avenue South
Moorhead, MN 56563
www.newriverspress.com

to Oriana
and to Yonatan

CONTENTS

the muse of OCEAN PARKWAY

I t wasn't love for nineteenth-century Russian literature that brought me to this Ocean Parkway living room in Brooklyn, just pure vanity. Out of the blue I received a call from a stranger who admired some of my stories. Nothing like this had ever happened before, and when he threw two plots at me, one at least ten years old, I was quite intrigued. I published in the most obscure places and never believed there were any readers out there, especially that rare kind who could remember one of my plots: a man rents out his apartment for afternoon trysts, and when he returns at night, he imagines the different women who've slept on his sheets.

I had completely forgotten the piece, probably for good reason, but Ivan Horowitz had always loved it, praising its Russian landscape, which was why he called. He would be honored if the "celebrated author, Joseph Riga," would come to a meeting of a literary circle that he headed. I begged off, much too busy, a habit of mine to stay away from literary discourses, breaks the rhythm … as a matter of fact I was just sitting at the typewriter.

A man in my position, Horowitz wanted me to understand, shouldn't be bothered with trifles, but this was different; I was invited to judge a novice's understanding of the genre as an honored guest. Membership in the circle was select, and though anyone could come to a meeting, only those who showed sensitivity to the theme of the night in question were asked to read a short piece at a later date that revealed a deeper understanding of the period. Entertainments and imitations were frowned upon.

In the end, imagining a roomful of Slavic professors and Russian émigré writers with connections in London, I consented. Though I had written enough stories to fill two thick volumes, nothing much had come of my efforts to bring out a book. Maybe I'd meet an editor in the room who loved literary circles and prided himself on a string of new talent discovered in the strangest places. "Would you believe I found Riga in Brooklyn talking about Gogol? Somebody's apartment."

As soon as I walked in the door, I had a change of heart. The place was like a museum, a European salon shortly before World War II, where embittered souls sacrificed their lives to art. Heavy drapes kept out the noise of traffic below and soft lamps near the thick sofa kept the rest of the room dark and gloomy. I expected Kafka and Brod to come out of the kitchen clutching a burning manuscript. The old mahogany furniture dominated the room and kept the conversation low, inaudible, private. When the cognac and Polish vodka were served with herring fillets and hard cheeses, it broke some of the tension, but the seven or eight people in the room still looked as if a short time before they had modeled for the severe aristocratic portraits hanging on the walls.

Ivan Horowitz introduced himself as the voice on the telephone, and pulling me aside, asked if I wanted to see a few very rare documents.

Thirty years ago he had carried on a short-lived correspondence with Dostoevsky's great-grandson. He showed me five postcards postmarked Warren, Michigan, where he claimed the young man had worked on a General Motors assembly line. He had it from a very good source that this man's insistence on being no relation to the other Russian, though he spelled his name the same way, was a peculiar habit immigrants had in shunning publicity.

I went back into the living room to eavesdrop on conversations and to get drunk. Mrs. Horowitz pushed a glass of something sweet into my hand and introduced me to the men sitting next to me. One of them told me he taught chess players the rudiments of Russian so that they could read international chess magazines.

"But personally, I'm looking for sex."

"Is that so?" I said.

"I have nothing to be ashamed of. I'm still healthy. My hair on top may be gray but the hair on my chest is still black and curly. I hear the women in Europe like older men."

"Though I've been there once, I really couldn't say for sure one way or the other."

There was a mad gleam in his eyes when he asked in a whisper, "Tell me, what's the best country in Europe for sex?"

"France," I answered without thinking.

"You mean it's better than Denmark?"

"It's the best."

"Isn't Germany better, not that I'd even bother."

"No, France is."

"After all these years?"

"Yes."

"And Spain or Portugal?"

"Not as good as France."

"The women there like it, they're hot-blooded?"

"Sure they like it, like other women."

"This country is terrible. You wine them and dine them and they won't have sex with you. So then you have to go and relieve yourself. So France is the best. I should go there?"

"It's the best, I swear it."

"And the food there? There's kosher food for a Jewish person?"

"Lots of food."

"Tell me what's damper, New York or Paris?"

"Damp?"

"I can't breathe. My sinuses."

"Damp?"

"Wet."

I escaped to another corner of the room and refilled my glass with imported Polish vodka, gulping it down in two shots. The earlier silence had given way to a strong murmur, not exactly passionate dialogues, but no longer were the faces carved from stone, the lips white and eyes drained. An older woman smiled at me and stroked her hair very gently. When I smiled back, she came over and asked if I had been relishing Mr. Block's insights into the Russian soul, especially its women.

"Who?"

"The man you were just talking to."

"Yes, very much."

"He's a great scholar, and very modest about his achievements. Though his dissertation is unpublished, several graduate students have already begun to quote him. I dare say his name will live on after all of us are dead. Begging your pardon of course. Mr. Horowitz has spoken of your fine talent."

"I just try to tell a story the best way I know how to."

"No need for modesty. As a matter of fact, my own life would make a great tragedy, if I could find the right man to tell my story in a novel. There is no problem when it comes to talking, but when I pick up a piece of paper the words just dry up. Do you have a moment?"

When I hesitated, she promised me 50 percent of the earnings.

"Just give me a few minutes before you say no."

"All right."

"Well, when I was younger I loved the stage. And I fell in love with an actor I've never forgotten about to this day. I still keep the *New York Times* review of his portrayal of Othello. 'Arthur Gordon was perfect, an eloquent sense of craft in his movements and the precise combination of longing and jealousy in his deep basso voice.' I waited for him after his last performance and in my bedroom he spoke about great parts for great actors. He begged me to listen to a monologue from his most successful play. I told him I loved his approach to despair on the stage and he complimented me on my abandoned nature in bed. There's nothing to be shy about. Our love was rare, perfect. He made love ferociously, like a boy of twenty, slept till noon, ate a huge breakfast, and promised to call the next time he was in New York. A week later, the plane he was in lost an engine a minute after takeoff and he was killed in the crash. For months I was hysterical. I couldn't eat, sleep, look at another man. I never married because of my love for Arthur. Am I a fool, a stupid woman? These thoughts and regrets must appear in the story. I don't yet know how to end the story except with my death. Can you help me write it?"

"I'll tell you what," I said. "Write a few chapters and I'll read it. Maybe then I'll have a better idea."

"Thank you very much," she said. "My name is Sarah Newman and I'm in the phone book. Call me in two weeks, better make it a month. I will have a freshly typed chapter for you."

Ivan Horowitz was discussing pain when the new woman opened the living room door very slowly. With awkward, shy steps, she selected a deep armchair in the corner of the room, as unobtrusively as possible, but everyone stared at her. Ten years ago she must have been a raving beauty.

"Am I late? I'm sorry."

"No, it's quite all right. Miss Lublin, may I call you Sonya?"

Ivan asked. "I was just remarking what play is without pain. Nonsense. It can't exist. But pain alone is no play. The great Russians would agree. Though not famous as playwrights, except two or three, they wracked us with painful stories. Have you any opinions on this matter?"

Flustered, she reached for a glass of cognac that Mrs. Horowitz had brought over, and after downing the drink in one gulp, looked up, still confused. "Were you talking to me? Oh, I see. Pain? I don't know. It's such an abused word. Can I have another drink? Thank you. I'm really sorry about being late, but I got lost on the subway. Do you want me to read now or should I wait a while? I'm very nervous."

Earlier I had been introduced to a master chess player named Arfel and he pulled me aside. "That woman, I hate her. She doesn't screw."

About forty, he was easily the youngest man there, his long hair still black and strong. Looking at him, I couldn't hide my amazement.

"You don't believe me?" he said.

"Should I?"

"Then I bet you don't believe me that I once played Nabokov blindfolded and beat him in twelve moves."

"What does one thing have to do with the other?"

"I want you to believe me."

I turned my eyes to Sonya Lublin. She moved close to a lamp where the light was brightest, taking out her notes. "I decided I would give neither a fiction nor a non-fiction reading. Just the truth. A few short sentences about who I am and what I think about." She hesitated but no one interrupted her.

"As a youth I read too many Russian novels. Now I'm past thirty and live alone on the West Side in a vast, empty apartment that, as a result of my fear of the landlord's whims and brutal anger, remains unpainted and unplastered. The hallway reeks of unusual smells, the memories of lost lives buried in the woodwork, and the bedroom, the only room I really use except for the kitchen, is as dark as the hallway closet with the same cramped smell and crowded space.

"In my mind's warped eye, every bedroom turns into Raskolnikov's single room on the fifth-floor landing and every street seems just off Nevsky Prospect, the most oft-mentioned street in Russian literature. Every drunk babbles with love for Mother Russia or hate for the dirty Jews. And the men I meet and fall in love with, well, if not actually repentant drunkards — I am always attracted to their tragic side, eulogizing faint, ephemeral losses. Souls of former serfs mourn for three days straight in Broadway saloons. And the cold Hudson wind is a Siberian frost, merciless and cruel. But most vivid are the faces of clerks, without eyes, noses, or lips, which abound in the subways riding towards jobs in the Civil Service."

Sonya sat down before anyone realized she had come to the end. Averting her eyes, she stuffed the page back into her pocketbook. Light applause followed. I turned away, embarrassed, and was glad to see that someone was serving tea and cakes. Like Russians, we broke off pieces of hard sugar cubes and held them between our teeth as we sipped the hot liquid.

Horowitz came over and asked for my opinion; I was about to nod acceptance, when I noticed Arfel across the room twisting his tongue obscenely in Sonya's direction.

"No," I said thoughtfully. "Her piece is too sentimental."

"I thought I heard an interesting little piece," Horowitz said.

"If you include her, I think you'll be compromising your own standards."

Horowitz looked bewildered. I added, "You don't want anyone to accuse your circle of being soft, where only the surface is read and what's between the lines is overlooked."

"No one can say that about us."

"I should want to keep it that way."

"I see what you mean. Of course you're right. An attractive lady. But not what we need." He shook my hand. "Thank you very much, Mr. Riga."

I excused myself and as I was putting on my coat, Sonya stopped me.

"Why did you vote against me?"

Her hand held onto my sleeve. "I know that you were tonight's judge and I think I deserve a simple explanation."

"Can we talk some other place? This is rather awkward."

"What's wrong with right here?"

Even though I should have been home revising my latest manuscript, I asked her if she wanted to go for a cup of coffee.

"Is this a pickup?"

"Yes, if you want it to be."

"I don't."

"All right then, good night."

I was halfway down the hall when I heard her yell for me to wait. Rather than stand in the hallway, I indicated I'd wait for her at the elevator. We creaked down in silence. On Church Avenue, just around the corner, we found an open, almost empty, luncheonette, ordered two coffees, black.

Without describing Arfel's tongue, I told her she was far too good and clever for the circle's antics and literary pretensions. I simply thought it best for her not to spend her evenings in the company of well-read madmen.

"What then should I do with my evenings?"

"I don't know. What about movies?"

"Don't be ridiculous. You know what happens to a woman alone in a theater. Right away there are ten men, all breeds and educations, who think it's their God-given right to screw you that night, after a perfunctory drink in the nearest bar. The first night it's always a cab, a tour of a one-room studio, admiring ugly reproductions, two quick vodkas to knock the protest out of me, and then perfectly horrible, masturbatory sex. Besides," she said after a long drag on her cigarette, "I don't like movies. It's all fake. Give me Chekhov any day."

"You could take a course. Better yet, give one. Or try different circles. Horowitz's friends are off the wall. Why bother with them?"

"You're a writer, aren't you? What's your name?"

She looked surprised when my name meant nothing to her.

"How could you tell I write?"

"I just guessed. Or maybe it's your moral platitudes about the world of books, as if it were different from everything else out there. So what if they might want to sleep with me? At least they don't work out in a gym twice a week to knock off a few perfectly innocent pounds. I don't like men who stop to look in the mirror on the way to the bathroom or keep nothing in the refrigerator except a bottle of cheap wine and eight varieties of salad oil without a trace of tomato or a piece of lettuce. By the way, I'm curious what a writer has in his refrigerator."

"I'm not really sure."

"Try. Start by looking inside the freezer."

"Ice cubes. Peas and carrots."

She winced. "Next shelf."

"Milk, eggs, sour cream, tuna fish salad, sour pickles, olives, a few slices of cheese, but I can't remember what kind, probably Swiss, I usually get that."

"Next shelf."

"Nothing."

"Are you sure?"

"Yes."

"Pretty conventional. But at least you have enough for breakfast. I suppose you have a few canned things. Any bread?"

"Yes."

"What kind?"

"Seeded rye."

"Wonderful. I like that, especially toasted. It makes a good tuna sandwich."

"If you're hungry, we could order something now."

"That's all right. I was just wondering."

"Don't be shy. Remember this isn't a movie theater."

"Crap. It's all the same."

"I'm not making any passes."

"So what? And if you were, would that be terrible? You think a woman doesn't like to feel desired sometimes?"

"Didn't you just say ..."

"All I said was that they were creeps. But it doesn't mean I didn't go with them still wanting something different. A woman hopes."

"We all do."

"What do you know?"

"I'm human, aren't I?"

She mimicked me: "'I'm human, aren't I?' Is that all you can say? What the hell do you write about anyway? Tell me, have you ever published?"

"Yes."

"Where?"

I mentioned several journals, nothing she'd ever heard of.

"I've known several writers myself. Quite intimately. But they're horrors. That pencil never stops. I might be sitting there bored about what to do Saturday night, and the next thing I know it's in one of his stories. I can't sneeze without him recording it. If I go to the zoo to kill an afternoon, he'll find a metaphor. If my apartment needs to be painted and the drapes hung, he'll disappear, talk about his bad back, his allergy to turpentine, but before my next period, *wham*, there it is, black on white. A little stroke here and there, and it seems like a different protagonist, but I know who it is all the time. What do you write about?"

"Different things."

"Yourself?"

"No. Mostly about old crippled Jews in Brownsville. But what I've really done is map out this imaginary world that I've peopled with bad and nearsighted poets, European revolutionaries, repentant and suffering sons, and bitter Kafkaesque fathers."

She wanted to read something I had written. Since I wasn't carrying any rough drafts with me, I outlined a plot of a story I was currently molding: several survivors in an unnamed city sometime during World War II, suffering a miserable hunger.

"The focus of the piece is the hunger, but the sense of place is alluded to. I'm dealing with the real feeling of archetypal characters in a nightmare world that turns surreal in the course of the narration. The three main characters react differently to the hunger, madly, I would say."

"I'm not sure I understand," Sonya said.

"Well, the language is very important. Very dry, very brittle."

"What's the theme?"

"I don't have any one theme that can be underlined in red ink. Let's just say this piece is a parody of the characters' wretched existence once it's stripped to the bone."

"Like Beckett?"

"I suppose there are certain similarities, but the tone and the way I work with words is completely different. After all, I'm a New Yorker, and I don't have his Christian guilt."

"I don't like writers who intentionally fracture their view of reality," Sonya said, refusing the menu the waitress offered us. "I hate these broken lenses."

I gently suggested that there was no one way to perceive reality, though I thought it best to refrain from analyzing the discoveries of French Impressionists after the invention of the camera. But she beat me to it when she criticized all the modernists for forgetting the Bible in their mad rush to scrape out a little meager landscape they could call their own.

"They're so greedy to be novel that they're blind to the ancient surrealism evoked by a despotic God, his humble, very human angels, and those screaming Babylonian poets in rags. And what about that dry, grizzly naturalism you get when the Hebrews are enslaved in Egypt, mixing mortar and cement in the hot sun. And when they're saved by Moses, it's the natural world gone mad. An epidemic of lice, frogs, water turning to blood, pitch black darkness, fire alive in giant hailstones. The plagues are nothing but the thread of sanity clipped from the conventional world. And where else can you find language like Ezekiel's vision or the heartrending melodrama of Joseph fooling his brothers, bowing down to the Egyptian Minister of Finance whom they don't recognize. Up from jail into Pharaoh's palace, his right-hand man. Name it and you got it in the Bible."

"I don't pretend to want to evoke an entire world," I said.

"Crap! Anything less is ego."

"But I don't even write about myself."

"That's what they all say. But scratch the surface and you'll find a bleeding ego and a twisted childhood. I'll be honest with you. If it's true you don't fill your pages with a day-to-day account of musings and reflections, then I'm glad."

"Why?"

"I have my reasons."

We had more coffee, but at that time of night the cake I ordered was no longer fresh. Between halfhearted bites, I stared at Sonya. I wanted to know if she'd ever been married, but instead I asked if she also wrote.

"Heaven forbid. Though once I tried my hand at translating."

"Only once?"

"Yes. It was a disaster. The writer was still alive, in his late seventies, and he approached me at some symposium I can't remember the topic of, after I'd made some trenchant comment, what a joke! Anyway I worked hard, and didn't even set a specific fee. Once he got his sheaf of poems back, he kept hounding me why I chose this word instead of another one he thought more appropriate. He began to sweat. I lost patience explaining nuances. I thought his English terrible but didn't tell him. He prided himself that friends of his, professors at Columbia University, had said he spoke English beautifully. I told him for a man who had friends at Columbia he really didn't need anyone else. A sham, he was a good writer, but so vain and afraid that my translation might detract from his noble vision. Now he's dead and the vision, untranslated, is with him in the grave."

"What language was that?"

"Yiddish. But whatever else can be said about these immigrant writers in America, no one can accuse them of writing literary conundrums to engage the intellect of bored critics. Prison is prison, no trimming. They stick to facts, describing suffering with real tears and pain."

Knowing next to nothing about Yiddish literature I muttered feebly, "Didn't Kafka know Yiddish?"

"Nonsense. And if he did, what's the point? Something you picked up in a fat journal. It's just propaganda from those insipid critics, always trying to carry Kafka on whatever bandwagon they're preaching at the time. All those twisted and damned critics. You and your cohorts have misread him for three decades. The man was a realist. It all really happened. The cockroach, the hunger artist, the trial. Every word is true. No suspension of reality, just the suspension of habituated and conventional reflexes. Kafka's stories are the ten plagues of Prague. Once you get beyond the surface you can't name one fantastic thing in his work. Don't read him for symbolism. It's as natural, as horrible, as the Nile turning to blood. He wasn't a guilty Catholic or a spent Buddhist, he wasn't an impotent clerk or a whining Jew."

Sonya's Russian piece was fiction, a bald-faced lie. She lived with her father in a cramped three-room apartment in a poor Brooklyn neighborhood overrun with muggers and thieves, and not alone in a sprawling West Side flat. Her mother was dead, too long ago to talk about it, and her father had turned religious in his old age, rarely leaving his spot in the kitchen except when he went to pray. She hated it when the *Times* did a feature story on the neighborhood's problems, focusing on a typical day in the life of the sexton in the old shul. The story was a stamp of death, a formal burial, stuck between a piece on a blind photographer's recent work and two recipes for squash. A week later the story was just dead weight, the neighborhood forgotten. Sonya wrapped a chicken with it and threw the rest out, without showing it to her father.

"My father has seen so much pain in his life. First in Europe and then in America. I had a brother who ran away from home. One card arrived from Israel, then six months later a letter with a photograph from Australia. He was wearing a sailor's uniform. We never heard from him again. My mother lived as long as she had a strain of hope that he was alive, but after a few years she just gave up. My father is old now, but he still curses everyone: the refugees for their greed and short memory and the Americans for their innocence and passion for pleasures. He'd like to see the police patrol the streets with German shepherds."

"That's rather violent," I said.

"Violent. What the hell do you know? It's the words of a desperate, broken man. I was wild myself once. After my mother died, I couldn't take coming home night after night to that ugly apartment, him sitting there with a cold glass of tea, spitting his rage at the world. He went through the *Forward* just to make fun of the writers' feeble attempts to say something about the events. How long could I take cooking for him and washing his shirts? I had to leave. And I did. But now there's nothing I wouldn't do for him, to make his life easier."

"You can't just live for others," I responded, unconvincingly.

"That's easy for you to say. You have your crappy art, a few published stories to nourish you for twelve years. I have my father, nothing else. What can I do? He has no one but me. At least let him have one joy in this world."

I was quiet. I didn't agree with her, but what could I say to change her mind?

"I love him very much," she said.

"Is that so?"

"You can't understand how I feel. It hurts me to look into his eyes and see a broken shell."

"I believe you."

"I don't know why I get into this every time I open my mouth. You're probably laughing at me. Here you want to get a chick into bed and she's turning into a melancholy bitch."

"I'm not laughing," I said, my eyes sober and thoughtful. "And I don't think you're melancholy. Not in the real sense of the word."

"Well, that's kind of you. But I see you left the bed part intact."

I had no intention of an affair, but didn't tell her that. To change the topic, I suggested dinner. It might do her good. She refused, saying that she ate only strictly kosher, not because she believed in the ritual, but out of respect for her father. "And let me tell you something. The only reason I'm sitting here with you is because you said you don't write about your life. You see, if I become your lover, and I say that very rationally without erotic intentions, you might write about me. Then what might happen, though I realize it's unlikely, is that my father reads the story and recognizes me as I made love to you without any clothes on, lying on a deserted beach, or in the bathtub, the skin wet and silky. Who knows what kind of obscene positions you'd embroider your little tale with. I could never face him after that. I'd just die if he knew about me through your lies."

"I'll never write about you," I said.

Though Sonya was near tears, her tongue was sharp. "You'd have to prove it."

"I could show you some of the stories I've published. They're in a bookcase in my living room."

"Your living room? You're just saying that to seduce me at your place."

"Not at all. There's nowhere else you can find those magazines. Some don't even publish anymore. One editor committed suicide and took five thousand copies of back issues with him to the grave."

"What about libraries?"

"I don't know. Do you think I wouldn't like that myself? If you want,

I'll send you a bibliography."

"Don't get angry. All I care about is whether you've ever written autobiographically or not. I can't be too careful."

"Believe me, Sonya, I never write about myself or anyone else I know. If I were having an affair with a woman, she could sleep for a year with me, eat blood and suck life, without chancing a vindication by me in print somewhere. After all I've been writing for fifteen years and not one word of anything I've ever published remotely indicates that I have that repugnant trait to drag up every scrap — parents, friends, lovers, childhood — to pinpoint my literary landscape. I'll tell you the truth, this kind of autobiographical fiction even insulted my critical sensibility in college, which sparred with Kafka, Beckett, and Borges."

"I'd hate it if my name became nothing but a bit of conversation, of the cheap sort, when you divulge dirty secrets about me to your guests."

"That would never occur, Sonya. I even have a theory about what can happen and what must never happen in one of my stories. When I describe someone — which is quite rare, since I don't care about gray hair, a gnarled face, or a yellow beard — what I do is shut my eyes and picture one of the characters I've met in my time, mostly strangers sitting in a cafeteria or the attendant at the park where I sometimes go after a good day's work. Even if I meet some of these people, they never appear as individuals, just as a kind of fabric." I told her about a sixty-year-old virgin I knew and another man who believed he was the greatest sufferer in human history, writing letters to CBS, the *Daily News*, *Status Magazine*, and Dear Abby. "I have no interest in describing people I become involved with. I don't fuse my life and the world of my fiction. I believe in invention."

"I'm safe with you?" she asked.

"I'm telling you the truth," I told her. "I hate turning a story into a confessional forum. It's against everything I've always believed in. Art is not the random facts of life, collected in chronological order, but the vision behind it."

"So long as that vision doesn't include me."

"I'm absolutely bored with writing about bed partners. For God's sake, even the sheets are more interesting in fiction, the goddamn hairs, the shade that doesn't work, the cold steam pipes."

"You promise?"

"I swear I wouldn't write about you. If you want, I can bring you notarized statements of other women who've slept with me that I never wrote about."

"Is it too late to call now?"

"What do you think?"

"I hope you don't think I'm crazy. But I have to make you understand what would happen if my father knew, if he recognized me in your story. I can't take a chance he might find your name on a slip of paper I leave behind near the telephone, and the next time he's in the library looking through a couple of periodicals he spies your name in a magazine."

"Isn't that rather remote?"

Her eyes were blazing. "I'm talking about my father's life. There is nothing remote when it comes to that. I have to account for all possibilities. He must never know that I know a writer. He's so suspicious he would do anything to find out where he publishes, even if it's under a pseudonym, and then look for evidence of my sleeping around. I love him too much to hurt him now."

"Why should he be so suspicious of you?"

"Who said he's suspicious?"

"I'm using your words."

"I didn't mean that. Oh, Christ. You don't understand a thing."

I sipped the cold coffee in silence, stealing glances at her tortured eyes. Was she a child of ravaged Poland, eating radishes to keep alive? Raped at twelve and abandoned to Europe's mad history at fourteen? I had seen her panic-stricken face in the brutal photographs of children shipped to the camps, her trembling body alone even among the hushed crowds at Warsaw Ghetto memorials. I saw her standing in the railway station in Vienna, five o'clock in the afternoon, then in Paris, reaching for a Yiddish newspaper, vainly hunting for one name among the living in the lost persons' column. Even after years of searching for a trace of her father in the wasted cities and towns — a wristwatch, an old letter, a good shoe on a young Pole's foot — she refused to accept her father's death.

"Sonya," I finally said, "I do understand. Only too well. Trust me and you'll see. All my stories are kept in one spot. You're free to walk into my study and reach for whatever you want. There's no way I can hide any piece from your eyes."

"Will you give me time to read a wide selection?"

"As long as you want."

"Even till dawn?"

"Till the following afternoon if you need it."

"You won't bother me while I read? Tell me to take off my sweater, or that I'll be more comfortable on the couch, or that I should get out of my uncomfortable dress and try on your bathrobe?"

"I'll be in the other room, making coffee."

"All night?"

"Reading, sleeping. Don't worry. I have things to do."

"And if I decide it's autobiographical and want to go home right then?"

"You're the judge."

"Will you call a cab?"

"If you want me to."

"Start now, it's raining outside."

Indeed it was. I wondered how she'd known, since her back faced the window. Perhaps my glasses reflected the downpour, but I didn't ask. Outside there were no cabs in sight. I suggested we walk to the subway, and if we spotted a cruising cab we'd hail it. By the time we reached the station, we were drenched. Drying off, she asked for a dime — she had to call her father and tell him she was staying with a friend.

"At your age?"

"I'm still young."

I got change for a quarter at the token booth, and waited nearly five minutes before she finished talking. Sonya seemed distraught, lighting a cigarette on the platform though it was forbidden. I told her at this hour every subway was patrolled by a policeman.

"Leave me alone."

"What's wrong?" I said, touching her shoulder for the first time.

"My father called me a whore."

"What for?"

"All I said was that I was staying with a friend, and he wanted to know why my bed wasn't good enough for me."

"Don't take it to heart."

"Look, if you called me a whore, a filthy tramp, I would wipe the floor with the paper it was written on. But that's my father. He called me that word!"

"Is it true?"

"What are you playing games with me for? All right. Since you gave me a dime, you now owe me $19.90. I'd like it in cold cash."

I ignored the remark. We spoke very little during the ride. Then as the doors were closing at Forty-second Street, she said maybe she ought to go home, but it wasn't said seriously. At Seventy-second Street, the next stop, she actually got up to leave. I held onto her arm and told her we were almost there; besides, it wasn't safe now to travel alone.

By the time I opened the locks on my door, I was a nervous wreck. The kitchen hadn't been cleaned for days. There was probably no toilet paper in the bathroom; the floors were filthy, the sheets soiled.

I concentrated. First I took her coat, then led her into the living room. I offered her a drink, bourbon. Immediately, she wanted to know why.

"It'll warm us up."

"I'm not cold."

"It's good."

"I'd rather have tea."

"It'll have to be without lemon. I'll just be a minute. Meanwhile you can start looking through the magazines." I pointed to the bottom drawer of the metal cabinet in the alcove where I usually worked on revisions. "You can see that I haven't touched or manipulated a thing."

As she gazed around the room, I felt cheap and dirty—last week's shirts on the couch, carbon paper on the faded rug, dust in every corner and cranny. I had lied about the contents of the refrigerator. There wasn't enough food for a decent breakfast; I counted three eggs and four slices of dry bread.

Upon my return with a cup of tea, Sonya absently reached for it, nodded thanks, and continued reading. Imagining love, I took a hot shower and scrubbed myself clean. When I returned to the living room, Sonya told me what she thought of my fiction, calling it damned, twisted, and aborted. The product of a diseased mind, this kind of scum belonged in the gutter along with other sensibilities warped by preconceived laws and fixed theoretical frameworks. Of course, I made one or two comments, but otherwise I chose not to dispute her taste.

"Did you find anything explicitly sexual?" I asked.

She put down the pile of magazines and for the first time that night looked calm. "You told me the truth. I hardly found a recognizable situation, and no real people. Everything just drifts. Lots of obscure symbols and mangled time zones. I suppose you know what you're trying to do but no one else does."

Her reading was an act of butchery, I thought, but as her fears slowly vanished I became aroused and kept silent. Next came the seduction, if I can call it that. Since there was only one bed in the apartment, it was just a question of time before we both disrobed and went to sleep.

———————

It seemed like hours passed. She drank her tea so slowly, then asked for another cup, smoked a half-dozen cigarettes, insisted on washing all the dirty dishes and cleaning up the sink in the bathroom. Then she brushed her hair, her teeth, removed her makeup in the dark, and finally crept into her side of the bed, wearing one of my shirts. Then silence, black everywhere, and after a few moments I could hear her heavy breathing.

"Sonya?"

Her body felt like ice though her skin was touching mine.

"Sonya?"

"Yes."

"Are you up?"

"Yes."

"Do you want to?"

"I can't."

Can't is can't. Afraid of another argument, I tried to fall asleep, but the bed felt like a fortress, the crumpled sheets spilling over the sides and the one cushion too small for both our heads.

My thighs touched hers and she didn't squirm off to the edge of the bed. Another inch and my tongue would be licking her neck, my mouth choking on her breasts.

"Sonya?" I whispered again.

"You said you wouldn't bother me."

"I'm not. I just want to know what it is."

"We just met."

"But you're in my bed."

"A bed is not a lay!"

Her words tore into me and I reacted like an attacked creature: a sharp twist of the head, lips into scissors, teeth into claws. When I was younger, I often went to lectures or poetry readings with the dim hope of picking somebody up, and when that failed, I settled for a few words with any woman in black stockings and white starving breasts under her turtleneck sweater. Lying in my bed at night, after climbing four flights of stairs to the two rooms I rented on the top floor, the woman's distraught face provided me with a body to make love to, my hand sculpting a ravishing two minutes. But I refused to dig up old fantasies with Sonya in my bed.

"I'm not a very happy person," I heard Sonya say.

"Should I call you in a couple of weeks?"

"Is it the few feels now and then?"

"I haven't touched you all night."

"So what." She leapt out of bed, tying the shirt-tails around her waist. "What the hell am I doing here anyhow? I must be crazy. You're up to something vicious. Oh, sure, you say you won't write about me, but how do I know you're not a madman who stalks the subway trains at night, pressing your filthy thighs against unescorted women?"

"I'm a novelist, not a deviant."

"That's what the last four said."

"Well, you read my stuff."

"College crap, undergraduate exercises. Whether you realize it or not, you write bad parodies. If I were you, I'd get my hack license and make an honest wage."

I was exhausted but I'd heard enough of her judgments.

"If you shut up for a second and listen, maybe you'll understand what I'm trying to do."

"Don't take all night."

"First of all, understand that I have no patience with details that confuse me. I get tired very easily from the endless descriptions of rooms, the biographies of lazy characters, the lies, the ins and outs of deceitful representations, the sick minds pursuing meaning, justice, and love while lamenting exile and anguish amidst a brew that wallows uninterrupted between the he saids, she saids, they saids, stating, arguing, obliging, replying as the days outside turn red, green, hot, wet, and cold, which leads the narrator to shift his point of view to the inevitable wretched umbrella and moth-eaten crimson scarf that protects the solitary figure against a nasty winter in the East End of London; and finally the dull comparisons between the Metro, the Underground, and our own BMT."

"That sounds far-fetched and exaggerated."

"It is exaggerated. And that's how they view reality. But the characters I write about are different. They're real, they suffer. They reconstruct their miserable lives until they have nothing left but a wretched parody of their own existence that condemns them to witness their own deaths. They are actors who mourn the demise of acting. They can't ever die of natural causes, commit suicide, or just vanish off the face of the earth. They must continually create their own hell, their own suffering."

I paused, reaching for a cigarette. "Their lives are empty; they feel it like a claw hanging around their necks, so that they are forced to seek any kind of nourishment. But the search for sustenance turns into an ironic quest that denies their earlier trials completely. They can't possibly win, they can't lose. They can only parody, burlesque. They aren't even allowed to moralize their hungers, and they can't invent a religion or a myth around the pain. They can only destroy everything mythic with it: a myth to kill myths, a hunger to hunger out hungers. To deny it, to mock it, a state of mind only balanced by the struggle between substance and air, facts and fictions. On the one hand, hunger is a normal state of affairs, people die, love disappears, sex vanishes, humans no longer function; on the other hand, there are those who cannot deal with hunger normally, that is, they complain, kill themselves, die off, but must find unique ways to deny their hunger. But they cannot deny it by calling it something else — the wrath of God, for example — but they deny it by turning it inside out on its head. They invent a system, a private world, which responds to the hunger insanely. Only the mad are not mad."

"Enough talk, let's screw."

Shortly after eight, I was roused from sleep by a neighbor's early raucous music. But once up, I decided on a hearty breakfast and went down to get cheeses, creamed herring, green vegetables, bread and rolls, and even freshly ground coffee. Back in the apartment, I scrubbed the kitchen table clean and arranged two settings. I felt good sipping my second cup of coffee while leafing through the *Times,* my eyes settling only on the innocuous stories, a curious lost-and-found item, an upstate auction, a loving description of a new seafood house near the waterfront.

Sonya entered the kitchen, coat in hand, and demanded coffee.

"Sugar or milk?" I asked quietly.

"Both. And make it quick."

Again I was shocked by her mood, but said nothing. Her eyes were ice and her hands fidgeted with the silverware.

"You owe me a hundred dollars," she said, putting down the cup of coffee. "I expect fifty now and fifty when the story is published. If it's a novel, my fee goes up to five hundred, and depending on sales, various subsidiaries, movie rights, foreign translations, and news syndications, I wouldn't be surprised if you'll end up owing me five thousand for the night. I have good friends in publishing so don't think you can hide anything from me."

"What night? What money? What rights?"

"You think I can't see through your pretenses. Your stories I understand perfectly. Absolutely vapid, two-finger exercises for the piano. But after today you'll have some blood to write about. You think I just pop into writers' apartments for the fun of it? My God! Do you know who I am? I'm Ramona in *Herzog* and Helen in *The Assistant.* I gave them human flesh to sink their teeth into. And I've also been the major character in many short stories, both here and Europe, and two English novels which never made it across the Atlantic. And all of them paid for it. I don't come into an impotent writer's life for nothing. Pay up!"

"I don't believe you," I said. "You're just not in the mood for a good breakfast. Maybe some dry bread and sardines would have been enough. Or just bitter black coffee and a pack of Pall Malls to go around."

She grabbed me by the neck. "I don't give a damn about your romantic pumpernickel and I hate the smell of cheese. It reminds me of decent writers gone to pot. I just want you to remember everything, every last detail since we met last night. And when it's a novel, just try to get out of paying me. I work hard for my money and this is my living."

"I don't have that kind of money."

"Give me a check."

"There's nothing in my account."

"What about cash?"

"All I have is ten."

"I'll take that now but I expect the rest later."

Extraordinary, I thought when she had left, a literary prostitute. Of course none of it was true. Sonya must have been reading the biography of a mad nineteenth-century courtesan whose life was threaded with writers falling in love at her doorstep. I realized then that I was congratulating myself, because who doesn't feel slightly proud after being with a woman who claims what Sonya claimed? But she wasn't the living incarnation of a character in a dusty century; she had spent the night in my bed driving nails into my world with screams and threats. Now she struck me as a ravenous witch. Suddenly I felt very frightened of her power. Spurred on, she could unleash a hatred vile enough to cause a man's suicide. I knew that if I ever wrote about her, no matter how well I disguised the circumstances of our meeting, I'd better use an innocent pen name, a simple R. E. Brown or L. Levin. Surely this was much more clever than transforming Riga into Rigman, Rigovsky, or DeRiga. I'd make the order of the syllables in the name so anonymous that Sonya, even if she read the story next month, could never unravel it.

joanna
LOVES
JESUS

J oanna loves Jesus. She has loved him for three weeks now, and has never been happier. The only problem is that Joanna is Jewish and her father, Rabbi Emmanuel Preshko, who heads a congregation of three hundred families in the Five Towns, isn't emotionally equipped for such revelations. But he stands next to his daughter's hospital bed transfixed, silent, scared. His wife's right thumb is pressed against his rib cage in an attempt to relay the message that she absolutely forbids him to give vent to the explosion building up inside his chest. Although his face is white, and at any moment he might begin trembling uncontrollably, the spectacle of their daughter's shattered body wrapped in bandages, tubes dangling from her bony arms, worries Roberta Preshko more than the possibility her husband might start clutching his heart and foaming at the mouth.

When they wheeled Joanna in, no one knew if she would live or die. After flipping over three times on the

West Side Highway, there wasn't much left of her Volvo, transformed into a potential two-ton Molotov cocktail. Luckily a Con Edison emergency crew, when they heard the piercing screech of wheels, dropped their tools and grabbed a ladder long enough to reach the embankment of the highway. Without questions or permission, they managed to extract the bleeding driver from the squashed wreck. Joanna wasn't conscious, and when she later learned about the three Con Ed workers, she smiled quietly and knew that the men were really angels sent by Jesus because Jesus knew that by the time the Roosevelt Hospital ambulance arrived the car would have burst into flames. The crash made the *Daily News* centerfold.

"Jesus made me kosher." Joanna is quoting a boy who used to stand in the back of lecture halls before class handing out pamphlets about being born again.

"Do you mean regular kosher or strictly kosher?" snips Joanna's younger brother, Joey.

Joey is famous in the Preshko family for listening to no one, but he knows a lot more than they think he knows. When everyone is out of the house on Sunday morning, he switches the TV channels back and forth, fascinated by Reverend Terry and Dr. Bob Schuller, or Jimmy Swaggart, sweating under the stage lights. When there's a Jewish program on TV he feels embarrassed. Perceiving the Jews to be void of passion, he's afraid to ask his father the rabbi why. When Rabbi Preshko gets angry, he has a unique way of meting out punishment: the guilty party must copy at least one column from the *Encyclopedia Judaica*, whose twenty volumes sit like a troop of guards in the Preshko living room, along with the collected works of Mordecai Kaplan, Abraham J. Heschel, and Erich Fromm.

Rabbi Preshko, biting his lips, doesn't understand what Joanna is trying to say. It's true that their home isn't exactly kosher, but then they're Reform Jews and they don't have to keep kosher like the Orthodox. He wonders what the hell Orthodoxy has to do with his daughter going out of her mind. He is watching his entire life flash in front of his eyes. If he can't teach his own daughter the truth about Judaism, what can he expect from the members of his congregation?

Finally he can't contain himself. "What are you, one of those Jews for Jesus?"

"Quiet, Manny." His wife's lips are smiling but her thumb is jabbing hard. "Save that for later when she gets out of the hospital."

"I can't wait, dammit. What the hell is going on here? One day my daughter is fine, and the next day she's in Roosevelt Hospital spouting about Jesus."

"Daddy, I'm fine."

"You're fine. Then tell me what the hell has gotten into you?" He wonders how he will ever survive this. His daughter has been through transcendental meditation, Rajneesh, bio-energetics, macrobiotics, Zen, and who knows what else, but Jesus is the last straw.

Rabbi Preshko bends down to speak in a quiet voice, "Joanna, tell me what happened to you. Are you under some kind of spell?"

"No, Daddy, I'm not under any spell." Joanna flinches as she hears the word. Where should she begin? Her chronology of that night is blurred. The man she loved heart and soul, a teacher of film at the NYU Adult Institute, turned suddenly poisonous and not only demanded back the keys to his apartment but threatened to call the campus police if Joanna ever showed up in one of his classes again. When she got into her car, sobbing hysterically, she drove with no concern for the speed limit, and the West Side Highway on a wet foggy night is no place to say goodbye to fifty-five.

She suspects her father knows about Leonard Glass — he's practically famous — but she doesn't want to bring up ancient history. For the first time in her life she feels happy, kind, good, and hopeful. Her pain is almost delicious precisely because it's what brought her to Jesus.

Although she is not too familiar with the fine points of her new belief system, she knows that being a Christian is merely the fulfilled part of being a Jew, but even with all her newfound courage, she is not quite ready to put it in those terms to her father. He would never understand that she feels Jewish and Christian at the same time. She barely understands it herself. She wonders if it means she will no longer be able to sit at her parents' Passover table. Although she is not crazy about the Seder, she doesn't want to cut herself off from everything. She has no idea what Christianity has to say about Rosh Hashana and Yom Kippur. Is it a no-no, or could she squeeze it in? All she knows about Jesus is what the night attendant told her. She is from Martinique or Grenada or Barbados and while watching her one night Joanna could have sworn a white halo embraced the crown of the black woman's head. When she later walked over to Joanna, a Bible clutched in her hands, and respectfully asked if the young lady wanted to pray, Joanna felt a quiver of electricity upon touching the leather volume.

Actually, the night attendant prayed for all the sick and wounded brought into her ward, but she was particularly taken with this fragile creature, her face nothing but bone and shadow, resembling photographs she had once seen of concentration camp survivors. She wondered if the child might be Jewish despite her Italian sounding name.

Mrs. Amanda Williams prayed so hard to move heaven and earth to heal poor Joanna Preshko that tears began to roll down her cheeks. Joanna, who had never seen anyone, certainly not a stranger, cry for her, felt as if she were basking in a different kind of light, and a sweet glow passed from Mrs. Williams to Joanna, particularly when she read passages from the New Testament, which seemed to Joanna achingly familiar, as if all of her life she'd been waiting for the melodies of archaic English.

Since then, Mrs. Williams has made rapid progress. Beneath Joanna's covers there are now a pocket-sized edition of the Bible (Old Testament and New Testament) and tracts and broadsides from Jews for Jesus, American Mission to the Jews, Christians and Hebrews. How will Rabbi Preshko be able to convince his daughter to abandon all that she's discovered about Jews and Jesus and Christians? What can he possibly say to her to match the idea of a Lord and Savior?

"Joanna, can you hear me?"

"Manny, I don't think this is the right time."

"Why not?"

Mrs. Preshko glances toward the doorway. Visitors have arrived for the patient in the next bed. They come in carrying an expensive bouquet of jonquils, forget-me-nots, and peach blossoms, and wake the elderly woman from her sleep to show it to her. Everyone smiles at both patients, and both patients smile back. Even Rabbi Preshko smiles. The new visitors peck the old woman, and then smile again at Joanna, and Joanna smiles back, as if nothing in the world had ever made her happier than being Mrs. O'Rourke's roommate in Roosevelt Hospital.

Not wanting to discuss family matters in front of strangers, Rabbi Preshko goes out to the hall in search of a phone. He calls his secretary and she reads him a list of telephone messages, which he pretends to take down. Most of the names are unfamiliar, which is not surprising. Rabbi Preshko is involved with half a dozen major committees on American Judaism and it's no easy matter to keep up with them. The one person he should call back is Davidov, his editor at Menorah Books, but with Joanna saying the things she's saying, that call had better wait. Davidov is editing a new series of thirty self-portraits in the American rabbinate, ten for each denomination, and Rabbi Preshko has been chosen to be one of them. The offer has raised his stock considerably, but for what? So he can include a chapter on Joanna's Jesus trip?

The rabbi pulls out a cigarette, but can't find a smoking lounge, so he settles for one of the stalls in the men's room where his eyes are assaulted by graffiti. One would think that in a hospital, where life is already so close to the perilous edge, the obsession with sex and violence would abate, but no — the graffiti could have come straight from the subway. Rabbi Preshko, whose job brings him to hospitals maybe a dozen times a month, never fails to be surprised at the paradox of finding this kind of language in a building where life hangs by a thread. He wonders if sex had anything to do with his daughter's conversion. Could she have fallen in love with a Jesus freak who twisted her mind around?

"No smoking allowed."

The starched white trousers and scruffy white shoes of a hospital attendant appear beneath the door, and the rabbi quickly drowns the cigarette, listening to the hiss of water entering the ember. With nothing else to do in the bathroom, it seems reasonable to get up and leave, but he's not sure what he can accomplish back in Joanna's room, so he sits, waiting, lost in thought, afraid.

Joanna's father can't fall asleep. Without the air conditioner running, whose hum disturbs his wife, he sweats like a kid after two hours of serious ball playing. It's the end of July, a rabbi's slow season, and most of the members of his congregation are on vacation. He knows that if he closed down the synagogue until the High Holy Days it wouldn't really matter to anyone.

Emmanuel Preshko came to the rabbinate late in life, though people assume because of his Biblical first name that he was destined for it from the day of his circumcision. In fact, history had been his first love, combining the excitement of fiction with the lure of reality, and he'd stumbled on the rabbinate more or less by accident. A graduate student at Columbia, he'd gone looking for a course on the Jews in the Renaissance (he'd always wondered if his name had Italian roots) and been directed to the nearby Jewish Theological

Seminary. Soon he made an interesting discovery: he could teach history from the front of a classroom, and see it reduced to dates and chalk marks on a blackboard, or he could teach from a pulpit and be involved in a living process.

To the surprise of his nonobservant father, who'd once played on the starting basketball team at City College, young Emmanuel finally made good on his name. He finished his rabbinical training at Hebrew Union College (Reform Judaism seemed to allow a rabbi more independence than Conservative Judaism did) and, after just one appointment in the provinces, was offered his present pulpit. Up until now, his greatest disappointment in life was that his wife, a cantor's daughter from upstate New York, was really antireligious and had married him, so he theorized, not so much out of love for the young Reform rabbi, but as a slap in the face of her Orthodox, Yiddish-speaking father, a simple man who never ceased to be amazed that people paid him to sing on days when he went to the synagogue anyhow. But this sorrow paled beside his daughter's delirium.

———————

The rabbi gets out of bed and goes into Joanna's old room, where he paces the floor and runs his fingers over the spines of her sprawling book collection — hundreds, it seems like thousands, of them. She was always a loner, a very private child, who was hard to control and excessively temperamental. In his eyes, however, his daughter is beautiful, painfully so. Unlike the other Preshkos, she has long, lean limbs, and deep, haunted eyes like the most expensive black olives — Jesus's sister, he thinks sacrilegiously. He's been spending long hours in her room lately, sitting at her desk, touching the sheets of her bed, looking for an answer to the question of how to get her back, and going over his life to see where he's failed: Were there things he'd said that she'd misinterpreted, and things he didn't say that he should have said? Would it be different if he'd stayed on at the Seminary instead of opting for the easier world of Reform? Had he made a mistake in the first place leaving the world of the academy for the more dangerous world of the rabbinate? There are no guarantees in life, but if he hadn't dressed his own historical yearnings in a religious mantle, isn't it likely that his daughter, who's obviously committing the ultimate act of rebellion against a rabbi-father, wouldn't be flirting with the other side now? As for himself, once the news gets out, he doubts if his career can survive the slings and stares. In effect, he'll become a lame-duck rabbi. To make matters worse, there seems to be no escape from the problem. Whenever he turns on his car radio, all he seems to get are stations selling Jesus. There is no end to it. Wherever he drives there are bumper stickers crying out, "Repent," and "I'm Going to Heaven, Are You?" and "He Died For Your Sins." It makes no sense to him. How could anybody die for the sins of anybody else? What does it mean? A person commits a sin, and that sin is redeemed somehow by the death of a man, nailed to a cross two thousand years before? It simply makes no logical sense to Rabbi Preshko to base a religion on this peculiar myth of crosses, sin, redemption.

Judaism is different. Everyone knows the Jews don't worship Moses, they worship God, or in more abstract terms, they worship Jewish history itself, the whole awesome curve of it. But not a person. So why is the world always hounding the Jews to switch their religion?

———————

Joanna's mother is impressed. Barely out of the hospital and still in bandages, her daughter has signed a lease for a refurbished walkup (sight unseen) on the Lower East Side in the faith that it's "exactly what she needs."

Mrs. Preshko has been visiting Joanna on her own but now believes her husband's presence is also required if Joanna is to recover totally. Rabbi Preshko resists.

"What kind of rabbi are you, if you can't face your own daughter?"

"She's not my daughter. In case you haven't heard, Jesus is her father!"

"Manny, you have a heart of rock."

The following Sunday both parents arrive bearing gifts of raw film stock, homemade marmalade, fresh bread, organic eggs, and several gallons of orange juice. They let themselves in through the unlocked door and are greeted by the sight of Joanna on her knees. The rabbi has a sudden memory of a foreign movie he once saw where the flagellants kneel their way to one of the stations of the cross, but it turns out Joanna is only looking for an earring.

"Are you sure it's not too soon to go crawling around like that?" Mrs. Preshko asks.

"I'm fine, Mom. Four weeks is enough time for bones to heal."

So cluttered is the one-room studio flat that Joanna's editing machines and Nagra tape recorder share table space with her bean sprout planter and an old-fashioned toaster that accepts the slices horizontally. A huge black and white still from one of her own movies graces the wall above her brick bookcases. Magazines, books, flyers, manila envelopes, stockings, and even underwear lay strewn about everywhere so that the only place to sit is an antique lilac loveseat not wide enough for both Preshkos.

The rabbi can't conceal his irritation, but his wife beams with admiration at how Joanna has managed, broken bones and all, to move into her new place. The mess, hinting at an exuberance of life, actually excites her. Not so the rabbi, whose eye falls on Joanna's first camera, an 8mm Bolex he'd been badgered into buying, which now lies abandoned inside a dried out Boston fern planter.

"How are you," he says stiffly.

"Praise the Lord," beams Joanna.

Rabbi Preshko turns white and looks at his wife.

"What did she say?"

"I said, 'Praise the Lord, the King, the One and only,'" Joanna repeats.

"I have to sit down," says her father. "Is this how you're supposed to refer to him?"

"Jesus, Daddy, Jesus. Say His name, the name of the Lord, the Savior, the only-begotten Son who was born to save us from sin."

"Is this possible?" The rabbi grabs for his daughter's shoulder but she pulls away.

Mrs. Preshko's face turns green with anger. "Manny, you promised."

The rabbi ignores his wife and looks at Joanna without flinching. "Have you forgotten that you're Jewish?"

"No, Daddy, I haven't forgotten, but for the first time in my life being Jewish means something to me. I'm one of the elect, Jesus's own."

"I can't listen to this. You're torturing me."

"I'm sorry, Daddy, it's just something that I spent a lot of time thinking about lately." Joanna closes her eyes, "It says in the New Testament ..."

"New! Did you read the Old, too?"

"Parts of it, please don't shout."

"In Hebrew?" The rabbi's voice rises, a defense attorney for the Hebrew God.

"You know my Hebrew isn't good enough, but I'm planning to start studying Hebrew again."

"Joanna, I may not be a very smart rabbi, but I do know that if you didn't read the Bible in Hebrew then you didn't read the Bible of the Jews. What you read was the Bible of the Christians."

"I don't care whose Bible I read. Jesus is the One. It all makes such perfect sense."

"Do you know what you're doing to us? To me?"

Mrs. Preshko feels the conversation is heading down a one-way street in the wrong direction. "Does anybody want some coffee? Honey, where do you keep the coffee? We brought some marmalade and fresh rolls. Wouldn't that be nice?"

The rabbi turns on her. "Can't you wait with all that?"

"It's all right. You talk and I'll perk. We'll just sit right here and have a nice cup of coffee, unless someone prefers tea. Last call for tea."

"Mom, did you hear what I said?"

"Yes, honey, I heard every word."

"About Jesus, I mean, the greatest Jew who ever lived."

"Yes, honey, if you say so, whatever you say, as long as you don't do anything crazy like you did with the car. Do you promise?"

"Mother, you're not listening to me. I'm talking about the greatest Jew who ever lived."

"Are you happy, Joanna?" Mrs. Preshko asks. "You look happy. Manny, she looks happy, doesn't she?"

"I'm the happiest I've ever been. Everything makes sense to me, my whole life, all the suffering, all the pain." It's hard for Joanna to explain but she has to let them know the truth about the New Testament, how each page speaks to her in a way the Bible stories have never done, so that she sees herself in the words, in the very shape of the letters. Reading Jesus's words makes her body soar, and gives her the feeling that she's being healed, and this healing is a sweet ache, like falling in love with someone new. The pages feel as soft as a bed of feathers, and the world she faces each day, which used to be so hostile, has suddenly assumed an air of gentleness.

There is a stillness in the room as Joanna describes these things. Mrs. Preshko is afraid to utter a sound, even to breathe, as Joanna concludes her monologue.

"Not only do I understand myself now, I also understand the Jewish people, Jewish history, why Jews have always suffered. Not only did the Jews give the world its law, but they also gave the world its redeemer, but because the Jews were blind to Jesus, they suffered and still suffer. It's really very simple. Without Jesus, a Jew is just half a person. The laws of Moses have been superseded by the higher laws of the spiritual kingdom of Christ, and these higher laws pave the way for the Messianic age that will be ushered in upon the appearance of Jesus. They even explain Hitler, because he represented the wrath of

God finally revealed at its fullest. All of that could have been avoided if only the Jews had accepted Jesus. We're being given one more chance, the final chance before the end."

The rabbi grits his teeth. "I can't listen to this anymore, Joanna."

"Why not, because it's the truth? You know where I was yesterday? At Grandpa's nursing home."

"You went to visit my father?"

"That's right. He's not just your father. He's my grandfather, in case you've forgotten. I had to tell him the truth. And do you know something? I think he understood. I told him to repeat after me that Jesus was the Messiah, and you know what he did? He kissed me with tears in his eyes."

"Are you out of your mind?"

"No, Daddy, I'm very much in my mind. Completely there."

"Roberta, I can't take this anymore. I'm going."

"You promised you'd come and be supportive," Mrs. Preshko pleads.

"That's impossible. My father is eighty-three years old, and the last thing he needs is a half-mad granddaughter ranting about Jesus. The man lived through a pogrom in Russia when he was seven, so why does he deserve this kind of treatment now?"

"Your father will survive. It's Joanna I'm worried about."

"I'm leaving."

"Manny, don't."

"Why not? Preaching Jesus to my father — is that normal? Come on, Joanna, where's all this Christian love I've heard so much about? And all that turning the other cheek. The only time a Christian turns the other cheek is if he has a knife stashed away in his boot."

"That's ugly, Manny. Now you sound like an Orthodox fanatic. Why do you insist on defaming people you don't even know?"

"For Christ's sake, Roberta, what's gotten into you?"

"She's happier now. Let her be."

"Are you kidding? She's losing her mind."

Suddenly a painting of a young bearded face seems to come looming out of its frame toward Rabbi Preshko, practically knocking him over. How could he not have noticed it all this time?

"Is that who I think it is, Joanna?"

"It's beautiful, isn't it?"

"Are you turning your house into a church?"

"As a matter fact, it's a Rembrandt reproduction. Does that make you any happier? The original is in the Met. Rembrandt used Amsterdam Jews as models for his religious paintings, so don't get all excited for nothing. If you don't like him as Jesus, just think of him as another Jew."

Rabbi Preshko is about to storm out when his wife stops him.

She drags her husband into the bathroom, and in a soft whisper, nearly crying, says, "I know only one thing: I want my daughter."

The rabbi puts his arms around his wife. "I understand. I really do. But if she's tied up with Jesus, she's not yours."

"Manny, she's ours. She'll always be ours. This is just one more of her phases, and if we make a big stink, she may really start taking herself seriously. Let's just forget about it."

Joanna sticks her head through the door with a final message: "I think you should know that I'm planning a long trip soon to the Holy Land."

Mrs. Preshko's eyes light up. "Did you hear that, Manny? Joanna wants to visit Israel. Isn't that wonderful?"

"Not exactly Israel, Mother, but the Holy Land. Bethlehem, the Mount of Olives, Nazareth. I want to spend Christmas on the Via Dolorosa. Not in Eilat, and I'm certainly not stepping into Tel Aviv."

"Joanna, do you know what you're talking about?" Rabbi Preshko asks.

"Yes, Daddy, I know exactly what I'm talking about. Christmas, December 25th, in the Holy Land. I think it would be a wonderful way to meet Jesus in the flesh, so to speak, on the earth where he once walked."

"I'm leaving. I can't take this anymore."

The image of his daughter in Jerusalem, tracing Jesus's steps, is so frightening, he has no words, no thoughts. All he wants to do right now is forget Jesus for a few hours, yet when he walks out the door, Rabbi Preshko finds himself on a bus heading uptown toward the Metropolitan Museum of Art, in pursuit of Joanna's Rembrandt.

Crossing Madison, he is nearly hit by a speeding truck turning a corner. The driver yells and curses, but the rabbi doesn't react. Although he's not superstitious by nature, he wonders if this brush with death could be a warning that he's barking up the wrong Rembrandt by entering the museum. But how can he turn back when he's only two minutes away?

Ignoring the Matisse exhibition, he makes his way straight to the permanent exhibits of the Italian and Dutch masters. Joanna's Rembrandt is not there, but the rabbi has no inclination to leave, and he stands gazing for a long time at ten centuries of Jesus. From one painting to the next, it is almost as though he can watch Jesus growing up from a primitive iconic presence to a martyr crowned with thorns, from a simple teacher surrounded by his students to a subtle mystic, from a man all alone on a mountaintop to an angry critic casting out the moneychangers from the Temple.

Finally he comes to a huge El Greco which seems to sum up the essence of Jesus through the centuries; the eyes have the gaze of sainthood, of one who knows, but won't say, one who never gets angry, one whose hands have never hurt another willfully. Was he a good son? The best. Did he do his homework when he was young? Always. Did he help old people cross the street? Certainly. Did he lust after women? Not on your life. Did he put on *tefillin*? Every day. And say grace after meals? Of course.

In the midst of these thoughts, Rabbi Preshko gets a stab of hunger. On his way to the cafeteria, he stops off at the art shop where, without too much trouble, he finds the portrait he's looking for reproduced on a postcard. Then, sipping coffee and munching on a croissant in the museum cafeteria, he studies the postcard and tries to imagine who the model might have been in real life — probably a Sephardi Jew whose family had fled the Inquisition. And was he paid anything for his services, or did Rembrandt tell the young man that this wasn't merely a painting, but an ironic comment on history? To facilitate the worship of Jesus, even Rembrandt must come to the Jews. The American rabbi sits there, amazed, realizing that what half the world sees when it stands before Rembrandt's paintings of Jesus is actually a portrait gallery of Amsterdam Jews.

When he leaves the museum, the sky is so blue that Rabbi Preshko feels he could be swallowed alive and wouldn't mind. Even the clouds, unusually white and vivid, have a razor reality, each one perfectly composed. For the first time in his life, Rabbi Emmanuel Preshko wonders if he's having a mystical experience. But before he knows it, he is brought back to Fifth Avenue by the inevitable hustle of city traffic, teeth of steel and rubber eating their way through the tough flesh of New York taxis and buses.

As the weeks go by, Rabbi Preshko grows more and more distant from his wife. He stays up until all hours, devouring everything he can on the history of early Christianity and its Gnostic roots, as well as anything he can find on "Hebrew Christians." He plows through the small print of Bultmann and Dibelius, rereads Buber and Klausner, and even goes wading into Catholic encyclopedias. In addition he discovers late-night gospel shows and becomes fascinated, wondering if this is where Joanna first developed a taste for Jesus. (He keeps the set turned down so Joey can't hear.) Watching one night as a new convert gyrates across the screen, then breaks down in tears — while scores of people in the audience follow his example — he wonders why in all his years as a rabbi he's never seen a worshipper cry.

He feels moved by the spectacle of such simple faith, reflecting a world so different from the horrors depicted every day in the newspapers—like the crazy item he'd come across just the other day about a club for necrophiliacs in Manhattan. With real corpses brought in from the Bowery, or maybe even killed for the purpose! With that kind of thing going on in the city, is it surprising that people should be drawn to something that looks as clean and innocent as the TV gospel preachers? Rabbi Preshko is worried. If a rabbi can see something positive in the gospel according to Channel 11, then what about Jews in the rest of the country?

The next time he finds himself inside his temple chapel, he shuts his eyes and tries to peer into his heart, but all he can see is Jimmy Swaggart swaying in front of the Ark where the Torah scrolls are kept, and he realizes that his own heart is like a museum, frozen and dusty, and that everything in this place is a lie.

For a moment he loses track of time, and of who he's supposed to be. He can't even remember if it's before the High Holy Days or after. But what does it matter? As long as the members cough up what they pledged last Yom Kippur night, that's all the board really cares about. Would they even care if his daughter started worshipping in the Holy Trinity Church around the corner?

As he keeps thinking, he realizes that he may have been waiting for something like this to happen for years. When he looks into his heart again, he fears that he doesn't love his family, not his wife and not even his children. Maybe he doesn't really care about Judaism, either, or about what's happening to the Jews here in America.

Are their lives any different from the lives of other Americans? Maybe Jews aren't practicing Christians, but they might as well be. Most of them work and go shopping on Saturday and rest on Sunday, and they're a lot stricter about observing Christian and American holidays than Jewish ones. So why shouldn't his daughter, when she found herself yearning for religion, have been drawn to the religion that so many Jews in America really live by beneath their Jewish facade?

In his generation there was still some sort of link to the past — a nostalgia for the old neighborhood, a memory of what an authentic Jew looked like — but what kind of choices did his daughter have available to her? Just the tepid, passionless Judaism with which she'd grown up, served up by a rabbi-father who'd never been able to achieve the living dialogue between history and religion that he had once aimed for.

Suddenly it's clear to Rabbi Preshko that Joanna went mad with Jesus not just for her own sake but to jolt her father out of his sleep. It's not Joanna reaching out to Jesus, but the rabbi himself, although he could never admit it. And since he could never have accepted such ideas as emerging from his own being, he must in some unconscious way have pushed Joanna toward the brink, toward the car accident that nearly killed her. At this moment he understands two things: he loves Joanna more than anyone else in the world, and no matter what she does, he will never withdraw his love from her. He also realizes that he will have to walk into a church and read from the New Testament, not as a scholar, but as an ordinary person seeing with his own eyes what it's all about.

———————

Rabbi Preshko couldn't have picked a more appropriate time for his travail. It seems that only yesterday was Columbus Day, and — after a lonely, brooding Thanksgiving — here it is already the second week in December. Joanna has gone off on her four-week tour of the holy sites, and from the moment he hears of her departure, the rabbi can no longer sit still in his office. Even as she's tracing Jesus's footsteps in the Holy Land, he begins to trace her footsteps in Manhattan, and comes across a town in the throes of a feverish preparation. Wherever he turns he collides into Christmas, blinded by the colors, bitten by the wind, wet from slush, knocked against by packages, importuned by the Salvation Army, and assailed at every corner by the incessant ringing of bells.

What is Christmas? Is it a religious festival or a national holiday? What can it mean to the Jews of America when the most festive day of the most festive season of the year — time of gifts and good cheer, and reconciliation throughout the land — excludes them from its embrace? He knows that most members of his congregation have Christmas trees in their homes, but who can blame them for wanting to be part of the world they live in, day after day, night after night? Don't most of America's Jews, despite the theoretical separation of church and state, really live in some sense like Marranos in their business and leisure suits, swinging their golf clubs and flashing their credit cards in this great free land? Do they take part in the seasonal cheer and good will because they are afraid or unable to live separately from the rest? And who in America doesn't want to feel an organic connection, to be at one with the earth, the winter sky, the month of December? Back in the old days when it was common to separate mind from body, blood from family, face from race, there was the possibility of being a Jew at home and a Gentile in the world. But now everyone wants to put an end to all separations. One land, one people, one God, one religion: America.

Rabbi Preshko is aware that he's writing his sermon for next week, and that it will be a good sermon, one which might even move a few people to burn their Christmas trees. But he doubts if he'll ever deliver it.

The next Saturday the Torah portion of that week is *VaYishlach*, with its famous tale of Jacob's all-night wrestling match with a stranger, perhaps an angel, who, before releasing Jacob, wounds him in the thigh. Ostensibly the story has nothing to do with December and Christmas, but as Rabbi Preshko stands in front of his congregation and begins to discuss the significance of Jacob's wound, he finds himself talking about latter-day Jacobs, and before he knows it, the subject has switched to forced conversions in Spain, Christianity in Portugal, the Inquisition.

The shift doesn't surprise his listeners; they've heard him introduced often as a "PhD in history, from a very prestigious university." But soon his usually calm lecturer's voice begins trembling and grows jittery and scratched, like the harsh pitch produced by a young violinist compelled to practice. In this new voice he begins to speak of Christmas trees and Santa Claus, launching into an attack on the Marrano Jews of America. There's a stunned silence in the audience, a sense of shock. Rabbi Preshko doesn't sound like a PhD any longer. He sounds like some sort of preacher, one of those terrible rural preachers who act as if they know all the answers.

"We are guilty, you and I, all of us. It's a sham, this religion, how we practice it. And if you think I'm not talking about personal experience, you're wrong. I haven't been able to talk about this to anyone, but my own daughter, Joanna — many of you know her, NYU Film Institute — has become a born-again Christian."

Rabbi Preshko is in tears. "I'm sorry for putting you through my own personal sorrow from this pulpit, but history has come home. There's a price to pay. A good Sabbath."

At the end of the service, Rabbi Preshko does not follow his usual custom of joining the temple president at the rear of the synagogue to greet the worshippers. Instead he slips out the back way, and without consulting his wife, hands in his resignation. He's not sure what he'll do with his life, but supposes he'll be able to land a job teaching history somewhere. It's only three mouths to feed now.

But the congregation won't accept Rabbi Preshko's resignation, and instead the board votes a lifetime contract for him. In the end, Rabbi Preshko accepts. His sermons are events. He becomes a more distant man, but at the same time the congregants feel that his suffering is good for them. Although they've never realized it before, they really do want a rabbi who can also preach and carry his audience toward a rip-roaring climax. Every year on the Sabbath before December 25th, Rabbi Preshko dedicates his sermon to Joanna, praying that one day she will return to the fold, to Jewish history, and he will look up from his notes to see her black olive eyes staring at him from the audience, her heart open, willing to believe that he loves her very much.

still life
WITH *SCAR*

E very painter in Brooklyn was dying to win the competition. For the first time in its history, the Brooklyn Museum was opening its Great Hall to native Brooklyn artists under forty for an unprecedented three-month show that was scheduled to travel across the country to the cities of Boston, Washington, DC, Columbus, Denver, Seattle, and Oakland. Not only would the show be the focus of national attention in major art journals and two weekly news magazines, but a $6,000 cash prize would be awarded to the first prize winner and two paintings of each of the ten finalists would be placed in the museum's permanent American collection.

Bernstein was no exception. As his trembling hands caressed the crisp announcement on the post office wall — flyers had been sent to every public and cultural institution in Brooklyn — his heart quivered. He was all aflutter, weak-kneed, and happy. There was no doubt in his mind that he would win, and the work he'd been producing in his room, the style he'd been perfecting for the past twenty months, a revolutionary turn-around from his previous concepts, would finally be redeemed. He had been going mad with fear that his eighteen-year-old vow was coming to an end and his fortieth birthday would find him teaching rebellious pubescents in a junior high school somewhere. But the forces had come to his rescue. This one was for him, alone. When it seemed that none of the clerks was looking in his direction, while his right hand browsed through the wanted posters, his left hand unglued the rules of the competition, which he innocently slipped into his pocket.

That Saturday, breakfast was again a thrill. Like the old days when foundations offered grants and he could afford a leisurely meal now and then, he ordered home fries, two eggs lightly over, juice, toast, coffee — life for under a buck. Spread out in front of him was the *Times*, and his eyes concentrated on the arts section where galleries announced new shows and reviewers invented new "isms" to describe recent schisms. He no longer kept up with the uptown scene, preferring quiet walks in the Botanic Gardens just across the way from his rooms to the frantic forays on Fifty-seventh Street alternating with the West Broadway glitter. Abstract expressionism, minimalism, conceptualism, it all boiled down to capitalism, and capitalism is really *who-you-knowism*. His father, an old-time socialist, used to say that art is an investment and people don't like to invest in strangers.

Bernstein wondered if his father could have been right after all these years. No, he'd insisted, quality wins out.

"But in the meantime you got to live."

"Food, shelter, paint. What else do I need?"

"Forget I mentioned a wife, but something simple. Insurance, for example. Doctors' bills. You think you'll never get sick, but wait till your arm says you want to paint and your teeth say 'Fix me'; I give you one guess who's going to win."

His father sent monthly checks to the Workmen's Circle to make sure Bernstein's teeth got fixed. Bernstein, embarrassed, held out till the pain spread to other parts of his body. He swore off chocolate, but swallowed M&M's whole to avoid potential cavities, and liked to set up a plateful next to his easel, his one indulgence after years of living frugally.

The luncheonette was owned by two brothers, recent immigrants from Greece, and while the waiter-brother cleared away Bernstein's dishes he sustained conversations with three customers on less than a hundred words of English that he probably picked up in some poker game or between an American whore's hungry thighs, despite a cigarette dangling from his lips. Not to be outdone, the chef-brother chopped onions, diced carrots, and slit celery stalks with one hand and with the other cradled the phone and yelled at the top of his lungs in Greek. Next to them, Bernstein didn't stand a chance. He couldn't win with fists and he couldn't win with words. The brothers belonged on Flatbush Avenue as if it were a suburb of Athens.

Bernstein remembered sitting at this very table a year ago when he came across the article on the op-ed page of the *Times* bemoaning the sad state of Brooklyn, one of the forgotten cities of the world, and its overlooked artists working in relative obscurity and almost total neglect because of the sentimental association of Brooklyn with incompetence. The author swore that Brooklyn possessed its own Rembrandts and Kandinskys, masters of color and form who, unless rescued from neglect, would die unnoticed only because when it came to producing slides or approaching a gallery, they were hopelessly naive.

True, true, Bernstein had muttered, aware that the author, a Brooklyn-born art historian teaching at Berkeley, was simply echoing what his father had always said. He means me.

From his windows on Eastern Parkway, the poor man's Fifth

Avenue, Bernstein's gaze swept across half of Brooklyn, a vast stretch of painter's sky that humbled you with eruptions of Renaissance light. When he first moved to this apartment directly opposite the Brooklyn Museum — because it was a changing neighborhood the place had sat vacant for almost two months and he didn't even have to bribe the super — it was like a doorway into heaven where different layers of reality opened themselves up to him: a magical green sea of trees rising from the hearts of Prospect Park and the Botanic Gardens; then way in the distance, the red-bricked walls and black-tarred rooftops where the only signs of life were a chimney spewing gray belches of smoke or a pigeon lost from its flock; and directly in front of him, an immense palace of art with massive stone walls so huge it looked as if it could swallow and spit out any state capital in the United States. He felt it was a godsend, a sign that finally he would be able to paint in peace. But the constant reminder of his inability to do justice to even one sky on an ordinary gray Tuesday afternoon made him wonder if he might not be better off to live in a cellar and paint by candlelight.

The week of submissions kept Bernstein glued to his window. From nine in the morning till eight at night, instead of working on his own canvases, he kept his eye on pedestrian traffic moving along the tree-lined boulevard. He was searching for artists bearing their work. But by the afternoon of the first day, there was no need to search for them. They came by car, taxi, station wagon, bicycle, motorcycle, van, pickup truck, but mostly they came by foot. At first, he tried to keep count, but it was useless. He had no idea, nor did he want to admit to himself, that one borough could possess so many painters.

His earlier mood of certain victory snapped. In a few days he'd have to crawl down the steps, bearing his own two choices, and compete with all the other "hidden talents" of Brooklyn. He began to dread the thought of losing. Desperate, he unpacked from storage three years of work, some fifty canvases, and spread them out along the walls in his studio, then his kitchen, then the bedroom, and finally, even his bathroom. As he surveyed the fruit of his toil, his mood swung from glee to gloom. Mostly there was a sour aftertaste in the pit of his stomach.

He wanted to call one of his old teachers, Gordon the Terror, whose cool blue eyes saw the false note of every brush stroke, but his old legs wobbled, and without forty bucks for a round-trip taxi there was no way to get him to come to Brooklyn, just as there was no point for Bernstein to travel to Gordon's studio without slides of his work — something he was always telling himself to take care of.

After eight each night, when the vans and the trucks had driven home, Bernstein allowed himself to leave his station at the window. He paced his apartment like a caged panther, feeling his strength leaving him. Pushing away a canvas, he stared at his face in the mirror. He had heard that by the age of forty a man deserves the face he's chosen to wear, and what he wore didn't please him. He looked dour most of the time, a fear in the corners of his mouth; his teeth, never strong, had aged badly. His chin could have used some sharper lines, although he had never grown a beard to cover up its fragility. Most people assumed he always kept his head covered with a cap of one kind or another because he was bald, which was true, but not the truth. His relationships never went much beyond the removal of his hat, and because few women he met could surrender to a man who made love with his hat on, he was alone most nights, preferring sporadic one-night stands to going through the story again of how a two-inch blue twist of a scar came to rest on his bald crown, and he would end up feeling numbed not by the bloody account of his second rite of passage at the age of three, which came in the form of a German officer's silver bullet splitting the red apple on his head, accompanied by an orchestra of Jewish prisoners playing the *William Tell Overture*, but by the women whose pity and tears in awe of his scar transformed desire into death. He preferred silence and secrecy. Even his closest friends knew nothing about the scar.

Bernstein, who kept his phone off the hook for hours at a time while working, hadn't spoken to a soul in days. His few remaining friends, Mel Lasker at the other end of Park Slope and Alan Korn nearer by on Atlantic Avenue, were no doubt scurrying about their own flats doing exactly what he was doing. He would have called them to help him to choose, but a paranoid fantasy warned him that they might do him in and pick the worst. There was Davidowitz who lived in Tribeca, which disqualified him from the Brooklyn competition, but he had broken off with him three years ago when his second one-man show featured nothing but models posing in the nude with tattooed numbers on their arms and barbed-wire jewelry hanging from their ear lobes. Bernstein, never a prude, called it obscene and opportunistic. But when he found out the numbers were actually Davidowitz's phone number, he threw the glass of wine he was drinking into Davidowitz's face and stormed out. They were not even on hissing terms.

Late Thursday night the ringing phone startled Bernstein. He jumped over three canvases and a half-eaten can of sardines to pick it up, but when he heard his father's voice, his stomach dropped.

"How are you?" the elder Bernstein asked.

"I'm fine," the son said. "How should I be?"

"You should be whatever you want to be. All right? Don't say I didn't say it."

"Who said anything?"

"Not you," said the father. "Not me. I just thought I would call. I didn't want to disturb you all week. I figured you were busy." He paused. "You wouldn't believe how many painters there are in Brighton."

"You know?" said the son.

"Don't I live in Brooklyn? Isn't my son a painter? So why shouldn't I know?"

"So how many painters are there in Brighton?"

"Enough. But don't worry. I can feel you're worried. Do you want me to come over tomorrow?"

Ordinarily, whenever his father wanted to visit he gave him the same story — that he had an important appointment in the city. He didn't like it when his father, a man who wore his seventy-odd years well, a retired house painter who knew something about brushes, came to poke around Bernstein's apartment and to peek at his work. It killed the day and he found that he couldn't work for six hours before the meeting and at least three hours afterward. But tonight he decided that his father could help. Let him choose the best. The call was providence. After all, it was his father, and not his teachers, mentors, or colleagues who indirectly led him toward his breakthrough.

"Don't come too late. Tomorrow's the deadline."

For the first time in a week Bernstein relaxed. Although the hour was late, he took out his easel, set up his brushes, shut off the lights, and lit a dozen candles at different levels so that the primitive light cast its glow over the entire stretch of canvas.

In representing the grain of a period when the only light on moonless nights came from candles, he discovered he was able to put himself into deeper touch with the period in question using the simple wax, flame, and wick alongside tempera and oil. The masters of previous generations, when tired of painting by sun or moon, had but one choice: the flame of a candle inside a dark cave or a secret attic.

Usually, Bernstein made his preliminary sketches directly from a photo, but tonight he allowed his mind to drift and his fingers to wander in whatever direction gravity pulled them toward.

Over the years, a virtual revolution had been taking place in Bernstein's work. Like hundreds of others schooled in the modern mode, Bernstein was a studio painter, determined to go inside of himself and find what he alone saw, a unique vision. His only compromise with the outside world came when, armed with a pad, he'd wander for hours in the Botanic Gardens searching for leaves with unusual designs, as intricate as the teeth in a set of keys. At home, he didn't render his discoveries until performing the ritual of tasting a fragment of the stem, chewing until the juice surfaced to his tongue. Only then could he begin the process of "magnification," his word for turning the veins and edges of a tiny leaf into a large abstraction, a struggle to give expression to the inner meaning of a breeze, the slightest movement in the leaves, even the shadows falling on it from the cigarette he held in his hand.

Refusing to inflict his vision of pure form and abstraction upon the world, he monastically chose to limit his gaze to a few trees, some shrubbery, a bit of sky, the beaks of birds, and occasionally, a brick wall facing his bathroom window in the rear. This was his world, but he could do bewitching things within its confines, and didn't hesitate to create twenty-one different shades of white in one cloud formation no wider than three fingernails on the canvas if he deemed it necessary. To Bernstein, paint lived. A successful painting not only had to look right, but had to smell right, even taste right. Bernstein's nose and tongue stopped at nothing, and when he was drunk, he swooned over the differences between pastels and yellows, grays and purples, reds and whites, blues and greens, adding a little wine to the pigment he tasted and painted, painted and tasted, careful not to swallow a drop of his brew accidentally.

The sweeping change in his work came about as a result of desperation. Almost penniless, foundation grants exhausted, Bernstein, who had never worked in an office and wouldn't have known how to do anything except deliver pizza or paint empty apartments, was reduced to doing street portraits. His haunt was Brighton Beach, where the arrivals of the Jews from Odessa had turned it into a honky-tonk boardwalk town eleven months a year. He considered street portraits little more than prostitution. For the price of a quick buck, he spat on his talent and spread his brushes for anyone who chose to sit down facing his easel.

———

One day the dapper gentleman sitting in the blue suit and white-on-white shirt sitting in the chair turned out to be Bernstein's father. Surprised, he dropped a pastel pencil and before he could grab it, it had rolled between the gaps in the wooden boards and disappeared into the sand beneath the boardwalk.

"Nice weather," the father said. "A little cool, but the sun is warm. And it's so fresh here, a wonderful breeze, beautiful waves. The life, huh?"

"We don't have to meet like this," Bernstein said.

"I'm here on business," the father said. "Strictly business. Why should I take my trade elsewhere when I have a son in the business?"

"I can't do your picture."

"Why not? I have a face, don't I? I have a mouth, ears, lips? Can't you do for me what you do for everyone else?"

"No."

"Ten dollars."

"Please."

"Twenty. I don't care what. Straight portrait or caricature. You do caricatures, don't you?"

Bernstein was quiet. "Whatever the customer wants," he finally said. "If that's what you want, that's what you'll get."

Doing the portrait of his father forced the son to look for long minutes at a stretch into the face of his flesh and blood, but instead of a realistic portrayal, Bernstein took the innocent features of his father and dipped them into blood, ripping apart the eyes, bludgeoning the nose, piercing the skull, until the final portrait of what he'd created on his own easel was what he hated in others, an abstract expressionistic face with orange nose, green serpent hair, and violet lips.

"Not bad," the old man said, after a few minutes of assessing the results, "but wouldn't you say it looks like you more than me?"

Bernstein was taken aback. He stared into the eyes and wondered if his father might be right. Without realizing it, had he stumbled into a self-portrait?

"If it looks like me," he retorted, "that's because we probably look alike."

"I'll take it," his father said, and wrapped in the $20 bill he handed his son was a packet of photographs. "Here are some pictures. Faces of real people. Your own family. Relatives who were killed — by Hitler, by time, by Siberia. I'll give you a hundred dollars for each picture you do, so there's no need for you to come to the beach unless you're here for a swim."

Without glancing at the photos, Bernstein said, "Look, I'm familiar with all the theories of the super-realists who paint directly from photos. It's really nothing more than another step in conceptual art, and I've always despised that too."

His father, well-read in the history of twentieth-century paintings, didn't want to argue theory. "An artist is an artist with his eyes, not with his mouth. Look before you talk."

"My mouth has nothing to do with it. I just don't buy what those *photographists* claim, that this form of realism adds a depth to seeing beyond what the eye usually sees by turning its energy inward — from life to photo and from photo to art."

"If you're insulted I mentioned a price, I'm sorry. But just take a look at these pictures."

"All right!" Bernstein said with a shout, "I'll admit the effect can be brilliant, if they'll admit it's vicious, spiteful, and yes, even masturbatory."

"They admit. They sent me a letter and said that we admit we're vicious and spiteful. I have it in writing. Now will you take a look?"

Bernstein realized that he'd been raving. While his father went off to the knish stand to bring back some food, he began to browse through the dusty collection, struck immediately by the power of the human face in an era before movies, TV, and the 35mm camera made it so common. Waiting for the first and perhaps only time in their lives in front of the black box of immortality, these black-and-white figures were somehow able to condense an entire lifetime into one snapshot, most probably, Bernstein reasoned, because they were forced to sit for sixty silent seconds without so much as a stir. Seventy years later, the world throbbing with color made these austere photos appear revelatory.

"Interesting," the painter said when his father returned.

"If you're hungry, eat," his father answered.

Bernstein, biting into a potato knish, saw that he had been dead wrong about the super-realists. What he really should have been condemning was their focus — Formica cafeteria counters, the reflections in a shiny Buick, a glass office tower — but the principle behind it was noble, even heroic: the artist making the choice to efface his own ego by a decision not to pollute the world with his abstract visions, but to use what was already available in the public domain, and yet make it new.

When Bernstein got back to his apartment that night, he wasted no time placing the photos next to his easel and then separating the tubes of color from his black and white tubes. The results were astonishing. On the one hand the image was the familiar icon of a previous century frozen in time. But something else in Bernstein's brush stroke clearly said that this was a modern composition. Perhaps it was the memory of similar photographs in family albums that created the painting's ghostly silence, as if these faces from the past were meant to be seen but never heard from again. Or perhaps what made it seem modern, ironically, was the use of black and white since the portraitists of previous centuries had explored every color in existence to capture the human face. Bernstein now became convinced that this concept of the black-and-white portrait could fix the break between the realm of the recognizable public world and the inner private realm of the artist, finally.

The competition didn't come a day too soon.

By the time Bernstein put away his brushes, the candles had melted and the flames had gone out. He sat in the dark, as if in a trance, staring at his shadow-painting. Across the way, the roof of the museum, where the statues of the seers from East and West — Sophocles, Pericles, Herodotus, Socrates, St. Peter, Isaiah, David, Moses, Lao-tse — kept vigil over the inhabitants of Brooklyn, was awash with its own source of light and some of it reflected down into Bernstein's apartment.

In a while the sky outside would begin to break. Then, when the dark purplish heaven gave way to a deep blue one, Bernstein could begin to discern a dim gray shape on the canvas. A two-inch scar on the top of the head trickled gray blood. The gaunt cheekbones swallowed any trace of flesh around it. But it was the eyes, staring vacantly into space and beyond time, that gave the painting its supernatural quality.

The cold empty eyes revealed the truth about the painting: this wasn't some spaced-out visionary in a state of high meditation, no, the man was simply dead and his eyes hadn't been closed, a corpse on a bed or inside a wooden box glimpsed directly from above.

Shock gave way to a thrill when Bernstein realized that he had taken his technique one step deeper into the mysteries of creation: instead of the resurrection on canvas of a subject long-since buried, he had turned the concept on its head — by actually painting a dead man whose soul had just left the body, he'd rescued the body from extinction, giving it life in a new form.

Right then and there he knew what he would be submitting in a few hours' time. The title came in a flash. He'd call it *Only the Dead Know Brooklyn*, after Wolfe's famous story. As for his second work, he arbitrarily chose the first painting he'd done in his black-and-white series.

Leaving a note for his father saying where he could be found, Bernstein left home early enough to be the first in line. When he walked through the doors, he exchanged his canvases, patches of paint still wet, for a blank application from a plain-looking woman with a drab brown dress and a volunteer button pinned on it. Her knuckles were strong and her fingernails chipped — a sculptor's hands. Bernstein smiled generously.

"Social-security number?"

Bernstein's eyes danced. "Am I applying for a job?"

"It's an ID number we put on the back of every work we get."

There were three other volunteers checking applications.

"How's business?" the artist asked.

"We expect at least a thousand today. Outside it looks like King Tut at the Met."

"The more the merrier." Bernstein meant it. "What's the point of winning if no one is competing?"

"I've heard that one before."

"Have a look. I don't mind. You see it coming and going."

"And so much of what I've seen, who knows what it was?"

Although Bernstein was usually more modest and let his work stew for weeks before anyone was allowed to sit in judgment, something in him craved her reaction, a total stranger. "Please?"

"I just go to art school here. I'm in my second year."

"It's all right."

She looked at both paintings, giving equal time to each one.

While waiting, he completed the rest of his application: name, address, birth date, education, brief biographical description (which he left blank), art materials, titles. The entire process hadn't taken more than three minutes, but she still hadn't said a word. He couldn't stand the suspense any longer.

"Well?"

"Nice."

Bernstein was respectfully silent. Maybe in a moment some comments would be forthcoming. When she remained quiet, he pressed, "Just nice?"

She offered nothing else.

"I see," he said. "All right, leave it at that. See you at the opening," he said with a wink.

He felt too good to let it slip away by the one word comment of a second-year art student, and refused to allow the word "nice" to crush his spirit.

The next month passed in a haze. Instead of painting, he took his first vacation in eighteen years by hanging out in the museum. He roamed from ancient Egypt to Mesopotamia to the North American teepees and huts of the Comanche and the Navajo. His eyes seized on an object, the shape of a letter in the Ugaritic alphabet or the symbolic presentation of an eagle on a deerskin, and he stored it away in memory for later use.

He ate simple lunches of rice boiled with milk and seemed a slightly changed man to the neighbors in his building as he held open doors and brought up mail to some of the elderly on the fifth floor. Once, when he ran out of sugar, he rang his next-door neighbor's bell, but she wouldn't believe him when he said his name was Bernstein.

One day the weather turned violent with thunderstorms and lightning, and when Bernstein arrived at the museum, he was one of the only visitors, and it looked like the enormous building was his for the day. In the past, the forbidding sky was a spice to his pleasure as he savored every second of traipsing through his private domain, but now he felt it was almost criminal that he was the sole person to walk in the palace. Rather than continue to linger there alone, he hurried out of the building and arrived home, drenched to the bone. For three days he wore a scarf indoors, but he had no regrets for his impulsive dash against traffic in the chilling rain.

In any other city, Bernstein knew that the boulevard below his windows would be one of the hot-rent districts, cafes and boutiques springing up out of the cracks in the concrete. In the back of his mind he felt a bit sad that this Brooklyn — quiet, anonymous, humble — which gave a painter the years needed to master his craft, might be lost for good when the ravenous hordes descended and picked it clean, evicting the old-timers like discarded toothpicks.

Then, on a Tuesday in February, the phone rang. It was the museum.

"Is this Mr. Bernstein?"

The artist began to tremble. "Yes?"

"Can you get over sometime today?"

A roar went off in his head. "What is it? Did I win?"

"This afternoon will be fine, around three. Department of American Painting. Will you find it?"

"Yes! Yes!"

Bernstein could swear he'd detected excitement in her voice. Even before the phone was back in the cradle, Bernstein felt a sweet vibration in his body and a delicious fragrance in the room.

It was a blessing — a major exhibition, trips to cities across the country, money in his pocket. He sat down to catch his breath. Maybe it was true — fame was better than exile, success better than secrecy. The proof was that the hum in his head had turned into a volcanic energy erupting inside every fiber of his being with the power to heal his own wounds, except the pain in his heart, which had begun to throb suddenly.

He told himself, while clutching his breast, that it was simply the result of all the excitement. He drew a hot bath, sprinkled some bath oil which he'd once received as a gift, and for the next half-hour, didn't move a muscle. When he emerged, he was a much calmer man. The dark room and the immersion in water released him from his vows. While bathing, he confessed his sins: obscurity in Brooklyn was a sham, a lie, a tough pose. The truth was that he'd always wanted to be as famous as Matisse, as elegant as Modigliani, as powerful as Braque. He wanted critics to visit his studio on Eastern Parkway and christen it the American Montparnasse.

This simple straightforward admission, after being locked inside for so long, brought Bernstein to tears. But it was a cruel twist of fate that the artist, who had never cried before, couldn't distinguish between the sweat of his brow and the tears of his eyes once the drops of liquid stopped flowing down his cheeks and came to rest just inside his lips.

For the next hour, sipping wine from a goat-skin flask, he walked around the Botanic Gardens begging forgiveness from the trees and the squirrels. His first love, a weeping hemlock, welcomed him with open arms. Outside, the tree looked like a small bush with tiered hedges, but creeping inside, he found himself in a private space, like a warrior's tent, low and carpeted, a protection from all the elements. Bernstein shared the last of his wine with the hemlock, and at a quarter to three, he brushed himself off and proceeded to his date with history.

———

Ushered into the offices of Twentieth-Century Americana painting, Bernstein was quite taken with the simplicity of the wooden furniture. He guessed Shaker, leftovers from the third floor: two rocking chairs, a rainbow-colored quilt on one wall, and even a spinning wheel. The desk, carved from narrow planks of oak, looked like a dining room table. The only thing missing were bowls of oatmeal. And except for an incongruous Levine hanging near the quilt, Bernstein would have never known that he was standing in the control room of a major American collection.

When the eyes of the man sitting behind the desk met Bernstein's gaze, they snapped alive, specks of yellow in a gray fog. Not that much older than Bernstein, he seemed to have aged early in life. His hair, gray and grizzled, was clipped close to the cranium and he wore a navy-blue, pin-stripe suit that fit like a glove, declaring the strength of his will or the skill of his tailor.

"You must be Mr. Bernstein," the curator said, pumping the painter's hand. "I'm William Robinson."

"I know. I've read your work on Hopper."

"Have you? That's wonderful. Please sit down."

Bernstein was shown where to sit and from that angle could see clear into the next room, stacked ceiling-high with canvases.

"Well, so you're Mr. Bernstein," the curator repeated. "It's good to meet you. I like your handshake. Good and solid. Not slippery like a lot of these abstract expressionists or stiff like the minimalists. But solid like a realist. Here in Brooklyn we're into realism, neo-, super-, neon-, what have you, and when our show is finally hung, you're going to see realism make a big break into the '80s. Uptown, they think this show will be some of kind of mish-mash, do you know what that is? Sure you do, you're from Brooklyn. That's what we're going to do, put Brooklyn back on the map where it belongs and not some joke that every critic thrashes around when he chooses to consider ineptitude. Guts, flesh, and blood are what it's all about."

Bernstein couldn't understand why the curator was talking so much. Could it be nervous prattle? He wanted to get on with what he had come there for.

Instead, Mr. Robinson pulled out a pipe and stuffed the bowl with tobacco he kept in a leather pouch. He lit up and puffed, waiting for Bernstein to say something. The painter, however, kept silent, suspicious as to why the curator looked so puzzled, occasionally twisting his lips as if he were soothing a pain in his gums.

"Let me be up-front with you," he finally said, glancing at Bernstein's file. "I have some good news for you and, I'm afraid, bad news, too."

So that's it. The truth comes home. He closed his eyes and tried to hide what felt like the beginning of tears. He saw the road behind him strewn with suicides and shadows and the road ahead adrift with losers and weepers.

"Frankly, you're a first-rate painter. Your work definitely has the mystery and authority of what we're looking for. It sings, if I can use the metaphor."

Bernstein wasn't sure what this meant, but it had the effect of lifting the blackness from his heart. Maybe the bad news was just a gentle warning about the condition of the canvas, an accidental cat's claw, or a flash fire that had ruined his work. Bad news, but this was life. Bernstein saw it as providence. If necessary, he'd rise to the occasion and, like a pro, recreate the conditions to reproduce the original.

"And the bad news?" Bernstein asked apprehensively.

"The bad news is that at some point an error was made in the screening process. But I want to stress that you are a first ..."

"An error?" the painter's skin crawled. "What kind of error?"

"Of course you know the exhibit is for painters under forty."

"But I'm not forty yet."

"You will be."

"Won't everyone?"

"It's not easy for me to tell you this, Mr. Bernstein. The screening committee should have never allowed your work to get up here as soon as they realized that your birthday, March 15, would make you forty years old by the time the exhibit opens on March 21. But somehow they made a mistake and your work ended up here anyhow. And before the error was discovered, you passed all scrutiny. Indeed it was a unanimous decision. We just didn't want you to get some bureaucratic letter in the mail disqualifying you because of the question of age, we wanted ..."

"You mean I didn't win?"

Bernstein's body left the earth. The trembling hands weren't his, and someone else's eyes were aflame.

The curator shook his head.

"But the day I applied I was under forty. Doesn't that count?"

"I'm afraid it's not enough."

"Yet the work was good?" Bernstein pressed.

The curator nodded.

"Then I'll get someone else to submit for me, someone under forty."

"I didn't hear that, Mr. Bernstein."

"Hear what? I can have a new application in an hour."

"I'm really sorry. But if you had any idea of the trouble we're having with submissions you'd understand. We had to borrow three full-time investigators from the Welfare Department to check the addresses that don't match up with the phone numbers. You wouldn't believe how many Manhattan artists tried to sneak in. Then we're being attacked by the Gray Panthers accusing us of discriminating against the old. Look, I'm over forty myself, but that's not the point. And every minority in Brooklyn wants proportional representation, as if art can be legislated. So what if I tell the board of directors you're doing important work, if they smell one infraction that violates the principles and by-laws of this competition, there's going to be hell. Let me be blunt, the funding of this show comes from a committee created to stress the vitality of the borough, its youth, and that Brooklyn is a living art capital, not some geriatric center where people paint part-time or when they retire from teaching or working in the post office."

Bernstein was incensed, his eyes spat sparks. "I've been a full-time painter for almost twenty years. I never taught. I never post-officed. Tell me, who is a better symbol of Brooklyn than me?"

"I believe you, but there's nothing we can do about it. I honestly sympathize. And I don't say this to everyone, but I'm sure things will break for you one day. Perhaps another competition."

"Do I look like an idiot?" Bernstein asked. "There's only one museum in this borough and this is it."

"A man of talent doesn't depend on one museum."

"Look, I may never have another chance. If you think my work is worth something, then do something. Don't make me beg. Do anything. Push up the competition a few days. Call it a preview. Put together a small invitation list, a semi-private opening prior to the major opening."

"Aren't you stepping beyond your bounds?"

"This is my bounds, mister. Eastern Parkway is my street, Brooklyn is my borough. I'm not leaving till I get a straight answer."

Enraged, Bernstein couldn't think clearly and he didn't care that his threat might backfire. He felt like seizing the crystal ashtray where Mr. Robinson's pipe sat and flinging it at the grotesque Levine staring down from the walls.

"Mr. Bernstein," the curator said, "I'd hoped that you'd accept our decision with the grace of an artist. Was I perhaps mistaken?"

Bernstein wasn't sure how it happened, but Robinson's question, uttered as if he were shooing away some fly that was threatening to land on his omelet, had a stunning effect on the painter's rage.

Bernstein stood up and, without another word, turned towards the door. Just before he crossed the threshold he considered making a final statement, something so dramatic that even after he was gone the words would linger in the room — but what can you say after being devoured by a civilized cannibal in a dark blue suit and a white shirt?

The click of his heels echoed down the long marble corridor, but it wasn't only his heels that he heard. When he glanced backwards, he saw two guards following him, no doubt summoned to make sure the disappointed artist didn't create a scene. Mustering every ounce of will he possessed, Bernstein managed to exit the building without uttering a single expletive, but once outside, a barrage of four-letter words tore loose from his locked throat.

When he got home, his father was pacing in front of his apartment building, stamping his feet and clapping his hands to keep the cold away.

"You were not in."

Bernstein was about to snap at his father, a cynical quip meant to reduce the old man's naive observation — of course he wasn't in, why state the obvious — but held back, hoping his father would interpret silence as a need for privacy.

"You look like you came from a funeral."

The older man, not about to abandon his son, the mourner, followed him into the building and although he usually managed two steps at a time, remained respectful and kept pace with the younger man's single, heavy-footed trudge to the third floor.

Sitting in the dark, Bernstein could hear his father fussing in the kitchen, the rustle of paper and plastic, the racket of dishes, the clang of silverware. He wasn't particularly hungry but food might dull the pain. As they sat eating sandwiches of soft and hard cheeses, tuna fish salad with bits of carrots, sliced tomatoes and onions, and a few black olives retrieved from some forgotten jar on the bottom shelf, the younger Bernstein informed his father that because he had missed the age limit by a hair — six days actually, he was disqualified from the competition. Thus the sad eyes; he was lamenting his brief fame, not even fifteen minutes and already banished.

"They had two goons ready to arrest me if I so much as made a peep." Bernstein reached for a paper napkin and wiped his forehead: the steam was going full blast. "It's finished. It's over."

The elder Bernstein put down his glass of tea. "Who's finished? Forty is a baby. Forty and six days, even a bigger baby." He took a long contemplative look at his son, nodding his head as if answering his own question. "Who knows, maybe someone made a little mistake on your birthday."

"A mistake?" Bernstein had no idea what his father was talking about. "What kind of mistake?"

"You have two."

Bernstein was waiting for his father to complete the thought. "I have to what?"

"Two birthdays. Your American, and your Hebrew. Maybe I never explained this. Every few years the Hebrew calendar adds a thirteenth month."

"A thirteenth month? Sounds primitive."

"Actually it's very smart. We go by the moon, a short year; the world goes by the sun, a longer year. So to make sure Passover always comes out in the spring and doesn't jump around all over the calendar, the sages added a thirteenth month every third or fourth year."

"I didn't know that."

"First thing in the morning I'll head over to Crown Heights and pick up a few calendars. And if it's true that you're not yet forty in the Jewish calendar, they'll give you back what they took away."

The younger Bernstein let out a sigh so agonizing it confused the father. "You don't want me to do it?"

"Did I say anything?"

"If you think it's wrong, then forget it."

"Shouldn't it be my decision?"

"Then make it."

"But is this how I want to win? I'll just embarrass myself."

"What's wrong with winning this way? Are you ashamed they'll think you're a selfish, sneaky Jew?"

"Please don't say that." But it was too late, a fuse had been lit and the son exploded, his fist slamming down on the kitchen table, upsetting his father's unfinished glass of tea. He felt choked, a tiger's rage inside the body of a stupid, dull sheep. "I can't take this anymore. This is America. If I'm selfish, I'm selfish as an individual, not a representative of my race or religion."

"Nobody is twisting your arm. If you're not a religious person, why use religion to win? Very noble of you to make sure no one accuses you of being sneaky."

The father took a sip what was left of the tea. "Bottom line, if this art exhibit is a game, it doesn't matter who wins or loses, it's all in the playing. But if the exhibit is war, then in war you fight with everything you've got. Decide what you're in, a game or a war."

———

Initially repelled by his father's "two birthdays," within twenty-four hours Bernstein decided it was war. After establishing that by using the Jewish year he wasn't yet forty, he found himself in the offices of Katherine Cobb, curator of the Folk Art department, her sun-dappled, straw-colored pageboy alive and springy each time she swung her head. She responded with an incredibly friendly, farm-country voice as he presented his arguments to her: that the museum could not, or should not, rescind an award it had already announced, an unethical and Philistinish act; and when that argument couldn't convince, he dramatically spread out his collection of calendars on her desk, explaining the concept of the sun and the moon in the Jewish year. According to the Jewish calendar he wasn't yet forty. Bernstein offered to bring rabbis as witnesses, but Ms. Cobb kept saying it wasn't necessary. Within a week she'd have an answer.

She was true to her word. Within a week a telegram informed him of the museum's decision to create a special category for a Brooklyn painter who'd never lived outside the borough, a Lifetime Residency Award, same prize money, plus a selection of his paintings to join the others for the national exhibition.

The news gratified but also disappointed; had his first-prize standing been restored, he would have called his father, not afraid to admit that he had taken his advice, but for some reason the Lifetime Residency award didn't sound very promising, almost insulting, as if he were a native breed without the guts to leave home. True, there was money and possible exposure but he had sacrificed his principles to win the war and not this skirmish on a forgotten field that no one cared about. Too tired to fight again, he didn't even acknowledge receipt of the telegram.

On the morning of the awards ceremony he came down with a burning fever, every bone in his body sore. Drowning in a sea of achy sleep, he convinced himself that chicken soup might be the best bet, and then ordered his body out into the street to the corner grocery for what turned out to be overpriced cans of a watery liquid, its resemblance to the real thing a manufacturer's delusion.

All day he fought a second war, infusing himself with endless cups of tea, but a darkening sky convinced him that it was a lost cause. Scheduled to start at seven, it was clear he would miss the great day's celebration. He felt weak, too weak for even self-pity, too weak to say a word to his father when he called to find out how his son was doing. At some point he awakened, the radio clock blinking 9:10. Lying there in silence and blackness, he attempted to distinguish between the darkness outside and the darkness within, wondering if he could ever paint these two darknesses — his next project?

He was about to turn over and slip back into sleep when he realized that his immune system had expelled much of the fever — he felt strengthened, strong enough to force himself out of bed. He dressed warmly, an extra pair of socks, scarf, a thick woolen sweater and a hat with flaps.

Flashing his invitation, he entered a brightly lit gallery off the side of the Great Hall. As far as he could tell, the first and second place winners were on the podium, thin-boned, dark-complexioned women, both with short spiked hair but with different bangs, one combed and the other zigzagged. Even at a distance of one hundred feet their smiles dazzled each time someone approached to offer congratulatory remarks. The chair for the third prize winner sat empty.

Then, off to the side, Bernstein caught a glimpse of the museum director's close-cropped head; he was listening intently to someone whose face was hidden but whose hands were conducting the conversation. He thought of approaching the director, locating a pause in the conversation and then asking if the decision to include Bernstein was based on expedience, or rather a rational understanding that he was an "authentic" artist.

As he was about to trek across the room, a tall bearded man standing in Bernstein's line of vision moved away and the painter's knees nearly buckled when he saw that attached to the gesticulating arms was his father's short thick chest supporting his large Picasso-sized head. Without thinking, the painter flung himself behind a pillar, crouching low, as if his father's blazing x-ray eyes could penetrate through ordinary walls. Anyone witnessing the sudden move on Bernstein's part must have wondered what had just taken place, who was he hiding from, and why.

For crying out loud, he belonged on the podium, not behind a pillar. He was an honoree, not some frightened creature that flees at the first sound of an approaching stranger. Recovering his normal breathing, he attributed the frantic speed of his automatic response to instinct, fear his father would brand him a hypocrite, a vague protest at home and then sneaking inside behind his father's back, a hungry rat willing to do anything to win.

Why didn't he recognize the obvious? His father was clearly right about the Jewish calendar; it had put him over the edge, here he was, a winner, his earlier protest an exercise in vanity. Turning around he took a second peek at the two; both his father and the director were in stitches, as if they'd known each other for years. Was it a round of priest-rabbi jokes, or were they sharing intimate bits of gossip about running a major museum and the endless stress of being father to an artist?

Moving hesitantly at first, then more forcefully, he headed straight toward the man — the men — who had made it possible. He didn't know what to say beyond hello, but even before he reached them the director looked up, the snapshot of recognition growing into the heat of a generous, glowing smile, incandescent. But that was nothing compared to the joy on his father's face. Between the two, Bernstein felt thrilled to be embraced by smiles as wide as the scorching sun, brighter. Or in this case, the sun of Robinson and the light of thirteen Bernstein moons.

miss FINKLESTEIN

B esides mine, there are two other apartments on the floor. An old crazy woman, the muttering kind, usually flashing red wigs, lives in the rear. And a brooding Belzer Hasid, his wife long gone and his children scattered from Manchester to Monsey, lives in the other. Though we're all Jews, none of us speak to each other. Not even hello, not even on the Sabbath. Outside, the street is dark, perpetually shadowed under the Williamsburg Bridge. I don't leave the building at night unless it's absolutely necessary. If I'm out of bread, I starve.

I have been here for five years. Before that I lived in Brownsville, Crown Heights, Jerusalem, and Paris. And Lodz, where I was born.

Every night I do an exercise.

I remember each bed I've slept in, and when I run out of beds (sleep still beyond me), I start on the nooks and crannies, all the different places where as a child after the war I lay huddled next to a stove, wrapped in an overcoat; and if I still haven't fallen asleep, I think of the different women I've slept with. This ploy never fails. Not that I still get erections so easily, but when it does happen I have fantasies about the old hag next door, Miss Finkelstein, thirty years younger, appearing in my room after she hears me calling her name. She mumbles French words in the dark, the seductress, and licks my ear. She must have brought in a phonograph because I don't recognize the music. A red lamp lights up the room. Lips a grotesque pink, the belly invisible under a black negligee. A beautiful gutter sound.

Are you a whore? I whisper.

Shhh.

What do you want with me?

Don't make a sound. I'll do everything.

Afterwards I always hate myself, and avert my eyes the next time I see her, wishing she were dead or paralyzed.

The old Belzer Hasid never speaks to me because in his eyes I'm an apostate. I smoke on the Sabbath and keep my head uncovered. A few years ago I used to bring women to my room. Passing me, his eyes drop to the ground. Even though he survived Treblinka, I've learned to hate him. Between him avoiding me, and me avoiding Miss Finkelstein, I'm caught in a vicious cycle, squeezed tight.

————————

When I leave my apartment in the morning, heading for the library a few blocks away, I pass Hasidim coming home from prayers. Black, silent, suffering creatures. Don't be so quick to believe that Hasidim are a joyous people, creating a dialogue between man and God even in their most mundane activities. Under the heavy black garments, white, untouched skin rarely sees the light of day or the sweat of summer nights. A decaying rot hangs over the streets and you can see it in their eyes, in their averted gaze. When I pass them at night, their bodies freeze. In the dark I look like a lean Puerto Rican, shoulders hunched, moving on the balls of my feet, cigarette between my lips, no coat even when it's freezing, the heat inside my blood hot enough to burn anyone who dares to step inside my private space.

In our strange times, they're more frightened in Williamsburg than they used to be in war-torn Europe. Suddenly, men and women whose bones and teeth hadn't gone up in smoke in the ovens or rotted away with typhoid, woke up thirty years later to find themselves along the more deserted stretches of Roebling Street, the unusual sacrifices for America's sins of the past two hundred years. I curse the slave owners but spit at God. Only a few months ago, Tennenbaum, a grocer on Lee Avenue, was killed because he had the nerve to ask why he was being robbed. Had he been caught hiding in a Polish field, he could have saved his life by bribing the farmer with a gold trinket he kept for such occasions, but here the leather jackets swoop down like angels of death, worse than the worst police state, because there is no ideology one can cling and claim allegiance to. The sin of the victim is the foul air he breathes, his heavy European accent, and the wad in his fat wallet, even if it's only seventeen dollars and change.

After months of being stared at as if I were also one of the threatening aliens, carrying a cold knife in my pocket and a viperous look in my eye, I drown myself in my room, avoiding the streets where the Hasidim live.

When I emerge, driven by guilt, I've turned myself into a devout Jew. Once again the madness begins. Shorn hair, a beard that begins to sprout, an old black suit and a black hat. Then a trip to the ritual bath. Sometimes it takes me days before I stop worrying about the Jews looking at me, sharing my secret.

I fast Mondays and Thursdays, dipping into the sacred books late at night. Winter mornings, even when it's only five degrees above zero, I battle the evil inclination and trudge my way to the synagogue. My voice throbs with prayer and my body sways from side to side, first slowly and then in a devoted frenzy. If I'm alone, the prayers turn to tears. Then a long fast for the sins of last year, breaking it with a piece of bread and a glass of warm tea. And what sins! Just for the record: greed, gluttony, and even the exquisite terror of hating the Jews I live amongst. But the sweetest thing to the Creator is repentance. No question about that. How is it written? Where the repentant stand, even the sages must stand back.

I sit for hours without movement, my head buried in a prayer shawl, and after the prayers, I beg for an hour in my mother tongue, the sweet supplications rolling off my lips. But this is just between man and God. Afternoons I collect money for the poor daughters of Safed and Jerusalem so that they can marry and live the lives of true and virtuous Jewish women. Any amount given I take, and I praise their worthy souls, one eye nodding at the Jew with a generous heart and the other eye nodding at God.

After a month I've become Reb Boruch Lodzer, and though I was born only a few months after the war ended, I look years older as I drag my body around, pain in my back, my neck on fire, my face carved into a dark scowl.

With my beard, streaks of gray throughout, I'm ageless. A boy of seventeen sees Europe in my face, hears Poland in my accent, respects my memories. And what memories! More often than not I spend the long Friday nights in a little shtiebel revealing secrets, an hour when everyone is hungry for any kind of story to pass the time. I make up tales about my father, the famous black-tempered Lithuanian in the Gerer Rebbe's hasidic court. But as soon as the temperature dips ten more degrees and a little vodka passes the lips, I start quoting from my father's dissertation, which paved the way for his appointment as Professor of Medieval History at Cracow University until he was stripped of his title because of a purge and was forced to mop up afterwards in anatomy lecture halls.

"But you just said ..."

"My father happened to be a brilliant man, a fervent Gerer Hasid, a master chess player, a direct descendant of Pope Innocent's translator of Hebrew texts. Did you know that Mendele Mocher Seforim was my brother-in-law's uncle and when Modigliani painted his first picture in Paris, my father told him to forget about tablecloths and stick with women. What's more he once played a game of chess with the real person described in Chekhov's great story about a Jewish madman.

"Did this Reb Chekhov come from Lublin?"

"He wasn't a Jew."

Returning home at night, I walk in the shadows, my head bent deep to my chest. I don't like nosey neighbors asking questions. I unlock the door quietly, my heart beating a touch too fast, and slip up the three flights. Once on the landing, I pray neither Miss Finkelstein nor the Belzer Hasid will burst open their doors and confront me. A while ago I put two names on the mailbox: Lodzer, my own, and Rezdol, which is Lodzer spelled backwards.

But after two months my religious mask begins to choke me. Since I see through everyone, I'm terrified that everyone sees through me. In the slaughterhouse, the babbling of the fishwives as they haggle for a few chicken necks, drives me furious. I can't control the anger I feel for these women who talk about Jerusalem like an old friend met on an ocean crossing and later will have intimate conversations with Sarah, barren in the desert. And then they expect me to believe in their legends with the same relish they do. Four thousand and twenty angels singing "El Moleh Rachamim" in chorus and if only one voice hums off key, the world will burst into flames and destroy itself. Or a tale about a saintly rebbe in the neighborhood who leaves this world every night for hidden realms where he's taught Torah from Jeremiah the Prophet's own lips. I puke at the thought.

A different madness has seized me, a disavowal of the first. A heretic, I hide nothing. One morning I sneak into shul and spit out accusations at the shamash. "If those holy virgins need money so bad, why don't they work for it, like everyone else?" On a minor fast day, a fat chunk of salami hangs out of my pocket. So, of course, I'm never called up to a reading of the Torah, and when the poor box is passed, they refuse my change.

I curse freely, spit at bus drivers, accuse cashiers of shortchanging me. No one escapes my wrath. Women make me ravenous. When I catch sight of a young woman leaving the ritual bath, her hair still wet and the skin flushed, I make vulgar remarks about the marriage bed. Dressed like a stage actor and mimicking a thick Budapest accent, I offer young girls parts in the latest play I've acquired rights to. In the reading room of the Yiddish library, I spout against the blind Jewish God for infecting his people with a ghetto mentality. The old socialists don't know what to make of my Galicianer accent, but I'm offered a quiet table in the corner and given a fresh notebook to try writing about it. I break chess pieces and fling teaspoons against the wall. Word has it that I butter my meat sandwiches and buy pork in supermarkets. The owner of a Chinese restaurant swears a European came in after dark, sat in the back and licked his lips over two shrimp rolls drenched in soy sauce.

I'm avoided like the plague and figure that rumors are spread about me by the younger generation. The Nazis are blamed for my delirium. Mysterious histories are invented: they forced me to eat living flesh; I saved my life serving homosexual officers; they compelled me, God forbid the thought, to violate the holy Tzisker Rav's widow.

Secrets feed on secrets. The rooms I live in don't help. Last night I wondered what it would be like to burn it all down, every bit of paper, every false document, every lie I've invented and embellished.

My apartment is a prison, a tiny walk-up, a fire-trap. No one forces me to live here, crushed by the guilt I surrender to every time I think about Miss Finkelstein and the old Belzer Hasid. I used to think that when they died, I'd be free. I fantasized a double funeral in the month of Adar, a cool wind chilling the hushed mourners. But that's nonsense. Wherever I'd go there'd be a woman on one side smiling seductively, and the bitter expression of the old Hasid on the other side, demanding my faith to an autocratic God stalking around madly from Aleppo to Brooklyn, invoking laws, issuing threats and punishments to his disobedient flock. It's as if I've turned the Hasid into my father and Miss Finkelstein into my mother, the treacherous guilt punishing me even in this hidden apartment that almost never sees the light, has three locks, iron bars on the window, a working peephole.

I pull myself together and check the schedule to see when the library opens on Tuesday. I work for a Jewish cultural foundation. They pay me to read obscure texts and supremacist newspapers, keeping a record of different atrocities committed against Jews. Since I spend most of my days in the library anyhow, the job, as long as it lasts or as long as atrocities are committed, is perfect.

Once a week I head uptown and drop off four or five pages of notes and pick up a check on the way out. Except for one invitation celebrating an Israeli critic's attack on the self-hatred in American-Jewish authors, I'm never asked anywhere and would like it to remain that way. I hate them, and hate myself for taking money drenched in the blood of the dead Jews. Sometimes in bed faces come to me, one after another, like black-and-white photographs stuck to the side of passing railroad cars which never seem to end. Screaming for mercy, I turn on all the lights for fifteen minutes before trying to fall asleep again. I've been living alone on South Fourth Street for three years. What am I saying? Am I forgetting things? It's more like five, at least five, maybe longer. Each morning I wake at nine or ten, eat a hard-boiled egg and bread for breakfast and spend the day in the library until it grows dark, reading, dreaming, and translating. After a while, steeped in the lore, I imagine myself living in Lodz between the two world wars, or selling candles and spices in Damascus 971 A.D. I especially adore the modest woman I'm engaged to marry in Yemen shortly after Maimonides sent his famous epistle in 1216 to the people of the city. I don't side with the early Maskilim at the turn of the century, but because I know English from school, I keep up a regular correspondence with Melville, guiding his Biblical studies. Sometimes I spend the Sabbath in the Vilna Gaon's house where I once fell in love with his daughter, a tragic creature who was never allowed to express her desires to be a writer. She married early and brooded.

Why bother with the ugly room I live in if I can settle so easily into an old bed in an old house at the side of the Dnieper River and wait for the Dubner Magid to appear at the window and picture the different levels of hell waiting for me.

I overhear the Writers Committee of the Warsaw Ghetto interview a potential candidate: an oral examination on recent trends in translating the untranslatable. I lived for two weeks in a prison cell with the grandchild of Reb Moishele Kutna who was arrested for plotting an assassination. I taught him terrorist techniques while he told me stories about his uncle, a melancholic. Together we wrote Hebrew poetry without a dictionary or Biblical references.

But then I noticed my mind take a morbid turn that I couldn't control. I debated for the right to read Hebrew novels in toilets and was stoned wherever I went. I saw myself spitting on worshippers entering a synagogue on Broome Street in 1911 and was immediately surrounded by critics who hated my essays and harangued by women who found me repulsive. From memory I recited snatches of Psalms, but they corrected the tune. Weeping didn't help, they only snickered. I retreated to other cities, Buenos Aires after the war, a little town in Podolia, the Jewish Quarter in Alexandria, but wherever I went, I was mocked. Someone always knew I was up to something, a threat to their peace, a ravisher of their daughters, an interpreter of dreams with a scheme up my sleeve.

Twenty minutes before the library shuts, I grow frantic. Three frail men sit at different tables. Two of them snore; one eats. The librarian stares at the clock. Except when I need a key to the men's room, I never speak to him. In the library every night is the same night. Never does anyone leave together; it's a silent rule to depart alone. As usual, I'm the last to leave.

Although I have enough money for a hot meal in a good restaurant, I never allow myself the luxury. What I do for supper is buy the same kinds of food a man named Leibish ate eighty years ago when he lived in the Riednicker poorhouse. I boil the same potato he did and chew on a piece of onion dipped in sour cream. I can see Leibish sitting opposite me in my kitchen, silently gorging down the meal. His story is in his eyes, terrified of everything, even the slightest change in the wind's direction. He never answers a question, never offers an answer, never says a word. On Yom Kippur, the holiest night of the year, instead of fasting he got drunk and raped his wife. When she found out that she was pregnant, she lost her mind, convinced her child would be born part beast, part devil, retarded, goat's skin, albino hair, owl's eyes. Leibish the Silent.

During the meal he never speaks, not even to ask for salt. So the potato I eat may not be a slab of meat, but I sink more than teeth into it, each bite teaching me to be patient, to wait until the silence yields a deeper silence, the silence between the silence.

———

It's after midnight and I still can't sleep. Tonight no exercise helps. I light seven candles, and seven flames flicker in the dark. I begin to say Kaddish. My eyes are wet and my heart feels like stone. Seven candles for seventy million dead, which is just a conservative guess. If I'm counting, I may as well count everyone: unborn children and grandchildren. I imagine the heavens bursting with lost souls clamoring for love, attention and revenge.

Ever since the war there just aren't enough Jews to embody the masses of souls who had to be held, comforted and given refuge almost immediately after the first shock of a Nazi death, a memory so terrifying that in the mad scurry of finding a child just conceived, two mismatched souls ended up in the same body, and somehow, unbeknownst to me, I'm playing host to two souls that hate each other, like Jacob and Esau, the guilty one whispering in my ear that I was never meant to love the first, and the other one punishing me every time I dare turn my head. Burn them? Starve them in a desert? Live in a Jewish monastery as I'm doing now while beating my breasts for sins never committed, but for which these souls seem to recall and refuse to forget?

The old Belzer Hasid, I'm convinced, hates me. I see it not only in his eyes, but in every single movement he makes when I'm nearby. It's as if something went terribly wrong with his life, an irreversible horror, and I've been blamed for it. If he were really a Hasid, why doesn't he show some joy — even if it's make believe? Does he think I'm an American goy sent to spy on him? A neo-Nazi? I could freak him out by showing up one day as a skinhead. Send him shivering into his apartment, fumbling for the locks. But am I a murderer? Do I want to send him into cardiac arrest?

If these thoughts won't stop, I'm a dead man. How long can I brood on the Belzer's eyes? How long will I need to convince Miss Finkelstein that I would never hurt her? But this means I have to act. My God! If I could only bring some love into their lives, I'd be a free man. Why should the Belzer Hasid live alone? Why should Miss Finkelstein sleep alone? They could share a life and, married under a canopy, bring joy to Israel. Once I brought these two wandering souls together, my terrible dreams would vanish. Once they embraced and stopped hating the world, the two souls inside me would sing and dance as one. And what a wedding celebration! Drinking wine squeezed from Galilean grapes in silver goblets. Enraptured dancing for the bride and groom, she in white, the madness stripped from her eyes, the gaudy mascara sweetened by Hebron dew and her own tears of love for this fiery stranger, garbed in a black, knee-length coat and felt hat, black eyes. I feel a beautiful joy as his bitterness yields. And at the moment when they're alone for the first time together, a profound look of delight as Miss Finkelstein and the old Belzer Hasid kiss and weep for all these lost years and finally embrace with desire and words of love. I would feel free, light, almost innocent.

———

Miss Finkelstein is still up. Through the walls, I hear her puttering around. I don't know who to approach first, but I imagine she'd be easier to talk to. She doesn't recognize me through the peephole, but after identifying myself, I hear the chains rattling.

I barely recognize her, and standing so close to her pale face, she doesn't look mad or frightening. Is it possible that she was beautiful when she was young?

"I hope you don't think it's strange for me coming to see you." I follow her into the kitchen. Packs of old newspapers are piled everywhere. Is she obsessed with the past like I am? She wears an old nightgown, buttoned to the very last button. But I can see the blue veins in her calves as she sits with her legs sprawled wide. Smoking makes her seem younger.

"We're neighbors," I said.

"What do you want to know?"

Not knowing how to spring the idea of a match to her, I keep staring. "Aren't you curious about me? Where I come from, what I do with my days?"

"Not really," she says. "Where do you come from?"

But I'm here to leave a hint about the Belzer Hasid's infatuation.

After all these years of living next door he's still very shy, but he feels that he knows her, knows what kind of woman she is. Later I'd tell the Hasid the exact same story. I know in my blood that I can be the cord that yokes these two souls, and though what I'm doing may seem to be no more than a flick of the wrist in the universal scheme, nine months from today Miss Finkelstein may shock everyone with the birth of a child. If anyone asked, I'd say call him Isaac. Even if he lived a quiet life, one day he might save a man from drowning and change the course of history.

Old hag, a Belzer Hasid's wife, mother of a child named Isaac — suddenly all these perceptions of Miss Finkelstein feel like heavy veils: isn't she a woman? And though many years older than I am, I want to ask her intimate questions: was she ever loved when she was younger? Taken to an extravagant restaurant and treated to roses and scents? Did she ever pick up a man and take him home on the first night and then, eating breakfast late in the morning, arouse him again with her hands under the table?

"Have you ever been married?" I ask, my voice as soft as a cat's purr. Yet I seem to have startled her. "I don't mean to pry."

"You're not prying," she says after a long silence. "My God, it's been a long time since anyone has asked me about him. Yes, yes, I was married. Not for a very long time, though. A terrible, terrible thing happened." She lights another cigarette and takes a deep drag.

"You see my husband was a young student and wasn't aware how the world works. He was terribly jealous. Even before the ceremony was over, he was giving everyone dirty looks. A very famous man was there, later to become the Vice-Minister of Religion in Israel, and you should have seen the looks my husband gave him. Instead of enjoying himself, he decided to review the marriage contract, going over the spelling and grammar. Before blessing the bread, my husband located the owner of the catering hall and insisted on seeing his fringed garments to determine if he was truly a religious man, or was only pretending to be one. But he didn't stop there. He criticized the crispness of the waiters' uniforms and checked every fingernail for dirt before the waiters dared approach a table, despite their white gloves. After a few weeks, my husband suspected everyone of sleeping with me. All he ever did was look for violators. His hair began to fall out. He grew old, wretched, depressed. Day and night he raved about my betrayals, and slowly it began to dawn on me that I had married a very sick man. He died in a mental hospital where they had taken him after he accused my own father of making a pass at me. That was the last straw."

"It sounds frightening."

"It's over. Listen, do you want to see my wedding dress?"

"Won't that depress you?"

"No, it was the only good night." She blushes. "It's the only night I could talk him into going to bed with me. One night and that was it. I took off the white and there I lay."

Ten minutes later I walk into her bedroom and there's a startling difference. In the white dress her body looks ripe and good. Her eyebrows are plucked, her face rouged and the lips red. The black wig she's wearing seems like real hair.

"This is how I looked twenty years ago."

"Twenty?"

"Maybe it was thirty."

"Do you ever want to get married again?"

"I would say no, but why answer so absolutely? God only knows is a better answer. And you?"

"I feel I'm too young."

"Too young? You must be pushing forty."

"Thirty. I look older. The beard."

"I don't think it's just the beard, but since when is thirty too young? You're a man aren't you? You have desires?"

"I think so, yes. I mean I have desires but it comes out so ..." What I want to say is that it comes out so twisted, but I leave it at that.

A bedside lamp glows and the yellowish light bathes her face. Before I know what I'm saying, I blurt out, "Do you still have desires?"

Her face reddens.

"Am I too blunt?"

"It doesn't happen too often, but yes, occasionally."

Teeth clenched, I fight the feeling of being drawn toward her with all my strength. If I'm here to create a genuine love between Miss Finkelstein and the old Belzer Hasid, how have I allowed myself to go this far!

"Do you feel anything now Miss Finkelstein?" I can't believe I've said it.

"A little bit." She raises both arms as if she's about to catch a bouquet of wild flowers picked in a virgin forest.

I move closer, putting my hands on her neck, gently caress her skin, as if my fingers were feathers.

She jumps, shocked. "What do you want? You're making fun of me. Don't hurt me."

"All I know is what I feel right now. I would never hurt you."

"I've been next door for years. You didn't see me. You didn't talk to me. You never looked at me the way you're looking at me now."

"I'm feeling things."

"Please don't turn this into a joke."

I guide her to the bed, my body rebelling against my mind. The more frightened she is, the greater my need to soothe her, to calm her terror. Ever so slowly, I begin to push my body against hers, kissing her neck, slowly guiding my tongue toward her mouth. At first it's shut tight and then, very falteringly, she opens her lips to mine. I feel delirious. The light is low. I pull off her clothes and though she's fat I don't care. My own clothes come off in seconds. She begins to moan and pant, her arms grab me, her teeth bite. I feel her desire and her desire enflames me. I plunge deep into her and feel the happiest I've been in years. A beautiful tension. I'm being pumped and hoisted, lifted above everything. I begin to lose control, I don't want to come so quickly but I can't help myself. I twist my neck and clench my teeth tightly, trying to think of the weather, the Broadway El outside the window, but it's too late. I let go, quick and fast, and suddenly after the third or fourth spurt, I become frightened. Oh my God! What have I done? I must run and hide, spit out her taste, wash her smell off my body. How could I have slept with this old woman? I want to scream that it was a mistake. To change everything back to how it was an hour ago, alone in my room. I want to stop this madness. I feel sick to my stomach. Oh God, I feel so broken, so ugly. How could I have touched her? How could I have put my tongue into her mouth? How could I have let myself come inside this wretched old hag? I want to puke her vile taste out of me.

At that moment I think I hear the door open. Has someone walked into the apartment?

Candles begin to flicker, I count seven flames. A white shroud dances in the sky. Blood pours from a candle. The moon laps it up like a cat, and then breaks into a perfect Hebrew, laughing at me, a thick dark mustache around its pale lips.

Out of nowhere, the old Belzer Hasid approaches me, a knife in his hand. Except for his fringed garments and yarmulke, he's stark naked. As he rushes through the prayers, the knife above my head, I'm too frightened to move, to beg for my life, to plead that I don't want to be sacrificed. But sure enough, the plunge of the knife. A scream, a taste of blood, but it's only my teeth biting my lips. I'm still alive. But there's a condition. He wants me to suffer for my lust, to beg forgiveness.

I beat my chest and confess. I lusted, I desired, I succumbed, I failed. Terrified of dying, I begin to weep. I lick the ground his feet walk on. I swear never to do it again. I bless his name and curse my own.

From the corner of my eye I see the back of the Belzer Hasid's neck as he steps away. In his right hand the slaughterer's knife, on my right hand the wound.

I rise out of the heap of soiled sheets. Like a drowning man I suck air. But soon my throat calms the passage. My mind grows quiet and waits for the pounding in the heart to still. From the corner of my eye I see that he's put down the knife and lifted a strong leather belt. In the morning I'll have welts on my back and bruises on my face. But it's all right. At least I'm alive.

As God is my witness.

dear
MR. G

2 April 2003
Dear Mr. G.

I hear you are making a movie about pain, someone being killed, crucified even. I have seen other of your movies and I liked it very much. And you are a good actor, and from your eyes, I can tell you are a good person. You know how to suffer, to make it real. I like the look of pain in the eyes. My question to you is since this is all make believe, like a fairy tale with good imagination, actors and cameras and very nice pictures, did you ever see the real thing? Would you like to? The people you should speak to are some people who went through the Nazis. Real flesh and blood. Like me. I could be a very good advisor. Right now I am not employed and would be happy to take on a job.

Sincerely yours,
M. Znessener

P.S. Originally from Lodz, Poland presently residing in Crown Heights, Brooklyn, N. Y.

28 April 2003
Dear Office of Mr. G.

I was very happy to hear from the people of whom I am interested in communicating. You cannot even begin to feel my happiness. I tell someone not very close to me, a jealous person, and she says, the big G will never have time to answer, and here I am answered. And it only shows that you are a good person. And real. This is much to admire. And as to Aramaic, I must unfortunately admit, that my own schooling did not go very far in this direction, of the *Gemora*, which I think is what you mean by Aramaic. Also a few places in the Torah, but where and what I am not exactly sure. For this you would need a religious person, and I, unfortunately for me, for us, I am not religious. In fact, I do not know the word for who I am, I know "agnostic," I know "atheist," but a person who believes with hate, in hate, and of hate, as they say in the Gettysburg, what can you call him? A hate-ist. When it comes to God on one hand, and then Auschwtiz, Dachau, Treblinka, what do we have left? Nothing but hate, not even hate, nothing, no feelings, nothing. This is my very clear belief, and if necessary I will even swear. But Aramaic, I am from a family where we all go to work young, and besides, in knitting, in making garments, in Lodz, which is, if you want to know, Poland's heart. No, Aramaic you will have to ask a boy in Lakewood, or these other yeshivas, this is a wonderful idea, I believe it is, to ask them to be Aramaic consultant. They are thousands of young boys who know much Aramaic. But may I suggest that if you need a person who speaks and writes the Yiddish language, I will be happy to translate. Yiddish, which is the folks' language of all the Jewish people, I am master in, if I am not to brag. Maybe your lead character should speak something in Yiddish, adding to Aramaic.

I know people in Old Jerusalem, two thousand and more years ago, do not speak Yiddish. But if your hero will speak Yiddish, it will show that you understand how similar the suffering. I suggest Yiddish. And why not the whole thing too?

> With appreciation,
> I am M. Znessener

May 25, 2003
Dear Office of Mr. G. and Ms. Klein,

Thank you for giving me much thanks. But this is more than interest. I must to admit that I have a personal reason: me, if this is the right word. Or maybe I mean <u>my</u> life. <u>My</u> story. In fact, when Mr. G finishes with this project, I invite him to come and listen to some of my stories. I can understand a person as great and famous and important as Mr. G receives from the people, all across the cities and towns, endless claims for making movies of different people and their stories. And he has even heard from people who have been through what I have been though, the Holocaust. To me this is not the right word, for me I call it the Destruction. The first word, Holocaust, I do not know what it means, but everyone knows destruction. In fact, I have a suspicious that in making his movie about J, you know the god of your people, not us, he really wants to make a statement about us, J's brothers, cousins, the whole family. The Jews, the simple yiddaleh. And maybe I'm exaggerating, that it's not us he is making his picture on. But why not the next movie. I know Mr. G is facing all kinds of people who tell him what to do, and what not to do, they forget he is an artist, and artist is not afraid of attacks. An artist is not afraid, period, except even if you are under attack, it sometimes makes sense to tell the enemy, in this case that's us, all of us who know something about suffering too, that he is really with us. And for this I have a simple plan, let the next movie be about me. I mean, why not? I will give the ideas life, some on paper, others in words, I am a good storyteller, and I have marks on my body, scars both on my back and front, and since my teeth are outgeknocked, one by one, my new teeth speak a big truth, and the little fingers on my feet, frozen from walking in snow for days. So I am not ashamed, and if necessary I will remove my clothes, all of it, to show where I have suffered, and where I think a camera would make a good shot. This is the plan. While Mr. G is making his Big movie, he will have a little movie ready to show when the attacks get big.

And if my story is not good enough, and why should it not be, I know many other people and their stories. I have only lost a wife and two children, but some people have lost 10 children, brothers and sisters, father and mother. Oh, I know that Mr. G's movie is about a man, and what he went through in his suffering. Nails in the skin. Beatings, whips, flesh like chicken pieces, chopped, cut, crushed. But what would you say if the mother of Jesus would have had ten children, ten beautiful little angels, or twelve, or nine, the number is just a number, and before they decide to put nails in him, they start putting nails in all the brothers and sisters, one, two, three, four, five, and so on, and if not nails, then dogs on the leash, or guns to the head, between the eyes. And not just any dogs, not a poodle or a Lassie or a sweet Bernard who comes to save you, but dogs that they are not giving food. If you didn't eat lunch yet, I am not interested in spoiling an appetite, everybody should have a good lunch first before reading this. So who suffers more, my little yiddaleh, or you know who? Please think not that I making a little nothing of the suffering, and yes, he died a very very terrible death. But if a man is still alive in a pile of bodies, and this I have seen, and he is crawling inside the pile, and the officer comes close, and pulls out the naked body, and gives him a one, two, right in his brain. And this is not suffering. But why should we compare lashes, the terrible nails in each child, in each body, in each flesh.

A second thing, and if you think that I am running away with myself, just talking, instead of listening. Believe me I will listen to you from today until tomorrow, but to listen you have to talk. So I'm waiting. But in the meantime, it was worse for the women. Because not only the killing of the body, but the women went through such shame, their bodies did not belong to them, even less than the men. I knew of an officer who would give his dog human flesh, and not just any human flesh but of a woman he himself had lain with. And to top it off, he liked to show this feast of the dog to the husband of the woman. Probably you think I am making this up, it cannot be. No human being could be so cruel. I agree with you. This was not a human being, I do not know what he was, or who he was. But to begin with not a human being, and only to do what he wanted to do he takes the uniform of a soldier. This husband did not live long, after he sees what he sees, how could he live? His soul is crucified, and for him the fence from electricity is a blessing. But he does not die so fast, so the Nazis beat him black and blue and red from blood, and I am myself certain that this beating was the best thing for this person, only this beating could take away a little of the pain this man is feeling. And every time the whip whipped and the stick struck and the rifle knocked, the man said "Thank G-d, o Thank You for the pain the body is feeling to help ease the pain in the soul." Do you understand what I must want to say? Do our people know less of suffering than the movie you are making of that other person's suffering? I saw with my own eyes a man who saw with his own eyes how this happened, who told me, and I must believe him. I would be happy to give Mr. G. the whole story, the name of the camp, how big was the fence, what kind of dog, everything you need to know to make it exact, and then maybe Mr. G. would use it, and then maybe he would be kind enough to contribute a little something to the man who saw this, and who did not want to talk anymore to anyone, but he did make me a request that when he dies, they should bury him not in New York but take the body to Poland and find a cemetery near the Auschwitz camp, doesn't matter Jewish or not, so he can be near to these people, the man he loved, his best friend. It would not have to cost very much, and since Mr. G. is a man with much power and publicity and all kinds of things that a person in the world needs today, he would be able to help. I have tried. But the Polish government is against more Jews buried near Auschwitz. They say the body will need a visa, and they do not give visas to dead people. Enough Jews have died, they say, but they are really saying that they don't want us to remind them. For Mr. G. it would be for him a wonderful thing to do, and he could also by this, be teaching young people the importance of fulfilling the request of a dying person. I am not a fundraiser, but if Mr. G. would be willing to contribute, his contribution will be honored, and if it's enough money, there will even be a plaque.

I am with appreciation,

Moses Znessener

June 18, 2003

Dear Emily and Office of Mr. G.

This is wonderful news. I will be sending your office not just the name but we have been thinking of making a testimonial dinner, and inviting important people. Of course it will be kosher, even though I don't care. Would Mr. G be able to attend as an honored guest? He will be on the stage, the dais, as I understand is its name. And the man who wanted to be buried in Poland will be there, so it will be our pleasure to introduce Mr. G to this man. We will be happy to have a rabbi who will argue against being buried in Poland because some of the people making the dinner believe in democracy, and everyone should be heard, even if you don't agree with them. Perhaps Mr. G will give his opinion. Even though he is not a Jew, as far as we know, still his opinion would be highly valued.

Yours in respect,

Moses

July 18, 2003
Dear Office of Mr. G.

Should I say that I am not pleased for a token? What would make me happy would be if Mr. G would be able to attend. Enclosed you will find my description of my life in the camps, I have decided that I must write it down before I die because I too have no children, and if not now, never. Right? If you want to use any description, I am all for it. You can make close-ups and far-ups, and from down in the pits to all the way up. I was in a room no bigger than my body, hardly, I couldn't reach out my hand all the way, and it was dark, and once an hour someone came by to remind me I was a Jew and he wasn't.

I remain,
Moses

August 12, 2003
Dear Office of Mr G. and E.K.

I cannot write you a brief synopsis because to me every word is important. I am bound by these words, I feel each one a piece of iron in my flesh. To send you a synopsis would kill what I created. But I admit I am not a real creator, just a copier of my memory, what it tells me I put down.

MZ

8/21/03
Dear Office of Mr. G.

I have been to the movies and I now saw the Passion of Melvin. Believe me I felt like my own body was being killed. This even the Nazis didn't do. And believe me, from someone who has seen the whippings, only a Schwartnegger could be whipped so much and live. It is impossible for a man to suffer so much. But a movie needs to be real and strong and ten dollars is ten dollars. I didn't count but if I am to guess, J was whipped two hundred and fifty times…this is impossible, and if I know nothing from the Torah I know they took forty lashes and made it 39, maximum. More than that a person dies. My mistake was eating food before, I could feel a throw up coming up. Lucky I had a lemon candy, and I took deep breaths. But in all honesty, I must honestly say we Yiddalech don't look so hot. We come out nice and ugly, a terrible people. Oi, this is hard to swallow, but America is a democracy, and I personally always believed in hard work and this movie shows hard work, it looks and feels very much like I am there, with him, in the same room. This is not easy. But all the Jews, so full of hate for this man. This is hard to believe. We Jews love to fight between us. You think in the camp we all agreed on what the German was. We didn't agree on anything. Some of us, the intellectuals, the big-shots, the first to give up, tried to understand everything and that means even the Nazi. Mr. G, your picture is wonderful but a lie of some kind. Okay, I have nothing against lies, we all lie if we believe enough. But you will be in big trouble soon, so I come back with my original idea. The best thing for you to prove a Jew is not someone you hate is to make a real Holocaust movie. The real thing. Schindler the movie of Spielberg was nothing, a few minutes of suffering here and there. The Jews in the background. But after your passion I know you are the best person in the world to make our movie. You are a genius. Don't say I didn't tell you this from the first to the last, to today, and to tomorrow.

I remain,
Moses Z.

November 8, 2003
Dear Office of Mr. G. and Emily Klein/Kline,

I am waiting for answer. I am a very patient and good person, by good I mean even more patient than patient, and it is weeks that you have not answered. If you think that I am writing about money, of this you can be sure that I am not. If you pay or do not pay, this is no concern for me. I can live with it, I can live without it. But I do not understand why you send me a bus schedule from Monsey to NY in Yiddish and want to know if this is a threat. I do not know why someone sends bus schedules to the great Mr. G. Did I make the schedule? Did you want maybe a letter of threats and worse. In Yiddish? Why they send you a Monsey bus schedule, to me, this is crazy. I have no idea. It makes no sense to me. Or to you. Unless they want to say that the Jews are alive and well in America, and Monsey is America. But I did not write it. Please answer.

Moshe, a friend

December 2, 2003
Dear Office of Mr. G. and Emily Kline,

Again not an answer, it is months already. I understand. Mr. G. has his own problems. His movie is big, everybody is talking, and do not stop from today until tomorrow. To be honest, every day I look for a letter from you. Even if you do not want my story for a picture, my life, or the lives of people I know very well. I hear that you are thinking to yourself, what does he know, what does he want, who is this person? This person is me, Moishe Znessener. Thanks again for your help. One thing, I am not asking for money. And if you feel bad that you did not send money for the dinner, we can live without a donation. But most of all what makes me sad is that Mr. G is the one person who if he understands suffering, should be able to look at my suffering. I mean just for a minute. Okay not a minute, make it an hour. But to look. What can it hurt? So please answer me.

Moshe, a friend, not an enemy

December 31, 2003
Dear Office of Mr. G.

This is the last day of this year, and this is the last time of my writing. If not now, when. So it says in the books. Is it a happy new year? You tell me. Yes, I can have sympathy for Mr. G. His movie is so big the world and the moon and the sun, everybody is talking. Some are jumping to the sky, and some are crying. I am not of the criers. I see something potential, something good. Soon I may see the movie again, but to be honest, I get sick from blood, even in the movies. So what else is new? When will it be in the theaters so I can go.

An old friend, remember?
Moshe also Moses Znessener

August 2006
Dear Moshe Moses Znessener.

We've just come across the correspondence we carried on with your office a number of years ago, starting in April of '03. Emily Kline is no longer with us, and that may be why there was a miscommunication. I hope you recall the circumstances, how you were interested in certain projects, and were thinking of a collaborative effort … well, as you can imagine, with events beyond our control, it became extremely difficult and totally inefficient to scatter our energies and creative efforts at the time, which is why we feel that right now an important opportunity has surfaced. Undoubtedly, you're familiar with some of the controversial statements that our client made during a recent encounter with the California Highway Patrol. As a result of that unfortunate incident, our client has expressed genuine interest in moving toward a new direction in his creative efforts, which is why we think that your recent proposals regarding a Holocaust generated film may be put on the planning boards. We particularly found the story of the Nazi officer and his dog an interesting episode. Our major concern is whether the community at large, and by that we mean the Jewish community, will accept a Holocaust movie directed and produced by our client, or whether such a movie might not be perceived as an attempt to hitch a ride on the sufferings of one group in order to produce another film of a type which some critics are labeling as a predilection toward sadism. The communal standing of your charitable organization is important to us, its validity in the larger community, and your own ability to substantiate the story. Is it based on eye witness accounts, and if so, were these accounts written down immediately after the concentration camp period or were they recorded years, or even decades after the purported events?

Roger Lear, Esq.

P.S. Going through our records we note that a check to your charitable organization never went out, and although a number of years have passed, please be kind enough to accept our small donation of a thousand dollars. Also, does your organization engage in educational efforts, such as seminars, classes, or lectures which are open to the public, and which we might be interesting in pursuing? If so, do you have a website where such classes are given online? We look forward to hearing from you.

We were also interested in the possibility of some publicity shots. What do you say to the idea if Mr. G came out to Brooklyn, met your family, your cousins, nephews, nieces, whatever. One thing though is that you look like a real Jew. None of this modern stuff, suit and hat, and a shaven face. We need somebody with a very Jewish look.

8/8/06

Dear Office of Mr. G. and Roger Lear, Esq.,

Very interested, and very glad to make our acquaintance. I will be happy to work in such a capacity. It should be excellent opportunity for all sides. Wish me luck and I wish you luck. Hello, California, good-bye Brooklyn, New York. So you see, I am happy that I took an opportunity to offer my services. If not for my letters, Mr. G would not know of me. Now we can talk to each other, and I can be a real help. My salary is something which is too soon to discuss. Maybe after we work for a month or six weeks. I am not in a hurry. We will talk soon about this. Our organization is small but strong, like me. Or how I once was. We offer everything, classes, one on one, two on two, the whole story. Also books and maps, and the story of the dog is true. One hundred percent. We have more than one testimony. Excuse me, could you explain to me a website, and then I can tell you if we have one, or no.

I do not have a beard but I will happy to grow one. As to whether I am Jewish looking enough for you, time and you will tell.

Sincerely yours,

Mr. Moishe Znessener,

International Chairman of Next to Last Generation of Jewish Suffering

happy

Being happy is not an art, it's a vocation. I was chosen to be happy, one of the chosen ones, one of the happy ones. My happiness used to be a secret, nobody knew why I was so happy, even I didn't know why. I sensed something special about myself but couldn't tell anyone. And then, because of Mendel, I was finally able to share my happiness. And this ability to share has made me the happiest person in the world. That's probably why I was picked to be the Messiah, not because I'm so clever, so good, so tall and handsome, a diplomat. I was chosen because of happiness, the happiest person in the world.

There I was, home alone one Sunday night, eating a broiled steak, home fries, a fresh cucumber, tomato, onion salad with olive oil. The radio was turned to QXR, classical sounds vying with the hum of traffic on Amsterdam Avenue four flights below, as well as the occasional wail of an ambulance or police car, life is...life is... life *is* what you want it to be. And what I wanted it to be ... was this feeling that I could pay the rent, buy my food, a paid up and bona fide member of the human race.

I was about to bite into the thick crust of a dark bread I'd picked up on the way home from my luxurious Sunday walk when the phone rang.

"What took you so long, Dave?"

No hello, nothing. "I was just sitting down to eat supper."

"Next time don't take so long." Anyone else, and I would have hung up immediately.

"Did you see the 'letters to the editor' section in this week's *Village Voice*?"

When I told Mendel I had stopped reading the *Voice*, he hinted it might be a good idea to drop everything and get a copy of the paper.

"I'm too tired."

"Do you know what MSG is?"

"Emes what?"

"MSG. Monosodium glutamates, a salt they put in food. Anyway, this letter concludes with a confession and an apology. Whenever the letter writer eats Chinese food with too much MSG he gets horny, and when he gets horny, he ruins good friendships. Anyone who has ever suffered the ill effects of this powerful salt is invited to an MSG ball on Saturday night to share experiences. Bring your own take-out order. No name, just an address on Bank Street." Mendel paused. "So what do you think?"

"What do I think about what?"

"Dave, what's wrong with you? Are you listening?"

At least once a year he gets some crazy idea into his head and begins scaring people. Before you know it, he's inside Kings County or Manhattan State or Bellevue, just to name a few. I was beginning to get excited.

"Every word, Mendel." I didn't want to sound too interested — concerned, even sympathetic, maybe shocked — but the fact was that Mendel's little episodes were my bread and butter. I should be embarrassed to admit it but I couldn't wait for his annual breakdown.

"Dave. A little secret. Believe it or not, this has nothing to do with monosodium glutamates."

"That's not what I just heard."

"It's a message, Dave."

This was vintage Mendel. It was turning out better than I could have imagined.

"Say MSG quickly."

"Are you serious?"

"Just say it."

"Emessgee, emesgee, emesgee, emesgee . . ."

"Can you hear it?"

"Hear what?"

"This could be it, what we're all waiting for."

"What are we waiting for, Mendel?"

"For a message, you idiot."

I bit my lips. "What kind of message?"

"There is a plan here. The way I see it four kinds of people will show up at this party. First, you got your actual MSG sufferers. Next, you got your Saturday night hustlers looking for a little action. Third — and now we're getting closer — you got those who know that the letter is a secret message that has to be deciphered. And finally, there is that select group of people who actually know why the message is being sent."

Wow! I liked Mendel's analysis. I remembered his last breakdown. Even though I didn't meet any women, I had loads of fun visiting him at Mt. Sinai, which was where he ended up after he approached a black nurse in the hospital cafeteria, claiming she represented the black fire on white fire with which God wrote the Torah. When she tried to get away from him, he put his white hand on her black shoulder. The security guard advised him to leave immediately, but Mendel insisted he was a personal friend of the founder of Mt. Sinai, Moses himself.

I liked the fancy uptown neighborhood, taking strolls inside Central Park, as well as dropping into the Museum of the City of New York, which was just a few blocks away.

"So you're coming?"

All I knew was that I would have preferred Mendel's breakdown at the start of the weekend. That way he could get himself a nice room, a decent view, and I'd have a chance to visit at least once before heading back for work. Since it was already late Sunday, if he was destined to end up in Bellevue, I could kiss a good night's sleep good-bye, which would mean I'd be a wreck when I showed up for work the next day. One thing about me is that I'm totally responsible; I never like to miss a day's work, no matter what hour I get to sleep.

"Okay, how about Sheridan Square in an hour. No, make it an hour and a half."

"That's my man."

I looked at my dinner. The juicy meat had turned cold, but if I didn't eat something who knows when I'd eat again. I decided to warm up the steak in a frying pan. It came out stringy. Tabasco sauce didn't help. I ate, wondering where I would be eating my next meal. Tasteless. I decided to pack a backpack of items that would come in handy if Mendel ended up checking into Hotel Bellevue. I threw in a pack of Kents, my brand, figured I could get his Winstons in the street somewhere. Then a couple of Milky Ways and some Reese's chocolates floating around in the pantry. I also found a John le Carré novel, and since he'd probably need a change of underwear I also packed that, as well as beach thongs because he hated the paper slippers the patients were made to wear. This way I wouldn't have to make an extra trip. All I hoped for was that I wasn't just wasting my time and lugging this stuff for nothing. At the last minute, I filled a pouch of almonds and raisins in case one of us got hungry—all that admissions' paperwork could turn into a long night.

The ring of the phone startled me.

"Dave, an amazing thing! Guess what MSG stands for."

"You just told me, monosodium glutasomething..."

"Messiah Son of God."

I loved it but I couldn't betray my joy. "Isn't that a bit much?"

"Nothing's too much for the Messiah."

I took a deep breath. "So what do you think it means?"

"Maybe the Messiah is going to make his appearance at the party."

I could rattle off a half-dozen other crack-ups, the black nurse in Mt. Sinai, that fire in his bathtub, going down on the subway tracks and taking a long piss, killing the cat he was supposed to be babysitting because he heard voices...As far as I knew this was his first Messiah breakdown, which kind of surprised me since he had Messiah breakdowns written all over him. There was something aristocratic about him—the aristocracy of religious dreamers, Hasidic revolutionaries, eighteenth-century kabbalists. Sure, we were both black sheep—but totally different herds. During every one of his hospitalizations, he would chart out his lineage, making sure I saved it in a safe place. I prided myself on my lack of lineage. Who needs lineage if you end up in the nuthouse; I came from simple Jews, glaziers, near-sighted tailors, shopkeepers, practical types.

Messiah Son of God sounded nice and nuts. This was it; my packing wasn't in vain.

"But why would he pick a party for monosodium glutamates?"

"Can you think of a better place?"

"I never thought about it one way or the other."

"Well you should."

"Did you forget that's not our religion?"

"Dave, this is not about religion, this is about who we are and where we belong. We're in the fourth group, Dave. We're it. We understand. We're the elite. Hey Dave, where should we meet? Uptown or downtown?"

"Didn't we decide on Sheridan Square?"

"That's my man."

Before I locked up, I clicked on a pre-recorded tape of evenly timed barks of a German shepherd, one hundred and twenty minutes of feisty growls. The man in the home protection store had told me it was a German shepherd. So far it worked fine — no robberies. Stepping into the corridor, I kept congratulating myself on how lucky I was to have a good friend who made it his business to end up in the psych ward, otherwise who knows what would have happened to me. Psycho wards happen to be one of my favorite haunts — as a visitor of course.

When I stepped into the elevator, I couldn't remember if I'd shut off the gas range or not. Instead of rushing back I decided it was time to confront my fears — all of them. From now on I would start signing petitions, join demonstrations, respond to telephone surveys. I'd even put my real name on the mailbox, removing the dash that turned Teitler into Feitler so that a thief, with his eye on a third floor window, would give the telephone operator the wrong name in attempting to find out if the intended victim was home or not.

Feeling good about my new resolutions, I came to the simple conclusion that without all my old fears I would be one of the happiest people in all of New York City, especially on weekends. So happy, in fact, that I knew it wouldn't last — someone would burst the bubble, *Hey scumbag, who gives you the right to be happy?* Of course, the best defense is a sour glance, tight-lipped silence, and head bowed under a great weight.

But it was all a show, the idea was to fool the enemy into lowering his guard. I'm sure I've succeeded. The enemy leaves me alone, why bother with some half-forgotten typesetter, a glorified typist on the Morganthaler. Most people think my job is stupid, which is why I love it. I sit in front of a green screen and type names for phone books all over the country, automatically alphabetized, from Abilene, Kansas, to Zion, Illinois. Somehow my brain is able to send messages to my fingers and keep track of the letters that need to be typed, so that the rest of me goes on vacation.

One time Mendel visited and expressed interest in typesetting. I looked at his puffy fingers and pointed out that you had to type about one hundred words a minute, with no mistakes. I realized that I was discouraging him even before he tried. He kept saying that if he got a normal job, he might live a normal life. During one of his breakdowns he wanted to move in with me. I coughed nervously, claiming my landlord would do anything to throw me out of my really cheap rent-controlled apartment and with Mendel around, he'd find a way to break the lease, claiming I was renting out a room.

What's more, in addition to his disability checks, Mendel sells a little grass on the side and the last thing I wanted was one of his disgruntled customers banging at my door in the middle of the night. His apartment is also rent-controlled but he's never happy, always complaining about money and drugs and women while I love my life. You won't get me to apologize for banality. It's my religion. Total predictability. So if I'm so happy, why am I wasting my time with Mendel, a real basket case, a psycho?

I was practically at the subway when I heard sirens roaring up Amsterdam Avenue a block away. My heart aflame, I ran back as fast as I could. There was no need to because the fire trucks were heading north. In the meantime I went back upstairs and sure enough the back burner was lit. I couldn't believe it. A loose piece of paper could have easily drifted in through the open window. I shut the flame, recording my movements in my notebook, so that if any doubts cropped up later, I wouldn't find myself getting on the subway again just to make sure I had shut off the damned gas range.

Mendel was late. I kept myself busy checking out the sights and sounds of Sheridan Square. Everybody looked like someone's fantasy — leather miniskirts, dog collars, frightening Goyaesque tattoos. Weren't they afraid of AIDS? The screaming voices screeching from the subway steps as the Number 1 line deposited new revelers every few minutes made it clear that despite the end of the revolution, here in the Village the night was throbbing with raw, ravenous sex. I suspected there were still private orgies with discreet invitations, but back then orgies were public events. Overnight the laws of sex had changed. No more phone numbers and dates, no more mister nice guy, no more seductions. With a woman at your side you were admitted into Plato's Retreat, a sex palace. I may not be too smart but even I understood that when AIDS buried all the public orgies where sex could be had without saying hello to your partner, Mendel was finished. Now the chicks wanted a Health Department Certificate, or the equivalent. With the rug pulled out from under Mendel's penis, he began to lose his mind.

But not me. Why? Because I was not feasting before AIDS, and the arrival of AIDS didn't start a famine. On the contrary, the fact that I looked plain and non-threatening worked, while Mendel looked like a cross between an Apache Indian and Charles Manson, a look that said you were a wonder in bed. But those days were gone, nobody wanted to deal with that kind of crap anymore. Guys like me were taking over. Not that I run around too much, but when the situation is right, I go for broke and pull out my health certificate. Okay, so maybe the women I meet are not exactly competition for Sophia Loren, but the fact is that one day this cockroachy kind of guy woke up and lo and behold he had turned into a perfectly respectable Mr. Franz Kafka, a sexually content office worker who no longer ran after women.

That's why I love my weekends. In the past I used to jump all over the place, crazy for sex, desperate. But now, once I get home, I nap, later a nice hot tub, soaking myself till early afternoon, defrost a steak.

I like to watch TV, it doesn't matter what's on. But I get a special kick out of Channel 13. I like their shows and I like the fact that I'm a member. I once sent them a small check, got my subscription, and I'm in step with the world, just the present, the eternal present.

"Hey, my man."

We hadn't planned it but Mendel and I were both wearing white shirts open to the third button, dark blue jackets, and jeans. I could smell the marijuana clinging to his clothes, like the remnants of a campfire in the rain. His eyes kept jerking from left to right and right to left, wired to every skirt in the street. Shaking, almost trembling, a film of oily sweat clung to his forehead.

"Ready or not, here I come." He stuck out his tongue like a rattlesnake and written in saliva-resistant black ink were the letters MSG. It would be a long night. I felt the raisins and almonds in my jacket pocket — good-bye Mendel and hello Bellevue.

"Well, I'm ready. Where's the party?" When I put my hand on his shoulder he pulled away, darting between traffic like a blinded cat. Reaching the other side of Seventh Avenue, he stopped in front of the bank where there was an ATM and a long line.

By the time the light changed, and I'd crossed over to Christopher Street, the line waiting for withdrawals had turned into a semi-circle listening to Mendel's harangue.

"Remember Noah's son, Ham? He was cursed. And do you know why? Because he shoved it into Dad, old man Noah, drunk from a night out on the grape — raped by the grape. Canaan came from Ham, cursed to serve his brothers but also cursed to be a slave. Anybody who thinks that he can live the gay life without becoming a slave is a fool."

This was dangerous. I couldn't believe that a few steps from the Bunker Hill of Gay America he was attacking gays. As more and more passersby — a mix between extras from the *Rocky Horror Picture Show* and the occasional suit and tie on the way to a restaurant—crowded around I feared a riot was a distinct possibility, chains, razors hidden between the teeth, broken beer bottles. I wanted a breakdown, not an ambulance to some emergency room to stitch up a knife wound in Mendel's gut.

Without thinking, I approached Mendel and told him we'd be late for the party. I was surprised when he showed no resistance. To make sure he didn't suddenly dart off, I removed my belt and looped it into his, and began to lead him away. I heard someone laugh, and then the *bow wow* of someone drunk, and then I was asked, very politely, if this was some part of a comedy routine.

"Yes," I said, avoiding eye contact. I took a side street, praying we weren't followed. Except for increasing the distance between us and that ATM corner, I had no idea what to do next.

"I had a vision," he said.

"Don't talk so loud."

"What are you, paranoid?"

I thought I saw two bikers, leather jackets on bare, muscular shoulders, staring in our direction. At the next corner I swerved right, onto Cornelia Street and only after we'd gotten to the middle of the block did I release the belt. "Do you realize that this is where Stonewall took place?"

"So what?"

"You're right next door to the holy of holies of the gay world."

"Free speech, Dave."

"Free speech does not include yelling 'fire' in a theater."

"Yeah, but if there is a fire in a theater, and you don't yell, you could be sued for willful negligence."

"Five more minutes and they would have strung you up."

"What about the truth?"

"Mendel. Live and let live."

"Gay sex is a game, a dick contest. One plays master, and the other plays slave."

I didn't say a word. I couldn't tell if he was serious or if he was losing it. Don't be serious, I prayed. Be nuts. But my prayer wasn't answered, at least not immediately.

"Listen, Dave, you think I'm crazy, but I'm not nuts at all. I'm brilliant, and you're lucky that I let you hang out with me. The time has come to speak up."

I decided he was crazy. In my experience there were entertaining breakdowns and crazy breakdowns, and this one was turning into something totally crazy. Nobody in his right mind starts up with gays.

But Mendel wouldn't stop. "Did you ever hear of Abraham Lincoln? There was a war between the states. No more masters, no more slaves. It's finished. But the one place where it isn't finished is right here in the Village. I'm talking about the future of this country. Do you want another Civil War?"

I didn't understand how the earlier part of the night when the breakdown was all about messages and messiahs had been transformed into this boring political nastiness. Maybe he'd had his own gay experience and was acting out, a public confession concealed in an attack. The change was scary but what was even scarier was the reappearance of two leather-clad bikers, their boots so heavy with metal I could hear their steps fifty feet away.

I pushed Mendel toward the vestibule of the first building I saw. "Where's that party? Bank Street, right? What's the address?"

"I don't remember."

"Well, look at the newspaper."

"There's no party, Dave. There's no newspaper. I just made up the whole letter to the *Voice*."

"What are you talking about? You just went through all these different possibilities about MSG. If it wasn't real, why did you insist I drop everything and meet you downtown?"

"You ever have a dream that felt so real you just want to move in for good? The dream began with a letter to the editor about a party in the Village, near the HB Studios, where I once saw a play, and everybody in the dream was upset about MSG, monosodium glutamates. I thought it was a great dream because I knew the letters carried a hidden meaning."

"But maybe there is a party."

"I dreamt it."

"So what." I knew we couldn't stand in this vestibule for the rest of the night, and just as I feared a man with a dog on a leash opened the front door. Luckily, the dog was tiny, no bigger than a sirloin steak.

"Can we help you?" The dog owner towered over both of us.

"Wrong address," I said, guiding Mendel out.

Mendel asked me for a match but I was busy checking the street for those bikers. When the coast was clear, I gave him a light. "Some dreams anticipate the future. Maybe you had a genuine premonition."

Head tilted, eyes wide open, he released a generous smile. "I'm the man, Dave. I'm the dreamer. Mendel, son of Joseph."

"Now let's find the party to prove you're right." I didn't know what I was saying — anything to get us as far away from Stonewall-Bunker Hill as fast as possible — anything that would assign masters and slaves to the back burner.

"Not so fast. The letter said to bring your own take-out order."

"Which letter?"

"In my dream."

"I think they'll understand if we don't come with a take-out order."

"No, Dave, if we're going to do it, we have to do it right."

I craned my neck in all directions, searching for a Chinese restaurant. "Let's try Greenwich Avenue, there has to be something." Sure enough we found a place, but true to the mood of the Village, instead of blazing neon and red Chinese dragons, the restaurant was dark and quiet, with lots of pale wood and what looked like a very expensive bar. We decided on two simple dishes, sesame and noodles, and beef and noodles. While we waited they served us tiny cups of chamomile tea, no charge. Even the take-out cartons resembled expensive china.

After paying twice the price charged in cheaper Chinatown, we headed toward Bank Street. Somewhere in the low sky over the Hudson, the moon looked like a skull. I turned away, afraid I was jinxing myself. I had no idea where exactly we were going, but statistically speaking, there was a chance that someone on Bank Street was having a party tonight.

"Look at the buildings and tell me if any look like the one in your dream."

Mendel shook his head.

"What about that one?" I was pointing to a six-story tenement on the south side of the street.

The building, from a distance, looked like a tenement but turned out to be a luxury apartment house — a dimly lit living room on the street level floor actually a gallery for early American crafts, baskets of pumpkins in the rear and tall brass candlesticks on the mantelpiece above the fireplace. The front door was locked. The same was true for the second, third, fourth, fifth buildings. Running out of buildings, I suggested we try another block.

Mendel walked to the corner, stepped into the gutter and checked out West Eleventh Street.

"Could be."

Even though it was almost midnight, a Laundromat was still open and a small crowd of people was waiting for their cycles to end. The shop was below ground level with steps leading down, but the steps that led up to the entrance of the building revealed wide open front doors. We rushed up, and sure enough the inner door wasn't locked. But a party? We began the climb, turning on each landing, our ears poised. Accused of trespassing, we could always claim we were students of tenement architecture, planning a book on the black and white geometric design of the tiles in the hallway. Then on the fifth floor, the sounds of Otis Redding filled the landing.

I knocked on the door that was slightly ajar, but there was no need to since it swung open by itself, virtually inviting us inside. As we entered, I didn't understand how we had the nerve to walk into a strange apartment. Part of me wanted to run back to Sheridan Square and get on the first uptown train. But part of me was curious what a real New York party might be like. And I could tell this was a real New York party because there was something democratic about the people's faces: no single age dominated, the very old wrapped in woolen sweaters despite the heat, and the very young with more rings in their ears than hair on their head, all so delighted to be in each other's company. The more quiet and shy guests checked the titles in the bookcases as if this apartment was really a bookstore on the fifth floor.

Walking through the long foyer, we passed the kitchen where a man stood biting into a chicken wing, the skin of his face stretched so tight against the bones he looked almost cadaverous. When he saw Mendel he broke into a wide, almost wicked grin, greeting him with a huge bear hug.

"Hey, you brought a take-out order, great. Listen, if it has anything to do with monosodium glutamates, your story might be the most painful one tonight and you could walk away with Miss Suffering, met by chance at the home of Lee Garber because a similar experience in life brought you two together. Lots of restaurants use MSG, but we have a special fondness for Chinese restaurants, so if your story begins with egg roll or lo mein, or what not, you get extra credit." Lee Garber took Mendel by the shoulder, "And you did suffer, didn't you?"

Mendel only nodded. Perhaps he was genuinely psychic? Walking into an apartment on a street parallel to Bank Street was one thing, but an MSG party? This was beyond coincidence. This was absolutely uncanny.

People stood around in groups of two or three, nodding, sipping wine being served from a huge punch bowl. One sip was all I wanted, and floating at the bottom of the glass were bits of cinnamon bark and grains of ginger.

I was hoping someone would explain what was going on, but all I saw were people with take-out orders in their hands, and Lee Garber assigning numbers to each dish, and then appointing a panel of three judges who would get to taste each of the dishes. After our take-out order was assigned a number, it joined all the other bags on the table.

There were eighteen dishes in all — our number was eighteen — and it took nearly half an hour for each of the judges to taste the different orders. In the end, the number nine was chosen, but the winner remained anonymous. To avoid a second round of tasting, Lee suggested they take the square root of nine. And that's how number three was chosen.

A woman sipping a glass of white wine began to weep. "I can't believe it."

Lee Garber bent over to reassure the young woman. "Don't worry. We love you. Just tell us your name."

"Anna Rubin."

"Say, 'My name is Anna Rubin.'"

"My name is Anna Rubin. All right, it was just another night and I was riding home from work, should I mention where? All right ..."

The second "all right" seemed too studied, too formal. Definitely something was going on. If there was any hidden message to the real nature of this party, I had to pay attention to every word she was saying, concentrating with all my might.

A woman carrying two drinks asked if I would like a refill. She wore a bitter, miserable frown, as if she'd been dragged into serving drinks. Even though I had never seen her before, I sensed that beneath it all she could also be in a state of pure bliss, hiding her real beauty. If that were so, I would leave with her. But unless I got a message loud and clear, I wasn't going anywhere. Just then she leaned over and whispered into my ear, "Messiah Son of God."

Oh no! Now I was in for it. It had happened. Mendel was not only a psychic, he was a prophet.

I looked at her. "Where?"

"Right here."

"Here? Who?"

"You."

Something froze inside my brain.

"You're kidding."

"God doesn't joke."

"Who are you?"

"My name is Nancy. What's yours?"

"Dave. Were you ever in Bellevue?"

"Never."

"What are you doing here?"

"Number seven. You want to taste it?"

"I'm nine," which was only half a lie.

"I knew it. You won. You won for a reason. You're the Messiah."

"I don't think so."

"You're the one who got the message. You understand the dangers of monosodium glutamates. You have a mission. It all adds up to one thing. You've met all the criteria."

"Is that all you need to be the Messiah? It doesn't sound right. What about angels, visions, transcendent light?"

"You've been reading too many books."

"I'm not the Messiah, Nancy. I'm just Dave, a regular guy."

"Of course you're a regular guy. The Messiah is the humblest person who ever lived."

"Nancy. Where am I?"

"You don't know?"

"Is this a party?"

"If you want it to be."

"For MSG sufferers?"

"Among others."

"Who made the party? I mean I came here with a friend of mine. He dreamt this party. He had some sort of premonition. Amazing. If there's any Messiah around here, you better speak to him. Mendel, I mean even his initials, MSG, make sense, Mendel Son of God."

Turning her head, she seemed to vanish into thin air. A few moments passed and then I noticed her carrying two drinks and whispering something into someone's ear. I couldn't hear a word, but I knew what she was saying, Messiah Son of God.

Where am I, I wondered? What am I doing here? Someone tapped me on the shoulder.

"I was worried about you," I said when I saw it was Mendel.

"That makes two of us."

"What kind of place did you bring me to?"

"Hey, Dave. Let's get things straight. You brought me here. Remember, I was doing fine in the street."

"But you were right all along. A woman came over to me, and out of the blue said those three words, and pointed at me, like she thought maybe it was me. Me? How did you know what MSG stands for?"

"Life is strange, Dave. You want to hang out here, or do you want get something to eat?"

"I'm asking you a question. Who are you, Mendel? Where am I? Who are these people?"

I began to cry, not sure what was going on. I didn't understand if Mendel was messing up my mind. Had someone put acid or speed in the punch? Maybe he really wanted to hurt me. All these people began to look weird; I had to get out of there immediately. But I couldn't move.

"Mendel, can you get me home, please?"

"Should I call someone first?"

"No, just get me home."

"Or maybe I should call the hospital."

"I don't know."

"What about St. Vincent's. They're the closest. Or maybe Bellevue. They have the experience. I can vouch for that."

"Why should I go to a hospital?"

"Dave, you're not feeling very well, you know that. But things are more complicated. The cops will have to take you there. You can't just walk in off the street. But for the police to come, they need a reason."

"What should I do?"

"The easiest thing is to remove all your clothes. That's the best thing. Someone makes the phone call, the police arrive, and the rest is Bellevue."

"I can't do that, Mendel."

"Why not? It's easy. Start with your shoes. It's the easiest thing in the world. Then socks. Pants. Look, just follow me. Look at what I'm doing. It's no problem."

Mendel began to remove his shoes and socks. And so did I. I heard someone say, "Hey what are they doing?" but we ignored them. Mendel was right. It was easy. I was tired, I just wanted to rest. From a distance I heard a siren getting louder and louder, but it was all right. The police would take me to Bellevue, and right next to me would be Mendel. They'd take us both. And later, when I would get around to telling people about this hospitalization, no one would believe me that it happened on the night when a beautiful woman told me that she thought I was Messiah Son of God, and despite the fact that I tried to tell her she was wrong, that I was a nobody, that I couldn't get my life together, she insisted that God moves in mysterious ways and that I was one of his chosen ones.

I bet she was right. Now I know why I'm so happy. Simply because I am chosen. Except I wasn't quite sure how that works out. I don't know any foreign languages, I barely know the Bible, just a few stories. Can it really be true that I will save the world? But it makes sense that

God would choose me. What's the big deal if God chooses someone who's a big success in life, in everything, a great being, like one of the prophets. It was time for the simple people, the plain people, just a regular guy who needed his sleep and his pills and his cups of coffee, and an occasional magazine. I would make a fine Messiah, when the time came. A happy Messiah — the happiest Messiah who ever lived.

THE
ghost
FROG

We have no children. About once a month I get *moyreh shkhoyreh*, a kind of Jewish "Gloomy Sunday" six days a week, not quite depression, more like a black desperation, "black" because there's no way out and "desperate" because having been educated in the sin-and-punishment world of the yeshiva, not being able to have children forces you to remember your sins. Even now, years after a normal Jewish agnosticism should have turned into a normal American hedonism, I fall sway to the old ways. I don't know if it's around the new moon, or the full moon, but when Brenda's period arrives, I crack like a soft-boiled egg.

In such a state, I avoid answering the phone in case it's Len or May asking us to baby-sit Lisa, their seven-year-old. We live in the same apartment building, the two most "Jewish" couples who always know which festival is coming up and which shade of guilt we should be feeling.

Lisa knows she has a key to my heart, but there are times when I can't look at her. It hurts too much. Usually, she runs wild in our kitchen, tasting ketchup, honey, tahini, even soy sauce. I say no to nothing, not even meat mixed with milk. Whenever her parents fall behind in their design deadlines, Lisa is escorted to the elevator by Len or May, she presses the number five on the panel, and is then met by a member of the Kotz family, Brenda or myself. The parenting manuals Len and May subscribe to encourage independent actions such as taking the elevator alone: what could possibly happen between "seven," where the Glicks live, and "five," where we live. What could possibly happen? Come on! Six could happen, I tell Len, but he laughs. There's always a "six," I insist. That's me. Fear of the sixes, fear of the mysterious stranger hurting a beautiful little girl with auburn hair, slightly slanted eyes, and a shyness that breaks your heart.

When Lisa sleeps over, she arrives with a library of story books, her Hug Me doll, and pink Care Bear pajamas abloom with hearts. When she hugs me good night, I have to make up all kinds of stories as to why I look sad. Lisa wants to name her next doll after me. I consider it a compliment. Until she gets the doll, she has a special pillow crocheted with the shapes of camels and horses and buffaloes, which she calls Samuel the Pillow.

I have not been the most important thing in anyone else's life for a long time. Brenda is too busy to hold hands, and I'm too embarrassed. If there's any difference between us, it is that she, a child of Yiddish-speaking socialists, believes in blind fate, while I, a child of Yiddish-speaking Orthodox Jews, still look for meaning to this madness.

I suspect the real reason why Brenda is so busy is if she had one free moment, she'd be forced to feel her pain, live with it, wrestle fate instead of accepting it. She says she can live without children, but I don't believe her. She says she's too old, but what's too old today? She says the doctors made a mistake in the tests, but all the tests say everything is fine. She calls it fate and goes off to work; I call it heaven banging my forehead.

She has two, not one, full-time jobs. She teaches during the day, sacrificing her sanity to undo the damage of the corrupt ghetto, and at night she retrieves some of that sanity by reporting on cultural affairs for WEVD, a station that broadcasted exclusively in Yiddish but now shares its frequency with other orphan languages: Korean, Greek, Chinese. Everyone is impressed with the no-nonsense, lion-maned, bilingual reporter who's rejected offers from both WNBC and WCBS radio, making her a WEVD legend.

Naturally, she is somewhat of a legend in her school as well. She can bring her students to a live radio studio, revealing a world that until hours ago had been totally sealed, and by lifting the veil of the inscrutable box with dials and numbers, she instills in her poverty-stricken charges a dream. The kids no longer see her as teacher but as a magician from another world.

She's even made it possible for professionals, like Lisa's father, a high-strung art director, to visit her class. He returned thrilled by how quickly the kids caught on to the principles of design and typeface. Like me, Len had never stepped inside a public school building in his life except to vote.

Before Lisa was born, Len and May and Brenda and I got together every second or third weekend, putting out a nice spread, all kinds of appetizing delights, wine, beer, homemade egg creams, while watching *The Honeymooners* and only afterwards would I think these gatherings may have had something to do with our childhood Friday night Sabbath dinners. But after Lisa was born, Len and May opened an independent studio in Chelsea, and studio became a euphemism for life. While Lisa was still a tot, they could bring her to the studio and keep her in the crib all day, but when she was old enough to wander around and trip and cut herself, the Glicks turned to the Kotzes.

At Lisa's first birthday, we felt like the proud parents-in-law.

We were Lisa's first choice of babysitters, sometimes taking her for an entire weekend while Len and May worked through the night and napped on cots trying to finish three projects that were all due yesterday. Devoted, warm, all hugs and *oohs* and *ahhs*, Brenda was the only person May would trust to be with Lisa for two days straight.

But now taking care of Lisa has fallen into my hands. Everyone agrees Lisa's very happy with me. Of the four adults, I'm obviously the least ambitious, a no-stress city job in the Board of Estimates, which I became eligible for by taking a few accounting courses, even though my B.A. was in English. That I've been trying to write fiction doesn't interest anyone anymore, particularly Brenda who's heard the story once too often. What do you expect when the "promising" writer is a year shy of his twentieth college reunion with nothing to show for his effort. A lot of people depend on Brenda and Len and May. They are part of the real world. While Lisa and I don't have the deadlines that people in radio, advertising, and publishing have, we have needs, so naturally we've come into each other's lives. She needs a babysitter who doesn't look at the clock and I need to be admired for my self-sacrifice and devotion.

We have something else in common—both of us love stories. I love Ruth Prawer Jhablava and Milan Kundera and George Eliot, and she loves *Snow White* and *Cinderella* and *Rumpelstiltskin*. Lisa's been able to read from the age of five, but she likes to hear the voice of another person.

We sit in Prospect Park on a wooden bench; one of the slats is missing. Strangers think I'm her father. It's the only time anyone ever smiles at me. In public with Brenda I'm rigid and awkward; wherever we go she runs into someone she knows. But Lisa knows nobody, nor do I. We watch the squirrels scurrying to and fro, kneeling for nuts, and although a cold November day with just a scratch of sun usually fills me with a hopeless dread, with Lisa a squirrel is one of the wonders of creation.

I try my hand at a fairy tale:

Once upon a time there lived a frog named S and a witch named B and if she hadn't needed a frog's heart for her witch's brew, they would have never met, married, and hated. After one hour with the frog she knew his tiny green heart fit the bill. The witch removed her cape, chiseled down her long nose, and costumed herself in the cloak of a princess, telling the frog that he was really a prince who'd been locked up inside the skin of a frog by a wicked witch. Since this was what the frog secretly believed all these years, the princess's revelation made him understand his fate, and he began to wait for the day when he'd again become a prince.

Lisa is not impressed with my fairy tale. She wants to know what happens next, and I tell her this is a psychological fairy tale, not much happens, except the witch and the frog fight all the time. I discover that explaining what psychological means is one of the hardest things I've ever done.

"That's boring. Who is S?"

"It's just a letter."

"And B?"

"B is the second letter in the alphabet."

"B stands for Brenda and S stands for Samuel," Lisa says.

"I just made up those letters."

"No, you didn't. You think you're a frog and Brenda is a witch. Why?"

Is this how a father feels when he realizes he's sired a genius?

"Don't you want to hear the rest of the story?"

"Only if something happens."

I like my fairy tale, even though Lisa doesn't. Maybe I should consider opening it up more to the world.

"Lisa, I forgot there's another letter in my fairy tale, an M." But she's fallen asleep. Her lips, four curved lines, brush an invisible pear.

M stands for my mother. She knew someone who knew someone who was moving to California. She understood that a certain kind of woman — her kind — would never marry me as long as I lived in a tiny studio, no kitchen to speak of. So she made sure that when the big day finally arrived, the bride-to-be would have a decent place to live in, and a locked building to boot. It just so happened that a Mr. and Mrs. Glick also lived there. I wonder if Lisa can understand the implications of people influencing the cause-and-effect of existence, how my entire life would be different if not for a stranger who moved to Los Angeles. I wouldn't be sitting on this park bench at this very moment, thinking these thoughts, aching for a child. Instead, I would have aches I never even imagined existed. Are there spheres of reality — little universes — where the implications of alternative decisions are lived, so that in addition to my life here in Brooklyn, there are other Brooklyns, an infinite number of Brooklyns, where Samuel Kotz never met Brenda, never didn't have children, never chose this moment to awaken Lisa from her nap?

———

We have become very close. I love how she takes my hand when we cross the street, heading for the museum. Inside the majestic hall I point out the tall columns and vast ceilings. She listens, she watches people, she asks questions. I forget that Lisa is only seven. Hungry, we head for the museum cafeteria where she invents imaginary conversations between the French fries and the ketchup. I whisper for the salt.

Later we come across a new exhibit of German expressionists loaned by the Federal Republic. Most of the painters died a good twenty or thirty years after the war, in Germany, and the dates strike me. Many of the works are grotesque. Lisa is fascinated by the colors, particularly the painting of a purple fox, which she says would make a beautiful cover for a book about fairy tales. If anyone other than the child of two designers had said that, I would have been astonished, but Lisa is just Lisa. Very little she does isn't astonishing.

"Samuel, if he painted a purple fox one day, do you think he ever painted a green lion or a red bear?"

"Or a gold frog?" I add.

"Like you?"

"Me! Am I frog?"

"That's what you said."

"But that was a fairy tale."

"Anyway, I like frogs. I like the sounds they make. I like Kermit a lot."

And she begins to make sounds like *drip, croak, vrip, drrrip.*

"Why do you like that sound?" I say.

"Because no one else can make it, not even a lion or tiger."

I weigh her words, looking for raw truth. I think she's touched gold. My mistake is trying to sound like a lion, when I should face my *vripping* frogness. A dark cloud turns white. I want to hug Lisa and lavish her with kisses, but I don't dare. The news is rife with awful reports about daycare workers who sexually abuse small children, some younger than Lisa. So I must be very careful when I'm with her. At most I hold her hand. But she has just singled in on an amazing fact. Frogs have unique voices.

I begin my tale with four words: I am a frog, alas, one of the first frogs in history who doesn't dream he's really a prince cursed by a witch. But straight away I feel the dialectic itch, and start on the ifs and buts. Maybe my frog is cute in theory, but in reality he still cherishes the vain hope of being rewarded a special recognition for his meekness; even though he himself is not of royal blood, he'll soon be keeping the company of lions, kings, and princesses.

I keep at it for days, scribbling like a madman about frogs and lions, frogs and monkeys, frogs and fishermen, frogs and frogs. I wonder if I could write about a frog who contemplates suicide. Rope or sleeping pills? Poor frog, even if he wants to pack it all in, all he can do is starve himself to death or sacrifice himself to a bird of prey.

———————

Brenda is away from the apartment much of the time, a conference way uptown at the Jewish Theological Seminary, something about literature and religion. Her odd hours allow me to work late into the night. All I really care about is becoming good enough so that Brenda Novak-Kotz will interview Samuel Kotz, the author of the new short story collection about cafeteria types, on her radio show and afterwards reveal her guest's real identity. We'd become the couple of the hour.

Brenda, in certain circles, has a growing reputation. She can get a ticket to the yearly sold out Elie Wiesel lectures at the last minute — for free! And if Roth ever reads in New York she'd be the first to know about it, a reserved front row seat. It should have been easy for Samuel Kotz. She'd wave her magic wand and I'd join the wrights of the round table, where the pen was the sword and the dragons were the empty white pages that had to be tamed. But she no longer seems interested in my work. Only last month she coordinated a panel comprised of young writers exploring their personal vision of the role of the Jewish writer as a modern-day prophet. True, all three nouns bothered me — *vision, writer, and prophet* — yet it would have been gratifying to be considered, despite shades of nepotism. A year ago I might have bought her yarn that the forum was limited to writers grappling with religious issues, but signs of dashed hope are all around us. She has virtually stopped reading anything I write, and when she does read it, her comments are brusque and brief. Little by little I'm beginning to believe it's the apartment, with a view of the lower Manhattan skyline that she fell in love with — I simply came with the lease.

From the bottom drawer of my desk, I pull out an unfinished draft, a suicide story I've been working on for ages. Brenda has never liked any of the versions — worthless, a waste of time. Who wants to read about suicide.

Who? I do! I'm very interested in why someone decides it's better to bite the dust than breathe it. My story is not a figment of my imagination, a projection of the unconscious, but based on real life — a close friend whose death I never completely understood.

It's way past midnight, a hot August night so humid my undershirt sticks to my skin. A thermos of black coffee sits next to me, as strong as Latin America. I'm getting close to the end, stripping down the piece to its barest bones, layer after layer until I can feel its skeletal shape.

In the next room, Brenda is fast asleep. Soon I will bring my manuscript for her inspection. I will wake her, but as usual she will not like it. Then tomorrow I will rewrite the story, and in a few days I will ask her to read it again. I fear that she will never like it, disapproving of every version. I will write and rewrite, and she will always reject.

This is my nightmare, how I've reduced my entire life to see if I can write the story of Kalman's death for Brenda's approval. But this is insane!

Or maybe it's not so insane at all. If my struggle with the story symbolizes the struggle with my marriage, then reviving the piece, making Kalman's suicide come alive, so to speak, might miraculously revive my dead marriage — and it is dead — a kind of reverse voodoo. The challenge is to breathe new life into the piece. Plain, simple life instead of obsessing over language, always trying to squeeze out a secret melody suspended somewhere between stressed and unstressed syllables, amplifying the inaudible breath hidden within the letters. To hell with trying to reveal the mystery of existence in nothing but sounds; it's time I get down to basics, the ABCs of suicide.

Out of coffee, I get up for a refill. A breeze, out of nowhere, teases me toward the window, but then I feel the breeze against my back. Turning, I accidentally knock over the empty thermos, sending tiny slivers of silvery glass all over the floor. I'm on the floor, trying pick up the broken glass with my bare fingers when Brenda opens the bedroom door. I point to the broken thermos, and without a word she returns with a broom and dustpan. I feel stupid, like an alcoholic caught hiding his whiskey in a thermos. I want to cry, but there are no tears.

"Aren't you coming to bed?"

"Soon."

"Aren't you going to work tomorrow?"

I don't say a word. Brenda goes back to bed. I go back to the page. The truth is I should interview her for the story. Kalman, shy around women, intrigued Brenda long after most people had begun to find him an intolerable bore.

He surprised everyone by applying to law school. But by the end of the semester he was back in Brooklyn, not a word as to why he quit. Thin as a rail, reeking of nicotine, totally broke, Kalman ended up in his parents' basement somewhere in Mill Basin. He needed very little money, just enough for cigarettes, coffee, the occasional subway into Manhattan where he haunted bookstores. But when his parents moved to Florida, something snapped.

Caught shoplifting, Kalman insisted that there was a fundamental difference between theft of an object which resulted in the depletion of the object's inherent value, and "borrowing" which resulted in no depletion at all. Kalman provided the judge with a detailed record of the books he'd "borrowed" from some of New York's leading literary bookstores, how long he'd kept them at home, and the dates he'd returned them, all in pristine condition.

The judge ordered a psychiatric examination; Kalman borrowed one of my jackets and a good silk tie. Even when the questions were provocative, he remained calm. Nor did he offer a word of protest when he was warned that all bookstores in NYC were now off-limits to him. Afraid of another arrest, Kalman began to visit old friends, often near midnight, with a list of requests for books. He also demanded all his old letters back, claiming he had copyrighted them. If informed there were no letters, he insisted on examining the files. He dropped in on everyone except us, which was strange because we were drowning in books, plus I had a batch of letters from his California days.

And then I found out why. From us, it wasn't enough to collect letters. One night fire engines roar up, sirens, flashing red lights, windows jerking open, where's the fire, where's the fire? A small army of men with hooks and oxygen tanks charge into the building, but they don't have to run any further than the lobby where a crude arson attempt is blazing. Not far away, Kalman is picked up with a quart of kerosene and a delirious look in his eye, and then rushed off to Kings County. This time he cannot talk his way out of it. We knew his days were numbered. Someone who starts a fire in the hallway of a Brooklyn apartment house where the floor is mosaic tile, the walls plaster, the stairwells steel, and there isn't a piece of wood in sight except the frame of a painting near the elevator, is either not serious or not all there. I knew he was very serious.

How he took his life belongs in *Ripley's Believe it or Not*. Ovens were lit, he swallowed pills, slit wrists, and he hung himself — in that order. A multiple suicide. The police, the doctors, the orderlies, no one had ever seen anything like it.

I keep working on the story. Religiously. Then one night I again feel a breeze entering the room. This time, before stretching my head out the window, I make sure the thermos is nowhere near me. Only then do I take a deep breath. I can feel the breeze struggling up Ocean Avenue, like a new-born creation, all the way from the Atlantic. Before I understand what's going on, I am drenched in some other-world sweetness. Not just the breeze, or the moon slipping across the August night like a yellow egg, but even the heavens seem to be spitting out a shower of silver grapes and raisins and tropical necklaces. *Ohhhhhshhhhhinnn*. I repeat the word "ocean" like a mantra, until the *shin* of Ocean merges with the end of time, and I know that if I don't regain control of my heart, it will shatter like the dropped thermos.

I close my eyes and rest. When I get back to the story, I'm not sure if I'm seeing straight. Something on the page is different, and then it crosses my mind that maybe the breeze isn't an Ocean Avenue creation, flowing for three miles against traffic — what if it escaped from the page itself. I peek at the language, snip at the words like a dog at a bone, swallowing paragraphs whole. By the time I get to the end I know the piece is finished. I feel alive, light, the exquisite ecstasy of escaping the gravity of the page.

Maybe I should wait until morning, but I cannot stop the pounding in my heart. I must wake my wife to test my ecstasy. And then to share it.

"Brenda?"

She stirs sleepily, pulling the cotton covers up to her chin.

"Did I wake you?" I touch her cheek. Her eyes open. She seems dazed.

"I think it happened tonight. The words just kept pouring out of me. Nothing I've ever done is quite like it."

"So important that you had to wake me?"

I don't answer.

"Okay, but get me a cup of coffee, strong."

Even before the water's boiling, she's already devouring the pages. "Must you glare at me?"

I retreat into the crowded kitchen, cluttered with cast-iron pots, spice racks, jars of every shape and size, and stare intensely into the dark, Brooklyn night. It has begun to rain, a soft, healing drizzle. Gazing out the window, I lose myself within the mysterious cloak of anonymity and silence. Across the way shadows of figures framed in brick and wood, like a flickering candle, stir from time to time. Who knows anything about anyone, who these people are, what their lives are like, their sorrows, their stories. It makes me feel sad, but it's the kind of sadness I love, peaceful, content.

When I walk back into the bedroom with a fresh cup, Brenda lifts her eyes. It's a long, silent moment, no one says a word, not a sound. I yearn for a smile, a dazzle of teeth, but her sea-green eyes look mystified, confused.

"I'm afraid not, Samuel. This isn't it."

The roof collapses. "Are you sure?" Unable to breathe, I struggle beneath the bricks, the wooden beams, the tangled electrical wiring.

"The character is a creep. It's impossible to sympathize with him. For all I care he should have done it years ago."

It must be past 3:00 a.m. But how can I go to sleep with a judgment like this hanging over the story?

"Maybe you're just too tired now. Would you look at it again tomorrow?"

"The story is off, period."

I know I shouldn't have woken her. Outside, the silence of Brooklyn is complete, as if some force has sucked up the sounds of the world.

"Tomorrow then?"

"Tomorrow." Brenda sounds drugged. "Tomorrow what?"

"Just ten minutes. Can you give it ten minutes. Or five, maybe just five?"

Before I hear a yes or a no, Brenda is fast asleep.

Am I obsessed? Instead of waiting until the morning, I open a fresh ten ounce jar of Yuban coffee. Despite the magical breeze, the silver grapes, the tropical necklaces, I start from the beginning. By the time Brenda has showered, I'm ready to show her a new opening. She reads the first paragraph between bites of toast, the marmalade so thick an orange mustache licks her upper lip. Right away she announces that the story is too depressing. When I plead that she give it at least a few more minutes, not twenty seconds, she insists that I stop concentrating exclusively on private pain, and should consider the news, ordinary human concerns. "Whoever gets too caught up in his own life has to step outside and consider other realities. It's so simple, how can you overlook it?"

I'm about to ask her if it's my life she's worried about or her own — since a major character in the suicide story is based on her, but

I maintain a guarded silence. One of the areas we've never discussed is how much of her life I'm allowed to put in my fiction. Would she consider it a betrayal if I described what she likes in bed, what I like in bed, assuming we went to bed on occasion. Or would she expect that I change details, so that if I love the way she once gave me fellatio, once and once only, its memory should never cross over to the written page? Do I have the right to invent a wife whose lips seek out her husband's penis, unlike the reality of our bedroom?

Fine, I shall consider her advice. I'll put away my story and start reading headlines. Atlanta has been in the news, children killed, a murderer loose, no leads. I sip coffee, hold an unlit cigarette between my lips, and think about a story someone could create based on this sequence of events. What if the police are looking for only one man, but it turns out that for every dead child there's a separate murderer. Uncanny, of course, but there could be a Cult of Evil with followers not afraid to carry out their master's orders. With a snap of his fingers this evil worship could put any city in America under siege, terrorize any town, even blackmail the government, simply by killing children across the land, and no one will ever know where he'll strike next.

Does this make better reading? Later that night, when I tell my wife the plot, she looks at me as if I'm nuts.

"You have a twisted mind, Samuel."

"But how do you know this isn't happening in Atlanta?"

"It's one person, one maniac."

"But what if it isn't?"

During the Atlanta episode, I feel fortunate that the Glicks trust us. But what if something crazy happens to me, a force enters my mind and commands me to do something evil? Do such things exist? That's what Son of Sam says happened to him. He worked in the post office. Most mass murderers are shy, quiet people who work at ordinary jobs, but their fantasy lives are elaborately twisted. I work in the Board of Estimates. There are inspectors who appraise property. I simply check figures. The appraisers are not required to know arithmetic. It's a stupid job. Without me the city would do just as well. I have an unhappy inner life with fantasies of grandeur; maybe I'm a potential murderer too. Lisa is the most beautiful thing in the world. But the papers are filled with people who kill the only thing they love. Who killed John Lennon?

––––––––

When word of Kalman's death reached us, Brenda refused to attend the funeral. There was only one scheduled eulogy. After the requisite Psalms, including those that began with each letter of Kalman's name, *kuf, lamed, mem, nun*, the rabbi employed by the funeral home spoke about the tragedy of a wasted life, an only son who had suffered much in his few years. But before we could blink an eye, the theme shifted from a young man's shocking death to a eulogy for the parents who, perhaps fortunately, hadn't lived to witness their son's death, Pinchas and Esther Jenkowitz, two people who had been through the suffering, the hell of Hitler, camps, hunger, thirst, beatings … rebuilding a life in New York. Any moment I expected him to ask for six volunteers to light six candles for the six million.

At one point he asked — almost pleaded — for anyone in the audience to say a few words. I should have sprung to my feet, not only because Kalman deserved his own eulogy, but to correct the wrong impression the rabbi had given of a wasted life. But I felt paralyzed, locked, my throat suddenly parched, my mind a blank, my legs chained. Was it shyness or absolute inexperience of speaking in public? It didn't matter. Glued to my seat, I couldn't move. I could have spoken about Kalman's erudition, overwhelming professors with his knowledge of Hobbes, Spencer, Joyce. Most of us used the public library but from an early age Kalman amassed his own collection, underlining everything, notes along the margins, dog-eared copies of Rilke and Kant — in German no less. Although he didn't write fiction himself, he insisted that I take classes after graduation. But not in an MFA program, rather individual classes at NYU or the New School or CUNY, thereby maintaining independence. And it was he, of all people, who encouraged me to take basic accounting classes that would qualify me for a city job, thus avoiding membership in any literary family. Making it or breaking it on my own, no one to blame, no one to tame.

With a few moving descriptions of Kalman's wit, brilliance, humor and yes, even his humility, I could have altered the mood by revealing a complex personality, a generous human being, a caring friend, a person committed to the pursuit of knowledge. Maybe I could have produced a tear, one sob of genuine regret.

But the moment passed, the rabbi stepped back, no one stepped forward, and the pallbearers were called to bear the body away.

Three days after the funeral, a letter arrived from a medical lab on Madison Avenue, an announcement that Brenda and Samuel Kotz were the beneficiaries of Mr. Kalman Jenkowitz's generous deposit of twelve vials of sperm to be stored in their frozen sperm bank for the next twenty years.

I had no idea what to make of Kalman's gesture. Was he saying that I would fail to impregnate my wife while he, even from six feet under, could do more for the next generation than I could ever do from six feet above? Or was it some kind of Iago move, a last desperate attempt to strike out, tempting me — gullible Othello — into believing that my wife had betrayed me, evil for the sake of evil, simply to cause a human being pain. Or perhaps it was true that he and Brenda had an affair, and these accusations being flung from the grave were the only way he could confess the truth. Or maybe it was a test of my character, knowing my pride would reject his offer while my humility should accept the fact that if I could not impregnate my wife I should step aside — no question of sexual undertones, simply the achievements of modern science.

I stared at Brenda, keeping my theories close to the chest.

After tearing the letter into tiny shreds, she announced that Kalman was much sicker than she had ever imagined. "Why in the world would I ever want to impregnate myself with his sperm!"

———————

Since I call my story "The ABC's of Suicide," I need to stick to the plain and simple. A sub-plot about a cyrogenic lab and liquid nitrogen, with a little digression about Kalman's macabre attempt at resurrection, will only confuse things.

Brenda does not yield — she will read no more suicide versions, refusing even to glance at the first sentence.

Not sure where to turn, I call Lisa's father at his studio and inquire if he's willing to look at my latest piece, but he's buried under a ton of projects. Lisa's mother, May, also begs off, never a fan of fiction. I then call up Nathan Lefkowitz, someone I met in a New School course. Although he edits a pharmaceutical journal during the day, he writes nights and most weekends. He agrees to read the piece, asking me to drop it off at the receptionist's desk. A week later we meet at a Broadway luncheonette. He orders fish, I settle for something light, hot chocolate and a cinnamon bun. Without delay Nathan goes for the autobiographical, he didn't know I had spent so many years in San Francisco. I tell him I was never there — it's fiction. He says "come on." When I repeatedly ask him if the story works on any level, he apologizes and says that ever since the company introduced flowcharts, it's hard for him to tune into the narrative inevitability of a story.

"Actually, I didn't have time to finish it, but I'm really curious about California."

I suggest that he can finish it now. He explains that he cannot concentrate when someone stares.

"But could you analyze some of the parts you did read?"

Nathan, buttering a slice of bread, narrows his eyes. "You want me to discuss your story, but why do you resist telling me what really happened to you on the coast? Are you that cheap with your life?"

I don't answer, my attention tuning into a rock song on the radio. I can smell cinnamon under my nose as I watch Nathan debone a piece of fish, chewing it like an intense, wary cat. Was I cheap? Or the kind of person who's afraid to throw anything out just in case it might be useful one day. Brenda once called me a penny-pinching accountant unable to balance his books. Instead of getting rid of the extra fat that I smeared my sentences with, loaded down with gobs of awkward plots and half-baked characters, better off in a trash can, I kept finding ways to sneak everything back in once I was sure no one was looking.

"I will say one thing." Nathan's face moves away from mine. "I believe that a character doesn't have the right to look at the world as unreal, bizarre, or fragmented unless he has an independent income and is willing to invest in his sensibility by founding a magazine, but until that day, the character should consider the possibility of a nine-to-five job."

Not knowing what to say, I nod. I don't want to be appear rude. Parting, I retrieve my manuscript, as clean as a new toothbrush. Splitting the bill down to the last nickel, we've become two strangers. Turning to Nathan to read the piece made about as much sense as stopping a total stranger in the street and asking if they'd be willing to donate a half hour in a new market survey, testing a new product, a piece of narrative, no experience necessary. Coffee on me.

Who needs Nathan?

Some would be intrigued, flattered, even excited.

Manhattan, where the stream of moving people discourages impulse surveys, surrenders to my desire to head home to Brooklyn where the pace is slower and the sky is wider.

Climbing out of the subway, I assure myself that a spontaneous survey is a legitimate method to test the market. To confirm that I am a genuine writer, I note the beauty in little things, a lone light in an abandoned building, a neon cocktail glass ablaze in a curtained storefront, the lit end of a cigarette butt cast away on the sidewalk. But mostly I look at women and feel lonely and sad. My wife is more beautiful, more alive than all of them, but something has gone terribly wrong. Instead of being in love, we are in hate, a state of mind that results from wanting to receive and not getting, or wanting to give and no one accepting.

A new theory about my suicide piece strikes me — that my story is nothing but a disguised eulogy for Kalman, to kill the guilt I must feel for not prying my mouth open when the rabbi begged for honorary eulogists.

Kalman, a major force in my life, advised me not to marry Brenda, pointing out that she was much too fiery for someone like me. When he tried to warn me of the consequences of a frog getting into bed with a lion, I was so upset by the violation of the privacy of the bedroom I wasn't able to listen to the substance of his words, the shock of hearing him compare me — my manhood, my sexuality, my authority — to that of an ugly bleeping, creeping frog while Brenda was a wild, sexy, powerful woman with a mane of hair that could make any other creature in the jungle step back in fear and shame. The only thing wrong about Kalman's prediction was that Brenda was a lion in life but not in bed, and I was a frog in both. Basically he was right, though. Brenda and I were two species who met, married, and grew miserable because at best, I croaked and she roared, mismatched from the first red pencil scratch.

No matter where I start out from I seem to end up near the zoo, this time its southern exposure, not far from the old Ebbets Field where the Dodgers once played. After waiting for the light to turn green, I find myself on a stretch of Flatbush Avenue I've never been to. The sky has darkened, a flash storm, the rain hard enough to threaten the manuscript I've brought along. I consider temporary shelter inside a small luncheonette. Peering through the window I notice few customers, most sitting alone at a table. Everyone looks sad, and I'm afraid unhappy people will use my characters for batting practice. One woman, the lean features of a starved dancer, scribbles madly, her ashtray filled with cigarettes. Another man, bearded like a rabbi or a Russian Orthodox priest, closes his eyes after pondering a difficult passage in his book. I'm about to enter when I notice an older black woman getting change from the cashier and dropping it into a round metal box. Then and there I decide she's my reader, sensitive and compassionate. We'll connect—both for friendship and moral support—across the black/white chasm, she for my stories and I for her charities.

Am I doing the right thing? I'll introduce myself, explain my objectives, and hand her the story. But she walks quickly. At Lefferts Avenue she turns suddenly, her umbrella wide enough for two people. "Are you following me?" Before I can explain, I hear a shriek from her whistle, and she's running, another shriek. I'm aghast, the light is green, but if I run back, I'll give myself away, as if I'm guilty. But guilty of what? Trying to ask someone to read a story I wrote. I must let them know that I'm not who they think I am. I am not a predator, I'm not a rapist, I'm just me, Samuel the Pillow, I make sounds, fine, healthy, innocent sounds, frog sounds. Everybody knows that frogs aren't dangerous. They're nice and funny, and green and cuddly, maybe ugly, beady eyes and green, green skin, but totally innocent. *Ddrripp, vrip, croak. Dripp, bripp, vripp . . .*

A siren sneaks into the night, getting closer and closer. Unable to distinguish between police or ambulance, I escape inside the first lit window, a liquor store. Not sure how to retreat gracefully, I point to a familiar brand and the next minute I'm hugging a pint inside a paper bag, close to my hip pocket. Somehow I end up where I started out from, the outer stretches of the zoo, drinking, smoking again, coughing up my lungs. But no matter how much I swig away at the pint, I do not get drunk. Although it's stopped raining, puddles on the sidewalk shimmer with swirls of yellows, greens, and reds on a brilliant liquid-like black canvas. Then the palette disappears and all I see is green, not kiwi green or lime green but frog green, everything covered by a green film, my skin, my tongue, my beady eyes, green, green, ugly and green.

Crossing Empire Boulevard, I croak a tune from a pond of muddy, murky waters. I don't know if I sound like a hippopotamus in mourning or a frog in heat, but people step aside, their eyes in shock, as soon as I get too close. All that's left now is to congratulate the proud parents. Sixty-eight inches tall and one hundred and seventy pounds. Bulging eyes, slight belly and very tender skin. Today I am a frog — it's official.

No, you're not.

I turn. Huddled in the shadows and smoking a cigarette in the rain stands Kalman. Not only isn't he dead, but the way he holds his cigarette reminds me of a sly and impish Humphrey Bogart, except Kalman is wearing a no frills baseball cap. No logo.

Kalman, is it really you? I must be drunk but who cares.

I've been trying to write this story about you for ages and nobody likes it, nobody wants to read it. And tonight I realized I was writing your eulogy, the one I never gave.

Save your strength. I don't need eulogies.

But do you understand why I've been writing your story for years?

Side Sui.

Come again.

You keep turning things around. The story is about you, not me. Face facts — it's you who wants to commit suicide. But instead of dealing with it, you pin it on me, from suicide to side sui.

Kalman flicks his cigarette into the rain, but it flies back like a yo-yo, landing between his lips.

But all those different ways: gas, pills, slit wrists, and hanging?

What the hell, something to add to the resume, everyone wants to be remembered, and all I had was a few weeks left to live. So why wait when I can go out in a blaze of glory.

Lifting his cap he reveals a skull utterly eaten up by the therapy, ugly patches of frazzled hair testify that his is not a Kojak number.

Advice gratis. Stop trying to write up my life. I'm not a suicide, I'm a brilliant young man who took a while longer than most people to find his real direction, and by that time it was too late, I became ill. Okay, I went a little crazy, but not much. And I had a good excuse.

And the vials of sperm?

You're the one with all the theories, you tell me.

Did you ever sleep with Brenda?

And what if I did? Basically she wasn't married since you were dead, you committed suicide long ago, except you forgot to bury the body. All kinds of widows in the world. That's what she is.

Am I dead now?

You better believe it.

And exactly when did I die?

That one you'll have to figure out yourself. By the way, do me a favor, rip your story into a thousand pieces. Besides, it's not your story anyhow, it's mine. Write your own suicide story.

Taking a long drag on his cigarette, he exhales smoke into my face ever so slowly. By the time my burning eyes adjust, his form begins to grow smaller and smaller, fainter than a pencil sketch on a gray pad. In vain I rush after him, failing to notice a taxi come to a screeching halt, sending a shower of rainwater smack into my face.

Maybe it was the whisky, maybe guilt, or maybe it was just another way to write a story without putting pen to paper — so much easier to trap a line of dialogue under a rainsoaked night — I decide Kalman's advice to destroy years of work is my own unconscious tempting me to sink into a sea of depression.

Instead I see myself standing outside the Gotham Book Mart in Manhattan, approaching anyone who looks reasonably intelligent and cleanly dressed. Intrigued by my dark good looks and curious about the anonymous stranger's manila envelope, one out of ten might say yes. Inside they'll find a self-addressed envelope and a simple form with multiple-choice questions.

But in the end I show the story to no one, though I still cannot bring myself to shred it, which is why the next time I happen to be with Lisa at the museum — one of our last September visits before her school year is in full swing — I'm still carrying the story in my backpack.

We are sitting in the museum's cafeteria. Posters of juicy hamburgers and sizzling French fries add color to the dull walls, but the burgers they serve are gray and pasty, and the franks look pale pink and plasticky, nor do the jelly donuts and tuna sandwiches on white bread entice.

For some reason I ask Lisa if she'd like to hear a story. She wants to know if it's a fairy tale. I say no. She wants to know if something happens. I tell her that she should be the judge. A persistent hum of some kind, maybe the refrigerator, makes it necessary for me to raise my voice if I want to be sure that Lisa hears every word. But first I bring her ice cream, and I get a coffee.

And then I begin to read:

"Everything was ready for the hanging, the note had been written, the rope tested not split under the weight of a 150 lb. man, and the stool placed right underneath ..."

"What's a hanging," Lisa says.

"That's the point of the story," I say. "Don't you want to wait?"

"If I don't understand a word, my mommy always tells me."

"Well it means that a person gets up on a stool, puts a rope around his neck, and takes his life."

"Why would someone do that?"

"Because they're not happy."

"Is that what dying is?"

"No, that's what suicide is."

She repeats the word. And then she says, "I think I once saw a show about it. About teenagers who aren't happy."

"That's right, except this isn't a teenager. This is an older person, like me."

"Is the name S and is there a person named B?"

"No."

"Good, I don't want you to do a suicide."

"I won't."

"You promise?"

I stop reading. Am I insane, telling a suicide story to a seven-year-old? I should be arrested.

"There's another kind of hanging," I blurt out, "and that's the one I meant. Come with me into the galleries. It's when the curator hangs a picture on the wall."

"I know that. My daddy does hangings all the time. I help him with the stapler. And we take the string in the back of the painting, and tie it on the nail in the wall. Is that what your story is also about?"

"Not *also* but *only*. What I said before was a joke, a bad joke. My story is about a painting that someone took which didn't belong to him and then he had it hung in his own house and then someone came and recognized the painting was stolen. It happened a long time ago, World War II, do you know what that is?"

"I don't think so. But I like it when you tell me things."

It's impossible for me to describe what I feel at that moment — pure love coupled with pure dread, how close I'd come to destroying the trust given to me by her parents.

For several minutes we examine a new show in one of the larger galleries, an assembly of work that traces abstractions in the world of nature. We stop in front of a Georgia O'Keefe, and I prattle on about how the curator chose to hang the paintings, distance, height, centralities. I doubt if what I say makes any sense, but my purpose is to juggle the word "hang" so often that my earlier use of the word "hanging" will be lost in the clouds.

Ten more minutes and I think we've had enough. "Ready to go?" I say to Lisa.

She doesn't argue. We could walk home but I want to get back as quickly as possible. Outside the museum I stop a cab. Lisa is bubbling about hanging paintings. I pray the cabby doesn't understand a word of English. He drives silently, stone-faced; even when I overtip he doesn't smile. As we emerge from the taxi, Brenda turns the corner, her arms weighed down with groceries.

"Hi, Lisa, aren't you the lucky one? Where've you been, Rockefeller Center?"

"The zoo, and then the museum."

"Wow."

All three of us ride up in the elevator together. When Lisa was younger she was shy around me, but now she's usually shy around Brenda. But not today. Lisa wants to show Brenda some drawings and so Brenda passes the last of the shopping bags she's still carrying to me. Inside the kitchen I prepare a pot of spaghetti, and then busy myself putting things away, the special green tea, the ginger cookies, the cheeses "imported" from Wisconsin, a world of delights that I never grew up with and still haven't totally gotten adjusted to. A little while later, upon Brenda's return, we're moving around the kitchen, much too silent for my comfort. I want to ask Brenda what they were talking about, but she seems totally withdrawn, sautéing onions without saying a word, peeling and crushing garlic while I cut up mushrooms and dice tomatoes. Are we a team, or two solo artists playing around with the marinara sauce? My shoulder accidentally grazes Brenda's breasts, deliciously soft. I lean over to kiss her neck, the first time I've touched her in weeks. Probably months.

"Not now."

Usually I don't say a word when she says "not now," but this time I'm angrier than usual. "Do you realize that 'not now' are the only words I ever hear from you?"

"It's only six o'clock in the evening."

"I love Lisa. Very much. But she's not my child. She has a father and a mother. I want my own child."

"Why?"

"Isn't it a natural urge to want a child of your own?"

Brenda doesn't answer, concentrating on emptying the bright red contents of a can of tomato paste into the frying pan.

"All I want is a child, and you make it into a sin."

I lean toward her but she pulls away. "We can't have children. It's out of our control."

Pushing aside the beaded curtain, she leaves the kitchen.

"Then let's adopt." I follow her into the living room.

"No. It won't make us happy. Look, I don't need a child who carries my last name. I have thirty children who are real to me. It fulfills me."

"But it doesn't fulfill me."

Her eyes challenge mine, like a guard facing down a prisoner. "I don't think I trust you as a father."

"How can you say that? Look at me and Lisa. We have a great relationship."

"Are you sure?"

Her eyes avoid mine, either composing words to withdraw her provocation or words to increase the flames. When the phone rings Brenda lunges for it, a gift from the gods, like the last life preserver on the Titanic.

"Not tonight," I beg, but Brenda, ignoring my plea, tears off the back of an envelope to write down an address.

After hanging up, she returns to the kitchen, checks the spaghetti and the sauce, decides everything is ready, then shuts off the gas. In the meantime I run some hot water over last night's supper dishes.

Without a word, Brenda leaves the kitchen. I don't lose a step as I trail behind.

"Couldn't whoever it was wait?"

"Samuel, enough."

"It hurts me, Brenda."

"You don't even know what you wanted me to say no to. There's a memorial for Allen Ginsberg where they'll be reading the kaddish, in Hebrew, as well as the kaddish he wrote for his mother. It should be a fascinating evening."

"Never one of my favorites. Besides he was a Buddhist, not a Jew."

"I can't believe you'd say that. You think you're a better Jew just because you went to yeshiva. That's so self-righteous of you."

I follow her into the bedroom. Indifferent to my presence, she slips out of her jeans and sweatshirt, sending me into a tail-spin, aching for what I can't have. Stretching, her bikini ass staring at me, she looks luscious. I watch her reach for the top shelf where she chooses a tight turquoise blouse and a short black dress with lace frills, fresh from the cleaners. A splash of perfume behind her ears and to the v of her cleavage, and the final touch, a rainbow jeweled bandanna around her forehead. Then a quick good night, and she's gone so quickly all I can do is ask myself why am I alone in the apartment and she's out there in the night sending messages in all directions except mine. Actually, I know why I'm not with her — simple old-fashioned jealousy, the pain of watching some man sidle up to her, his shyness vanishing as she throws her head back, sharing a laugh, touching his arm, an innocent touch, a not so innocent glance, craving everyone except me, her suicide-story husband.

Breathing in Brenda's fragrance, I sit still for a long time, fighting the urge to run after her. The smell of her scent arouses desire while awakening fear, fear that I might hurt her, accusations of betrayal, my rage out of control. How long can things continue this way? Brenda's lawyer will turn my desire into a form of sexual harassment, and before I know it I'll be sued for making a pass at my own wife.

I decide to catch a bit of fresh air when the phone starts ringing. First a call from the *Baltimore Jewish Times,* then Eric Grossman, a lecturer of Yiddish film, then the archivist from YIVO, and someone at the Ninety-second St. Y is putting together a klezmer festival and is wondering if WEVD could be the co-sponsor. Everybody is busy, diligent, sincere. I'm at the door when the phone rings again. My first reaction is to keep going, but what if it's Brenda, calling to apologize. I answer with a soft hello.

"You did a bad thing to me. I'm not allowed to talk to you."

"Why? What did I do, Lisa?"

"You teached me about suicide, about hanging."

"Taught. Anyway, I didn't teach you about suicide."

"My daddy says I shouldn't talk to you, so I am calling to say I can't talk to you. Okay?"

I rack my brain trying to recall if in any way I explored the concept of suicide. Then it hits me. "Exactly what did you tell your daddy?"

Lisa repeats the opening sentence I read earlier, she knows it by heart, word for word, her voice trailing off exactly at the point where I stopped. What an incredible memory.

"Even if I can't talk to you, can I still name my next doll after you?"

I mutter something, but the joy is gone. "Good-bye, Lisa," I say and hang up.

I could make up a story as to how I came to read that particular sentence to Lisa, nothing serious, slipped in for a second and then was gone, and then rush upstairs and apologize to Len. But I doubt he'll buy it, certainly not before probing me and my devious mind.

Again, the phone rings but afraid it might be Len, I choose to let it go. The ringing won't stop. By the sixth or seventh ring, I hear his raised voice, picture the hate in his eyes, accusing me of fooling around with the mind of an innocent child, and no matter what I say to deflect his anger all my attempts are in vain. I fuel the blaze. And then a barrage of four letter words before the final exhortation never to approach his daughter again. If I do I'll be brought up on charges. How could I have been so stupid, mentioning, even for a moment, the word "suicide." This is not something a normal person discusses with a child.

Within hours Brenda hears about it from Len and May. What I've done is shameless, disgusting. She will not believe me when I tell her I'd only read one sentence to Lisa, a fairly innocent sentence except for one word, "hanging," in effect a formula: *Everything was ready for the hanging ... everything was ready for the wedding ... for the funeral ... for the Olympics ...* But my defense won't penetrate. Not even eight years old. Have I lost my mind? Explanations fall on deaf ears. Guilty as charged! And if I claimed I loved Lisa, she'd laugh in my face, demeaning my love, how I loved only myself, intoxicated by a child's total trust that made me into an almighty creature in an innocent little girl's eyes. And that I was a very strange person, and even if we could have children, never with me, I would never be allowed to father her children, even if we could. Before she stormed out of the house her final words would encircle me in a flame of hate, piercing my manhood, "Don't ever come close to me, don't ever touch me again." And all this because of one sentence, one stupid sentence that escaped my lips.

Reaching for keys hanging on a hook, I must leave at once, first grabbing a bottle of something strong to melt away the pain and fear. Kalman was right and I was wrong. I should have burned the story to a crisp, torn it to shreds. From time to time, I slip into the entrance areas of apartment buildings. With each swallow, I count my losses. I've lost Lisa, I've lost Len and May, I've lost Brenda as well. And every single person in our building who hears rumors about Brenda's demented husband, kind-of good looking but very strange.

My direction is east, then south along a piece of urban artery that cuts through Prospect Park, risking the long empty stretch that leads to the zoo. Nothing but cars and headlights here. Who is that man walking alone? If I'm banished from my own home where will I live? Even less genteel Washington Avenue would be too expensive on only one salary. But there are lots of things to be learned by living near the zoo — eating habits, mating habits, roaring habits. If I concentrated with all my might, I might actually pick out the trumpeting of the elephants or the snarl of tigers. When it's absolutely still, not a swish of tires for blocks around and the wind just right, I might get lucky and hear the haunting *vrippp* of a lady frog as she surfaces to the top of the lily pond in the Botanic Gardens, and we'll proceed to croak our love across the dark and silent highway. It'll be wonderful, almost like living in the country without ever taking the subway out of Brooklyn.

But better than living near the zoo would be living in a furnished cage inside the zoo itself. Would it be that unusual for at least one zoo in the world to exhibit a human being as part of the evolutionary landscape, a mammal among mammals? I see myself in my little private cage, some days half naked, bucking around and then foraging for food, other days in suit and tie and typewriter, attending to business. Or perhaps an exhibit that functions as a commentary on the suppressed need or desire on the part of some creatures to de-evolve, moving back in time to a pre-historic age, from Samuel the Human into Samuel the Frog.

I must be half-mad. Maybe if I offered to pay for my lodgings, the zoo would take me in, not as an exhibit but as a rent-stabilized tenant. Then if Lisa came by with her parents, the initial awkwardness would be followed by her proudly pointing out to other visitors that she had once personally known Samuel the Human.

No, half-mad is too generous. If I prefer a foul smelling zoo to a roof over my head and a pillow beneath, I must be totally under the spell of my insane fears, dreading Len's violence and Brenda's contempt. And then it dawns on me, me as in Human and not as in Frog, that it was Lisa who called with the news that her father forbade her to have any contact with me. But wouldn't it have made sense for Len to call me himself? The very moment that Lisa reported to her father on our little cafeteria workshop, reading a story that began with that infamous hanging, he would have exploded. What's the meaning of this? He gets me on the phone, and comes storming down. How would he leave such an important confrontation to a seven-year-old?

When I get home I dial Len's number, ready to hang up if Lisa answers. But it's Len and when he hears my voice, he sounds almost thrilled.

"Hey, how're you doing? Sorry I couldn't talk to you earlier. By the way, I wanted to thank you again for today. You're really great Sam, what would we do without you?"

"Lisa is a wonderful child."

"Tell us about it."

"By the way I think you liked Ginsberg, and there's a memorial for him tonight, a Jewish one, kaddish and all that. If you're interested ..."

"Thanks, I appreciate you thinking of me but I'm in the middle."

"Well, maybe next time."

"Listen, I know it's early for Thanksgiving, but keep it open. We're having a big bash. May's brother is coming in from Oregon ..."

How could I have been so stupid? When I get off the phone, there is no doubt in my mind that Lisa invented her father's anger. Lisa, I am sure, never breathed a word to him. I must have frightened her to death, not because I introduced her to the notion of suicide, but because of S and B, even though I denied it. She was afraid my story was autobiographical, secretly sharing my suicide plans with her.

But something doesn't make sense. Lisa is only seven years old. Even a genius couldn't invent such a plot, making up a tale about her father being angry with me. I know she's precocious, but this is beyond precocity.

Playing back what happened earlier in the day, I recall the elevator ride, the three of us, Brenda going up to see Lisa's drawings. It hits me — it was Brenda all along. Horrified that a third-grade teacher's husband could be accused of "raping" the mind of a child, she didn't waste a moment, giving Lisa instructions, simply telling her what to say to me, attributing the remarks to her daddy, which is exactly what Lisa did. All under the guidance of mastermind Brenda, who told her never to speak to me again.

My stupid story! I can no longer put off Kalman's request. All I have to do is step out on the fire escape, my fingers as thorough as any shredding machine, the wind carrying off the evidence of Kalman's suicide to different parts of the borough, somehow arriving at the boardwalk in Coney or Brighton, and then on to the Atlantic Ocean, a private ticker tape parade. No one will know who it's for, who is being feted and why, who it is standing coatless on the top-floor fire escape, bowing like a Zen monk, as a silent roar ascends. Except for one problem. There is no wind when I step out on the fire escape, and if I start tearing pages someone in the street will look up, see the madman, and quite possibly, and quietly, alert the police.

There are other ways to bury a story. I call up Len to borrow a toy shovel, inventing a story about a neighborhood project of planting tomato seeds tomorrow in the park. As an afterthought I ask if he happens to own a copy of Ginsberg's "Kaddish"; I would love to borrow it.

Two minutes later May is at the door with the package, explaining that Len just got a call from California. I promise to return everything tomorrow or the day after at the latest. Within thirty minutes I'm in a section of the park not visible to Flatbush Avenue traffic, attacking a spot of soft earth. Another ten minutes or so and I have nice little grave. Is it strange to bury my stories as if they had once been alive, these suicide variations, pushing them deep, deep into the earth?

Afterwards, I read from Ginsberg's lament for his mother, the sound of traffic the only chorus. His words feel eerily perfect for this late night burial. By the time I get to the end I've forgiven Brenda for preferring a Ginsberg memorial to making love with me. If she could see me at my little grave, would she lament with me or turn away, disgusted? Or have me locked up with Naomi Ginsberg?

In late November there is a phone message from Len reminding us about Thanksgiving. A week later Brenda and I come to their door bearing a tureen of pumpkin soup and a bottle of wine from the Golan Heights. Lisa, dressed in a Pocahontas dress and a crown of white feathers, pulls me over to the side while Brenda continues on into the living room. I'm still holding the wine when Lisa, speaking softly, says, "I like it when you teach me things, but don't teach me about suicide."

"I won't ever again."

"You promise?"

I'm about to say "and hope to die," but stop myself. I would kiss her forehead but don't want to risk someone's disapproving stare. When she again says, "you promise?" insisting on an answer, I'm absolutely convinced that she will never say a word to anyone. It's our secret. It makes me feel strange, different, unique, sharing such an intimate secret about death — and love — with a seven-year-old.

"Yes, I promise." But then I remember that there may be one other person who shares the secret, my wife Brenda. If it's a three-way secret, it doesn't seem to bother Lisa. She takes my hand, pulls me toward her, says that she missed me, and asks when I will take her to the museum again.

"Whenever you want," I answer.

The meal lasts for hours. Everyone praises Brenda's soup and my Golan wine. When it comes to the "good-byes" and the "we must get together soons" and the "see you soons," we're the only couple who need not step into the cold November night, simply walking down the stairwell. I wonder if Brenda caught Lisa's conversation with me. Perhaps she pulled her aside afterwards, reminding her of her father's warning. Or perhaps Brenda is so high on the wine that she didn't notice Lisa and I conversing, and will let me make love to her tonight, the night she finally gets pregnant. Or the opposite will happen, she will finally confront me about reading my suicide story to Lisa, officially requesting a divorce, in effect telling me that she will never sleep with me again for the rest of my life.

As to Kalman's second request, not to write about his suicide but to write about my own, I think I know the opening sentence, well, maybe not the opening sentence but the general theme, a fable for adults in the form of a children's story about a frog who wants to take his life, an idea I once juggled with but never explored, a tale of a sad frog who discovers that he is the only frog in the world who will never become a prince, a frog who will always remain a frog. He grows so sad that he doesn't want to live. But for the life of him he doesn't know how to die. Perplexed, he approaches one animal after another but not a single creature knows how to commit suicide, although a skinny crow suggests he starve himself, making death inevitable. But the frog knows it won't work because his inborn instincts will never allow him to stop eating. Finally, the frog meets a human being, let's call him Samuel, and Samuel suggests that he will teach him how to take his life on the condition that the frog will come back, in some form or other, to tell him what death is like, sharing the mystery of penetrating the beyond. After they make their solemn pact, witnessed by a cawing crow and a silent fox, Samuel instructs the frog in the correct fashioning of a noose from twigs and branches. Later when the frog takes his life, Samuel the human waits for the frog's report to arrive either in a dream or a vision or a chance encounter with the frog's ghost. Nothing. He waits earnestly, anticipating news from the world beyond death. He waits and he waits and he waits. Nada. And to this day he still waits, realizing that the only way he will ever pierce the mystery of the beyond is with his own death, and for that piece of knowledge he is not yet ready to step onto the stool and leap — and never will be.

made IN CHINA

I t didn't happen overnight, but little by little, Karen began to feel awkward whenever she and her daughter Rebecca found themselves around older Chinese people. Younger, college-educated professionals who were on the same wavelength posed no problem, sometimes joking how the Jews and the Chinese, both a people who valued learning, were into marrying each other. But old-timers speaking little English and dressing as if they had just packed away their Mao jackets made Karen feel ashamed, a modern day lily-white kidnapper who could fly off to China and return with a living human child of a foreign lineage.

If it were up to her, Karen would never leave the liberal Upper West Side where they lived in a rent-stabilized Riverside Drive apartment, small but functional, the envy of all their friends. But she was also a good daughter and good daughters visit elderly parents at least once a month, and it had to be tonight, a Thursday, because next week she had meetings practically every day and the week after that Karen's mother would start cleaning for Passover, concerned not only about the tiniest crumb of bread but any product with even the slightest questionable ingredient, turning her kitchen into an armed camp, which meant that a child not old enough to be trusted to remove cookie crumbs, potato chips, M&M's from inside her pockets or mini-knapsack — namely Rebecca — was not to walk past the front door.

Squinting as she smoothed her eye-liner, Karen instructed her daughter to put away her beloved Kewpie immediately. Karen then checked her watch — if they left within the next five minutes, they could still manage the circuitous route to Flatbush. It was complicated, much longer than the faster B train, but about a year ago she decided that if the Grand Street stop in the heart of Chinatown made her feel uncomfortable, there was no reason why she couldn't take an alternate route.

"Honey, did you hear me?"

"I don't want to go. Do I have to? Daddy doesn't have to. Why doesn't he have to?"

"Daddy is very busy. You know he is a lecturer in a college and he wants to become a professor, and to become a professor he has to work many long hours."

That was the standard story everyone was told, how David ended up in Baruch but dreamt of NYU, or any school with a decent Jewish studies department. But dreams cost, and the cost was that David's research kept him from joining Karen when she visited her parents. Except once, and that was only because he was off to a conference at Brooklyn College. During the subway ride he kept questioning why the long way, at least half an hour longer than the B train that required no changes, no transfers, no confusing tunnels and passages and stairwells at Atlantic Avenue, just straight and easy, and after a while, the train climbs up out of the darkness and there are trees and backyards and swings on both sides of the train. That was fun. That Rebecca loved. Yes, he was a great father, very sensitive to the world's pain except to the pain of his own wife, when she shared her feelings and fears, insisting on a prejudice correction workshop to work on her warped perceptions. One of the reasons why he fell in love with Karen, he often claimed, was that she was tabula rasa, ready to imbibe all the ecumenical values he'd picked up during his decade of volunteer tutoring in a Boston urban commune. She had been thinking of studying architecture but he insisted the world didn't need another architect. Homes yes, but not home designers. And that's how she ended up teaching, a multi-cultural rainbow if there ever was one, going back to school at some point, writing a master's thesis on the aggressive and prejudicial immigration laws of 1924. And as to why she fell in love with David, it was because of the afterwards, how he curled up like a little boy, holding her tighter than she'd ever been held, almost swallowing her alive. And now that there was no longer an afterwards, just the act itself, she had little to hold onto … except Rebecca.

"Grandma is waiting for us."

"You go."

"But she loves it when we come."

"That's not true. She loves it when we leave."

Karen was shaken by Rebecca's words, but also delighted by her daughter's wisdom. Except it wasn't Karen's mother who couldn't wait, it was Karen herself. By the time she got home all she could do was sit in the darkened living room. The pain in her mother's gray eyes which concealed a lifetime of frozen tears always felt more real when they were not in the same room, memory more real than flesh and bones. Immobile, Karen wouldn't move from her spot until Rebecca came in to play, or to hug, or say that she was hungry, the perfect granddaughter even if the grandmother hadn't yet discovered that love was thicker than blood.

In the end, she bribed her daughter with the promise of a rich, thick, foamy, bubble bath when they got back. But getting Rebecca to actually leave was another story. Ignoring her mother's pleas, she kept trying on pyramid shaped dresses for her Cupie doll. Exasperated, Karen was about to seize the doll when her office called; they had just been alerted to a news-breaking story about illegal immigrants and identity theft, Karen's specialty in the think tank where, because of David's encouragement, she had been hired to demonstrate how the hysteria created by anti-immigrant lobbyists conflicted with the facts, methodically gathering statistics about people who specialized in eluding statistics, applying the research skills she had garnered in graduate school to prove that these illegal immigrants, no matter where they came from, were characterized by a strong moral backbone and deeply ingrained family values.

Somehow her latest report had been accidentally deleted, and key legislators in Albany needed to be contacted. That meant waiting for the computer to warm up, locating the file, and then emailing them to verify that they had received it. When the report's arrival was confirmed, Karen checked her watch again, calculating there was still time for the longer route to Flatbush, but just then Rebecca chose to disappear into the bathroom, locking the door behind her.

When she finally emerged, Rebecca looked twice her age, pink blush, plus traces of powder puff on her cheekbones, and more than a dab of red lipstick. She had even used eyeliner. Karen shuddered to think what a grown man might imagine upon encountering this little Chinese Lolita whose dramatic eyes, the color of black onyx, were born to stun, practically shaming all else in the room. And so different from Karen's Leah-like eyes, ripples of blurred darkness behind thick lenses.

"Were you using my make-up?"

Ordinarily Karen would have told her she was beautiful not only because the adoption guidelines advised the frequent use of verbal affirmations as part of the bonding process — it was simply true. But should a six-year-old be complimented when she was throwing off her entire schedule?

"Honey, wash your face. Quickly."

Only six, Rebecca was already more intrigued by make-up than Karen had been at the age of sixteen, when she suffered a corneal ulceration after her first attempt at contact lenses, painful red eyes and a green discharge that lasted nearly two weeks. Disgusted by the pus, she chose thick eyeglasses rather than another bout with contacts. Rebecca was so different and not just when it came to incipient femininity. She was bright, loved by babysitters and delivery boys — cute, curious, precocious, loud … and unpredictable. Having Mommy-child conversations with dolls one minute and dabbing on some perfume the next.

By the time Rebecca emerged a second time, her face wet and her hair moist, Karen had to choose: either she canceled the planned visit, enduring the guilt she'd inevitably feel, or settle on the shorter route, the dreaded B train, and accept dread as part of the visit.

She chose dread, praying for a quiet Grand Street rush, or at least no paranoid moments. But just as expected, a crowd rushed in, hauling heaping bags of downtown delicacies and exotic vegetables — bok choy and baby scallions and black Chinese mushrooms, sea-cold oyster shells, fat juicy duck parts, rich portions of roast pig.

Karen tried to quell her growing panic by clutching her daughter's hand. Instead of seeing individuals, each with his or her curious, intense and unique face, all she could see were vacant and empty stares, focusing on nothing. Rebecca cried out in pain; Karen had been gripping her daughter's hand with all her strength.

Even though it was not a warm night, drops of sweat were working their way down her back. She didn't recognize herself. She caught her racist panic and, like a hissing grenade, hurled it back to the enemy, in this case her own terrified heart. Was she the prejudiced one, or had she somehow internalized her mother's wordless question as to how a child born in some Chinese village could ever become the granddaughter of a woman whose roots were in cold, dark, anti-Semitic Poland?

She loved Rebecca more than life itself, a happy, scrappy child whose favorite dish in the world was French toast made with challah. Both Karen and David understood the need to preserve the Chinese part of Rebecca's heritage, furnishing her room with Chinese artifacts, encouraging her to play with other Chinese children in Riverside Park near their apartment. David's theory was that Chinese people were grateful that these poor little rejected girls were being given a good home in America. Nodding her head, Karen listened to every word but could not erase the feeling that at any moment Rebecca might be grabbed, the kidnapper justified in doing what he did because he was only rescuing a little Chinese girl from this woman, an older, bespectacled caretaker, preoccupied with her *Times* crossword puzzle, a modern-day kidnapper herself.

In theory, yes, it was conceivable. But Karen's therapist, Lenore Rich, cautioned against too much theorizing. As far as she was concerned, one's worst fears always came true, *always* and *all ways*, and if Karen was afraid that some Chinese guy was going to kidnap her adopted Asian child of six, she better face those fears head-on, otherwise the kidnapping was going to take place at some point in her life, one way or the other, if not physical then emotional or spiritual. Lenore was not interested in justifying or rejecting Karen's fears. The cause could be traced to her mother, her father, her husband, her eyeglasses, her high school, or the price of tea in China. Didn't matter. If you're uptight around old Chinese people and not young ones, hang out with the old ones, if you freak out when the subway hits Grand Street, hey, haul your ass down there, first thing. And if it's Chinatown in general, start hanging out in Chinatown on a daily basis. Her therapy in six words: the *what* and not the *why*!

For some reason the subway began to slow down, eventually coming to a complete stop. Peering through the window, Karen saw nothing but faint white lines along the walls of the dark tunnel. Could the third rail's power source have been switched off because of an emergency? She waited for the conductor to announce that they would be moving shortly. Minutes passed. What if they'd have to evacuate the car, using the catwalk to find an emergency exit, groping in the dark — not the kind of experience Rebecca should be having on her way to visit her grandmother.

Finally the train started up, but after about a hundred feet, stopped again. Craning her neck, Karen was able to discern a subway platform through the window. She felt relief until she realized it was an abandoned station, the mosaic lettering of the station's name obscured by graffiti. A peeling gray ceiling exposed steel girders the color of charred wood, and the station's once-white tiles were blackened by time and last decade's movie ads. Karen intentionally inventoried what her eye observed, something to hold onto when she wanted to remember the day the B train halted in a dark tunnel and exposed a rusty slice of Transit Authority history. Then she remembered where she was, and why she should be afraid.

Sitting next to them in the vertical part of the corner seats was a young Chinese man, wearing a cheap black leather jacket and a baseball hat with the name of a trucking company. After staring at Karen and Rebecca, he folded his newspaper and began doing odd things with his face, moving his ears up and down as if attached to a puppeteer's strings. Rebecca, hiding behind her mother, peeked from time to time.

Karen wanted him to stop, to leave them alone. If he was trying to be funny, she didn't like it. The details of the young man's face seemed to fade as he made his lips disappear, twisting his nose until it looked like a potato, then shutting his eyes until he was practically eyeless. Gradually Rebecca's shyness turned into excitement. Karen was getting angry. Why did he have to get involved in their subway ride, even if it had come to a dead stop? Couldn't he just read his newspaper and mind his own business? Karen blushed at the ferocity of her thoughts. She couldn't stand herself this way, so unlike her, so obnoxious — what if the Germans looked at Jews on the trams in Berlin with the same disgust that she was looking at this man.

From inside one of his shopping bags, the young man extracted a cone of waxed paper. Loosening the top he shook out a bunch of round red balls that looked like candy or home-made gum. He dropped one into his mouth, then began using his tongue like a juggler, his agile tongue flipping the red ball as if it were on fire. Finally the fire was put out, and a delighted grin spread across the juggler's face as he bit into its mysterious center. When he handed one of the balls to Rebecca, her mother, afraid pig-fat might be one of the ingredients, forced her to return the candy, resisting her daughter's tears and pleas. "Please Mommy, Mommy please." Some passengers masked their curiosity by burying their faces behind walls of reading material, but Karen knew what they were thinking, how this stupid white woman didn't trust candy from strangers! But this man was no stranger. He was Chinese for God's sake, part of Rebecca's past, though not part of her future if she could help it. But could she? What if he was trying to get her to fall in love with him by exhibiting such warmth and friendliness? Until this moment the thought of whom she might marry never crossed her mind. True, Rebecca was still too young to comprehend how she had been removed from one world and deposited in another, but the day would come when she'd realize that her egg-shaped face, designer cheekbones, and oriental eyes told a tale different from the one she was taught in her ecumenical pre-school where she already knew about Thanksgiving turkeys and the pilgrims and Martin Luther King and Chanukah lights and Christmas trees and Kwanzaa. There was no reason why Rebecca wouldn't be drawn to someone from her own race and since virtually all the Chinese infants put up for adoption were girls, the only Chinese men available would be non-Jews.

"Me China, she China, you no made in China. Who you?"

Was he talking to her? Made in China! What the hell did he mean by that? Usually it was a put down, a nasty reference to second-grade goods, cheap junk. If a white person had said such words, she would have freaked out, attacked back. Although he said what he said with a wide smile, Karen was trembling. Maybe she had been too quick to consign her fears to the attic? Well, one thing for sure, she was not going to ask him to repeat it. All she knew was that she had to get off this subway car immediately.

Miraculously, the train began to move, gradually picking up speed. Within two minutes they arrived at the DeKalb Avenue station. Grabbing Rebecca's hand, she rushed out just as the doors were closing, and mother and daughter found themselves on an almost completely deserted platform. Karen didn't move from their spot, a good two feet behind the yellow safety line, until the departing train disappeared. With no idea of an alternative route to her parents' home, she could either wait for the next train or take the stairs up and hail a cab.

Rebecca was angry; Karen watched her lower lip disappear as she pouted. Could Karen have misheard the man's accusation, nothing more than his incomprehensible accent. What if he were only warbling sounds to amuse Rebecca, a Chinese bird song?

"Rebecca, there is a store upstairs I need to see."

"Ouch, you're hurting me."

"Rebecca, please, I'm sorry. We had to get off because there is a store upstairs."

"What kind of store?"

What stores were near DeKalb Avenue? There must be a record store, and wasn't there a Macy's around here somewhere? She needed to calm herself down, get a grip. "I'm very hungry, Rebecca. Maybe we'll just eat something."

They walked into the first fast food place on Fulton Street, Burger

Heaven, where both the customers and the counter people were all black, not a Chinese person in sight. She ordered a Coke and Rebecca wanted a hamburger. "No, honey, you can have French fries or a fish sandwich. But not hamburger."

Rebecca ignored her mother, walking up to the counter as if she were marching in a parade. "I want a hamburger, please," she said to the young girl dressed in a green and orange uniform. "I want to work here when I'm big, may I?"

Karen canceled Rebecca's order. "I told you that you can have French fries or a fish sandwich. Or both."

"You're mean," Rebecca snapped. "And you're ugly, too."

Horrified and embarrassed at the same time, Karen was about to slap her but somehow the accusing eyes of the Chinese "puppeteer" on the subway restrained her arm.

"What did you say?"

Rebecca began to cry. Karen wanted to hug her, but held back, afraid the hug would be misinterpreted, a reinforcement of Rebecca's insult rather than a reprimand.

By the time the cab dropped mother and daughter off at the Schechter home, her brain felt locked, a confusion of dangling deliberations: to ignore or to punish? And precisely what kind of punishment? Clueless, she did nothing, rationalizing her inaction by blaming Rebecca's outrageous behavior in the restaurant on her own behavior earlier in the subway — rushing off the train like a madwoman. This was the first time Rebecca had spoken to her this way.

On top of everything, her mother was in bed with a bad cold. With the windows closed, the smell of sickness was thick and oppressive. This was not a room Karen wanted to be in. Against her better judgment Karen took a deep breath, inhaling her mother's inhalers, a trail of eucalyptus — no doubt Ben-Gay for her muscles — accented by something sour and old, rank bed sheets that needed to be washed.

"Why didn't you tell me? I could have brought some chamomile tea."

"Tea I don't need."

"What then do you need?"

When her mother didn't answer, Karen called Rebecca to say hello to Grandma, but Rebecca took one whiff and announced there was a bad smell in the room. "May I open the window for Grandma?"

Over seventy-five, Karen's mother was aging rapidly, her gray hair dull and thin. She never went to a beauty parlor, never had it cut professionally; instead her husband, a retired tailor, used his skills with the scissors. For Rebecca's sake, Karen's mother explained how a closed dark room allowed one to sweat easier and sweat was the best thing for a cold. Her accent, however, rendered her explanation beyond Rebecca's comprehension. When Mrs. Schechter finished speaking, Rebecca repeated, "May I open the window for Grandma?"

"Of course honey, just not too much, because she lives on the ground floor, and cats can come in if it's open too wide."

After raising the window about an inch, she said in her sweetest voice, "May I please be excused?"

Karen nodded and then addressed her mother. "She's crazy about this new book David bought for her, the ABC's of food, everything from avocado to zucchini, and it all pops up."

"This to me is a first time. What's this, 'may I please be excuse.'"

"We had a guest over, a darling little Indian girl from her class, and after she finished eating she was so polite, and said, 'May I please be excused.' Ever since then Rebecca has been saying that."

Karen had added the words, "darling little Indian girl" to test her mother, goading her, an excuse for Karen to storm out if only one word was said about entertaining non-Jewish children, a way to prove to herself that her escape from parochial Brooklyn paved the way for discovering a larger world where she engaged all sorts of people, including Egyptians, Iranians, Syrians. For a while she'd been involved in a Palestinian-Jewish dialogue group. No one could question her cultural fluidity.

Even in the dark, Karen could feel her mother's eyes shooting sparks, right into her frightened heart... until it dawned on her that it was she who was angry. It was *her* fears, plain and simple. The hard truth was that her mother was more anarchist than racist, mocking at values valued by the world. When she needed the world to listen, the world was deaf, so now no one could expect her to extend herself to every Lutheran or Muslim or Hindu just for the sake of being nice and positive and cheerful. Karen's mother coughed a deep scratchy rattle. When Karen brought her a glass of water, she pushed it away.

"Did you see a doctor?"

First she nodded yes, then she shook her head as if to say no. "All they know is tests, blood, urine, lungs, heart, machines, cameras, colored fluids with needles. Why never a doctor who looks at you, examines different things himself, with his own eyes, and then says this is what's wrong, and this is how you can help yourself."

"Ma, why didn't you say something?"

"I'm saying now."

"What's wrong?"

"Nothing, nothing. Please, the soup please. It's Thursday."

It was hard for Karen to comprehend the world her mother lived in, as if her father's farina-potato-cream-onion soup on Thursday night had been handed down from Sinai — otherwise the world would collapse. And this pickiness about food from a people who in fact had seen the world collapse. Now they become finicky about food!

Karen asked Rebecca if she wanted to peel the potatoes on Grandma's brand-new potato peeler, but Rebecca was too absorbed in her book to even look up. Karen then asked if she wanted to watch her dice and slice, cut and boil. Rebecca did look up but declined. In the middle of the page that pictured "f" for falafel, Rebecca announced that she was hungry and could she have some of Grandma's salmon fish cakes. There were none, and without so much as a groan, she happily settled on Melba toast and cottage cheese.

As Karen cut and chopped, she began to feel calmer. Maybe it was difficult growing up in a home where she bore daily witness to her parents' pain, but still, she felt lucky that her mother could bequeath to her a variety of culinary secrets, such as the exact moment when to add the sour cream so that it wouldn't curdle, giving the thick soup a tart and luxurious texture; her mother was an excellent guide.

With the soup on the stove going full steam, Karen's mother, wearing an old blue bathrobe, came into the kitchen, wiped her feverish forehead with a towel, and asked her daughter what was wrong.

Karen shook her head. "What should be wrong?" She went to check her face in the hallway mirror. The streaked make-up had been wiped clean in the cab, not a trace of tears.

Usually Karen lied when her mother confronted her directly. She could invent a story — how she and David had a fight just before she got on the subway. Her mother had liked David until she found out how much he disliked Orthodox Judaism. Although she knew of her daughter's marital difficulties, she never even hinted at the possibility of divorce — even an atheist is better than sitting home alone — but David's rejection of religious traditions made him the nearest address for anything wrong in Karen's life.

"Okay, I'll tell you, but I don't want you to worry. A young Chinese man who seemed to be very nice, making faces, amusing Rebecca, and then he said this ugly thing to me, 'Who you?'"

"'Who you?' I don't understand."

"That's just part of it. Like who do you think you are. Me China, she China. I think he was asking who am I to adopt a Chinese child? Who am I to be her mother?"

"Didn't I tell you again and again to take a car service?"

"And didn't I tell you it's crazy to take a car service when I have a monthly transportation pass."

"Money isn't everything."

"That's not how you raised me."

"Move to Brooklyn."

"I spent my whole life trying to leave and you want me to move back. Besides, Rebecca will be attending P.S. 87."

"This I never understand. Your husband is a Hebrew professor and you send Rebecca to a goyish school."

"First of all it's not a goyish school. It's simply an excellent school, one of the best in the city. If a landlord has an apartment available in our school district, he'll mention District 3 in the ad. Even more important than a river view."

"Don't you want her to know Hebrew?"

Karen guided her mother back into her bedroom where Rebecca couldn't hear them.

"Of course we do, we're just afraid that in a Jewish school she'll stick out like a sore thumb. Not only is she adopted, but she's also from a different race." Karen was speaking so softly her mother had to move closer, their cheeks practically touching. "But in a public school there are so many different cultures she'll just be one of five other Chinese kids in a cosmopolitan class."

"So why did you pick a Chinese?"

"I didn't pick a Chinese. And how can you speak that way? Rebecca might hear you."

Compared to David, Karen's role in the adoption process had been minimal — David filled out all the applications, made arrangements for a social worker to file a home study report, scheduled fingerprint sessions, FBI clearances, certification from the state authorities. He even located a translator for all the forms that could not be submitted in English. But the hepatitis vaccinations that she and her husband were required to take caused Karen to go into anaphylactic shock. They considered postponing the trip, but the agency advised them that once a couple received their acceptance letter any delays could put the application into peril. Since Chinese law didn't require the presence of both parents, David went alone. Karen's theory was that had she actually landed on the Chinese mainland, slept on a Chinese bed in a Chinese hotel, drank Chinese tea, ate Chinese broccoli, visited the Chinese orphanage, the trip would have functioned as a "pregnancy" pause, for even a one-month pregnancy was better than nothing. Thus the great day found her resting in the bedroom, strongly advised by her doctor against traveling to the airport terminal, surrounded by David's parents who had flown in from Toronto, and no one from Karen's family there to greet the new grandchild.

"Who will she marry?"

Karen didn't know what to say. "I don't want to discuss this now."

"If you put her with Jews, she will come out Jewish. If she goes to public school, she will come out public."

"Ma, the discussion has to end now."

"If it's money, your father will make a contribution to tuition."

"Not now."

"Believe me if you send her to public school, she will always be Chinese."

"Ma, she is Chinese."

"But Jewish. Jewish-Chinese. There is a bat mitzvah. And that's that. She goes to a Jewish school, she meets a Jewish boy. And life goes on. Is that so bad?"

"If she goes to a Jewish school, she could hate every Jewish boy she ever will meet because they might ridicule her."

Listening to herself, she heard a stranger, a liar, her husband's mouthpiece. For David, a Jewish couple raising an Asian child was one of the historic wonders of the twenty-first century; of course he could afford to be buoyant. His parents, if they needed flesh and blood grandchildren, had David's sister in Safed, Israel, currently up to number five. But for Karen's Holocaust survivor parents there were no other grandchildren — her brother, who abandoned Brooklyn for Bangor, Maine, had never married — and a little Chinese girl wasn't exactly the future they envisioned when they got married in a displaced persons camp in Germany in 1946. For Mrs. Schechter, her daughter's infertility was one of the curses of Hitler's legacy.

Kissing her mother good-bye, she promised to look into acupuncture, as well as other natural remedies, but her mother said not to bother. "I suffer the way I always suffer. With a Jewish doctor."

Her father arrived home from synagogue just as Rebecca and Karen, stuffed with supermarket specials that his wife had picked up since their last visit, were going out the front door.

"So soon?" Her father placed his hand on the crown of Rebecca's head, but she pulled away, hiding behind Karen.

"It's late, and we were here for a while," Karen explained. She resisted asking Rebecca to kiss Grandpa. Without being asked, her father pushed $45 dollars into her hand. "No subway now, please."

———————

Even before her key was in the lock, David opened the door, ushering his wife and daughter inside. Without saying a word, he pointed to the wall clock hanging next to the tall, narrow bookcase devoted exclusively to the Steinsaltz Talmud and various Midrashic collections, both in Hebrew and English. "You should have been home an hour ago."

"A subway delay."

"Why didn't you call me?"

"I could ask you the same thing, David."

In the meantime Rebecca started removing her clothes, asking for her bubble bath.

"Sweetheart, I'll be with you a minute. You know how long it takes to fill up a bath at this hour. And we have to make sure the water is hot."

"Don't you think it's a little late for a bath?" David asked. "She has school tomorrow."

"I promised." But when she checked, the water flow was weak and not terribly hot. One of their rent-controlled building's quirks was an ancient boiler and occasionally, late at night, the water was lukewarm. Maybe she should heat up a few kettles — couldn't hurt. On the way to the kitchen, she found David holding Rebecca, lavishing her with exaggerated, splashy kisses. He then asked his beautiful little girl if she would mind very much if she had her bubble bath tomorrow?"

"Yes, and a double yes," Rebecca answered.

"Well, let's say it'll be a double bubble bath. Did you ever have a double bubble bath?"

"What's that?"

"Double the bubbles. Thousands of them. And different colors."

"How many colors."

"Five. Yes, five beautiful colors for the bubbles." David hugged her. "Now let's get ready for bed, sweetheart."

Rebecca ran off to bed, leaving her parents facing each other. "Why did you contradict me?"

"Is that what I did?" he said, confused by Karen's tone.

"I promised her a bath tonight. And you turned it around, as if my word is meaningless."

"It's not meaningless, I'm just looking at the hour."

"It wouldn't have taken that long. But now Rebecca knows my promise is meaningless, and your promise is meaningful. You always do this to me."

"Do what?"

"Forget it. Forget I said anything."

"What's wrong with you? These trips to your mother are a disaster."

"It has nothing to do with my mother," Karen snapped. "Something happened on the subway, and we had to get off in the middle and find a cab on Dekalb Avenue."

Reluctantly, she described the Chinese man and what he said to her, insisting that as a non-Chinese woman she couldn't be a mother to a Chinese child. David asked for details — the man's age, how he was dressed, traveling alone or with a companion. Listening to Karen's response, David shook his head. "Sorry, you read it all wrong. I'll say it again: the Chinese people admire what we're doing for their children. And if they knew the significance of her going to P.S. 87, they would lavish us with gifts and honors."

Karen was sick and tired of David's glorification of this legendary public school. Right now she couldn't give a damn how many parents were trampling over each other in order to finagle their children into this school district so that by the time they were ready for high school they understood electromagnetic devices or were able to advance theories predicting the intricate dance of bees. What she wanted from David was an embrace, holding her tight and saying, "Everything will be all right," but he didn't move from his desk, his pen poised between his fingers as he spoke, his eyeglasses perched on his forehead ready to return to the bridge of his nose when she finished speaking.

"Maybe you didn't understand what the man was trying to say."

"I know exactly what he said. He said 'Who you?' in a degrading fashion."

"Let's not go there. You think that's what he said. But how do you know it's not a Chinese word? *Hu Yu*, or *Ha Ya*. Or anything. Maybe it means the opposite of what you think it means — like, *We're all Chinese*, in the sense that we all take care of each other. Who knows what he said?"

"David, did you realize that everybody adopts a girl?" Karen knew her fears could lead to sparks, and sparks to a blaze, but if she didn't express them, she would choke.

"And?"

"Which means there are no Chinese boys who've been adopted."

"I don't follow you."

"So what will happen when Rebecca gets older and it's time to get married?"

"She's just six years old, for crying out loud!"

"David listen. Because no Chinese boys were put up for adoption, there won't be any Chinese Jewish boys for her to meet and share her life with, zero, zilch, anywhere in the world."

"Get a hold of yourself. Why can't she marry a white Jewish boy, like me? There are plenty of us around."

Karen was exhausted, craving sleep, but at the same time her mind was racing. "Why didn't I think ahead? Why didn't I see what was inevitable. She's going to marry a Chinese goy."

"That's an ugly thing to say. Can't you stop? For all you know she may turn out to be a lesbian, and not marry anyone."

"I can't stand your cynicism." She gave him an icy cold look. "That man on the subway, I felt his hate, his superiority, his certainty that I would never be as close to her as he already was. What if she falls in love with a Chinese man, moves back to China, and we never see her again."

"That's absurd. Don't drag me into your paranoid fantasies. I refuse to go there."

David returned to his papers, but Karen insisted he listen, although she wasn't sure how to phrase her objections in a way that would penetrate his stubbornness.

"If Rebecca attends Manhattan Jewish Academy, she'll not only get a good education, she'll also learn how to bake challahs for the Sabbath. She'd learn about Jewish time, about another calendar in addition to the Gregorian one, she'd learn about Israel, and ancient peoples, and Mesopotamia, and Abraham and Sarah. She'd learn about her namesake Rebecca. Is that so bad?"

David's gaze didn't budge from his page.

"How can you be so cruel?"

"We are not raising Rebecca to be Jewish," he whispered.

"But you're a Jew, a professor of Jewish studies."

"It's my profession, not my religion. Why are you so bent on sabotaging our efforts to raise a normal child in a good New York neighborhood who will be attending …"

"Let's give her something in addition to mainstream culture."

"If we add anything, then it should be Chinese culture. We should find her a teacher of Mandarin, not Hebrew."

"I'm going to take her to shul on Shabbos."

"I've never seen you like this."

"She's my daughter too. Not just yours. Don't I have a say in her life?"

"We had an agreement. We are not a religious family. Period."

"We are not a religious family, semi-colon. Not period. And if my daughter and I decide that we do not, for the duration of twenty-four hours, listen to the radio or answer the phone, why isn't that just as good as the game of baseball or chess, each with its own set of rules?"

"I forbid you to do this to Rebecca."

"We both" — Karen was barely whispering — "adopted her."

"Did I just hear the word 'both'? If I'm not mistaken, that includes me. I will not co-operate in your little game. Do not expect me to make kiddush and bless the bread."

Shaking, as if a cold wind had swept through her, Karen slipped away, seeking shelter. She found Rebecca fast asleep in her room, clutching another of her Smitty dolls, half-troll and half-angel. Without waking her, Karen managed to remove her Oshkosh overalls and to dress her in pajamas. She kissed her forehead and, for a moment, felt so weak and scared, all she wanted to do was climb into Rebecca's bed and hug her to death.

She was angry at David, so stubborn, so self-righteous. She watched him working in his makeshift study in the L-shaped hallway corridor where he'd installed his computer on a narrow, custom-built desk after his office became Rebecca's room. As far as she was concerned, David was incredibly blind, an ox unable to lift its head as it plows the field. Her mother was right. For a professor of Jewish studies to be so against Judaism was pathetic. To calm her nerves, she considered a cup of tea, but remembering the bath, ran to shut the water off — just in time, a mere two inches from overflowing. When she tested the water, she was surprised — it had turned hot.

She locked the door — no need for all that water to go to waste. Before stepping into the tub she examined her face in the mirror and decided that she had beautiful, bedroom eyes, mysterious and inviting — and if the world only saw rippled pools of blurred darkness because of the strong prescription of her eyeglasses, that was their loss. But her forehead was too high, her face too narrow. She then stared at her pale breasts, gravity and middle age had reduced the distance between her milk-dry nipples to her thick-fleshed stomach. Why didn't David ever suggest that she diet? Probably because he wasn't interested enough. In fact, he never suggested much about her physical appearance, not the clothes she wore, the jewelry she didn't, or the style of her light brown hair, parted in the middle, and cut in the way that accented her jaw line. Why couldn't David be more involved with her life, not only the category of her moral choices? Had David been there on the subway maybe that man wouldn't have been so rude. They would have been a family on the move, protected.

She then lowered herself into the bath, letting the hot water lap gently, but instead of feeling filled by the warmth of the stillness, she felt drained, everything whole and good escaping from her body. She couldn't get that man in the subway out of her head. What if he had grabbed Rebecca's hand and simply run off just as the doors were closing? If she could never see her daughter again, she wouldn't want to live. She felt a chill — the bath had turned cold. Had she fallen asleep? Drying herself off quickly, she felt no cleaner than when she'd first entered the bath. Stepping into a robe and slippers, she returned to the bedroom where David was busy reading. He didn't look up as she slipped into bed.

The next day, after dinner, Karen told Rebecca about a new game, how starting Friday night they would not be watching TV, but only reading books and playing with her dolls, and they wouldn't put on the light.

"Why mommy?"

"It's a game."

"Oh, who wins?"

"It's not a game where you win or lose. It's just supposed to be fun. It's like every day we do things one way, and then one day a week we do things differently. Like we won't ride the elevator, we'll walk down the steps. And the day after tomorrow we will go to this big house where there is a singer in Hebrew, and a speaker and then they read from this very old book. Except it's not a book with pictures, but wrapped up in a purple or blue curtain with gold letters."

"Will there be any children?"

"Lots."

Friday night, feeling sluggish, with a runny nose, Rebecca asked for her favorite video, *Yes I Can*, about a choo-choo train. She also wanted tea with honey and lemon; Karen had totally forgotten about setting aside hot water for the Sabbath. How many years had it been? She couldn't believe that she had forgotten so much. But the next morning Rebecca was up bright and early, bursting with energy, reminding her mother that they were supposed to go to this place where there was singing and music.

"No music, honey, just singing."

"Why?"

"Because it's one of the rules of the game."

Eyeing his wife and child getting dressed, David asked Karen if he could speak to her for a moment. In the kitchen, with the door closed, he asked her what she was doing.

"We're going to shul."

"Why are you going against my expressed wishes?"

One more word—anything—and she'd tell him to fuck off.

But he remained silent, waiting for her answer. Finally she said, "Excuse me, but I didn't realize this marriage was a totalitarian country where you're the ruler."

David's face turned hard, a snarl of disgust. She had never seen anyone look at her with so much loathing. Maybe she had gone too far, it was just too risky. She needed to back off, elegantly. She wasn't Orthodox, so why was she using Orthodox practice to make her point? Maybe she could find a Conservative synagogue, even Reform. Absurd to bring Rebecca to a synagogue if David can't stand anything that smacks of religion. In the end only their daughter would suffer.

As they were about to walk out the door, Rebecca's fingers slipped out of her mother's hand. She rushed back to her father but David was still seething in his anger — he barely touched her. "Daddy, can you come with us?"

"Another time, sweetheart," her father said.

Karen knew how much David hated being put on the spot. "That's all right honey, Daddy has a chapter to finish, and I think he's meeting the chairman of his department." Karen reached for Rebecca. "Sweetheart, we'll be late."

It was a radiant April day as mother and daughter made their way to the subway on Broadway. A sharp wind whipped the debris into a whirlwind, the spiraling shreds of loose paper inches above the sidewalk concrete. Rebecca, delighted, gave chase. While they walked, Karen explained that the singing and dancing had been cancelled, and instead they would be taking the train to Chinatown.

"What's that?"

"A nice neighborhood."

At that hour mother and daughter had the subway almost all to themselves but when they got off at their stop, Grand Street was already pulsing with shoppers who must have risen at the crack of dawn. And the smells, a rich garlicky layer tempered by incense snaking out of a yellow and gold Buddhist temple stuck between stalls of fish hawkers with piles of crabs and shrimps and lobsters so fresh they looked like the midnight catch of ocean bound trawlers, the salt of the waves still licking their shells.

"You see this street, Rebecca, probably it's a little bit like where you were born."

"Where am I born mommy?"

"In my heart, sweetheart."

For the next half hour they stared unashamedly, walking up and down Mott Street and Pell Street, Bayard Street and Grand Street, yet no one looked at them, not even a curious glance.

Rebecca said she was hungry and Karen bought a pound of apples and some exotic red pears. Afterwards they found themselves walking on East Broadway, and in front of a mustard colored brick building braced with Hebrew lettering, Karen realized that she was standing in front of a Lower East Side synagogue. She considered going inside but decided against it. She was sure there would be no children inside, probably no women; she didn't want Rebecca's first synagogue experience to take place in a deserted women's section.

Across the street from the St. Teresa Catholic Church, they stopped in front of a street corner park. A sign on the mesh wiring, which Karen read aloud, warned: "Park off-limits to adults unless accompanied by a child."

"I'm a child," Rebecca said.

Inside the park a few gray-and-white haired Chinese men and women were babysitting for their grandchildren. When Rebecca said "Let's go on the see-saw," to one of the little boys, the other child answered in Chinese, confusing Rebecca, but somehow they figured out how to see-saw together.

Surrounded by little Chinese boys and girls, their voices screeching happily, Karen tried to picture Rebecca's future husband. Closed eyes helped, not to mention the rays of the sun heating her bare arms. It was as if she had immersed herself in a bath of sunlight, and as she held her breath, images from an unknown future were being dragged into the present. She wasn't sure if her husband would be Chinese or Jewish, or even Japanese. But it didn't seem to matter. Let the little one just fall in love, real love, not what her own parents had, or her brother in Bangor had. Deep down she feared she and David had never succeeded in having children of their own because there was something flawed about their love.

Just then Rebecca glided over to her mother, abruptly ending her reverie. Startled, it took a moment for Karen to re-orient herself. Was she actually sitting here in the heart of Chinatown, her eyes closed, not gripping Rebecca's hand?

"Mommy, I'm thirsty."

"Honey, do you want juice, we'll buy some soon."

"Do you have ice cream?"

"Rebecca, I'm not a freezer. We have to go to an ice cream place."

"Then what about candy?"

Karen checked her hefty shoulder bag. Sure enough, after digging around all the way at the bottom she came up with two caramel candies wrapped in cellophane, giving one to Rebecca, saying it would be nice to give the other piece to the little boy who'd been playing with her. But when she handed him the candy, the grandfather rushed over and pulled the wrapped candy out of his hand. The boy started crying and his grandfather picked him up roughly, storming out of the park.

Surprised by the old man's show of force, Karen worried about Rebecca's response, but without losing a step, she rushed toward the swing, legs lunging toward the sky, head bowed to the earth, as if nothing had happened.

Karen decided not to tell David about their day downtown. Let him think she'd been to synagogue with Rebecca, let him stew in his own anger. She'd once Googled him on ratemyprofessor.com, amazed at how well loved he was by his students, passionate, caring, patient, brilliant, the ideal teacher, a classroom experience not to be missed.

But his life in the classroom never made it back home.

David was tying the laces of his sneakers, his hair still wet from the shower he had just emerged from, when Karen and Rebecca walked through the door. Rebecca rushed up, found her way onto her father's lap, and began to tell him how they walked and walked and saw so many people who were eating so much food, and she wanted to eat ice cream, but there wasn't any, and they sat in the littlest park in the world, nothing like their park on Riverside but it was still nice and she wanted to go back, and then Mommy gave her and a little boy candy, but he had bad teeth and his grandpa didn't let him have the candy because the grandpa was very strict.

"I thought you went to synagogue," David turned to Karen. She said nothing in response. David, his relief visible, smiled, and she was about to tell him that there was nothing to be relieved about but then changed her mind. There was no rush. Soon enough they would do what they did best — talk about their fragile future, probing whether or not it had reached a dead end, despite their love for Rebecca. David would come up with statistics and psychological studies proving that a child needs both parents. She would respond that the best thing for a child was for the parents to love *each other*, and he would say something about the parents loving the *child*, always focused on the child, and not the parents.

Right now she felt exhausted, what she needed was a long, hot bath, an hour of total privacy, the room lit only by a few candles lining the ledge of the small window. She would lather herself gently with lavender soap, letting her skin soak up the subtle scent, and then maybe, just maybe, whatever it was she'd felt the other night draining out of her would somehow find its way back inside, back to where it belonged. And she would think about that man in the subway, the man with the potato nose, and he wouldn't frighten her. Maybe he was actually a scientist, or a doctor, maybe he was a child psychologist who was really happy that she had adopted Rebecca, and if she ever saw him again she would smile her beatific smile, removing her eyeglasses so that he could see her face clearly, and he would recognize that she was a good person, a good mother and a good daughter, even somewhat attractive, nice-looking, honest, genuine — and then she caught herself, shaking herself awake when she realized that she was composing a personal ad to a total stranger. And then she smiled at the cunning wiles of the mind, leading you in directions you had no idea you wanted to be led. Why not? Why fucking not?

new stoned CITY

Hauling his suitcase down the long narrow hallway on the fifth floor, Lenny stops in front of 5F and rings the bell. He feels wretched, eyes red from a long sleepless night, skin crawling with imaginary bugs, his tongue a slab of raw liver. When the door finally opens he doesn't know how to respond to his mother's tears so he hugs her lamely, telling her he's glad to be home. Has it really been twelve months?

Mrs. Goldberg is shocked by her son's appearance, but what disturbs her even more is the sour smell in his mouth — or is it coming from his body? — a pungent odor, reminiscent of bleach and urine. This last year has not been kind to her son. Lenny, in black jeans and battered leather air force jacket, gives the impression of someone youthful when he enters a room, but after a few moments, it becomes evident that his pencil-thin body is not the result of a health food diet. For some reason his back seems curved, as if his spine doesn't have the strength to straighten itself out, his long dark hair stringy and lifeless, his skin pale, and his straggly beard resembles a battered broom. In contrast, Mrs. Goldberg feels robust, in the bloom of health. She is a short, wide woman with dark un-plucked eyebrows, her sensitive eyes the color of ripe avocados, and her face remarkably free of wrinkles. Since she covers her hair with a bright blue kerchief, not even one gray hair visible, she looks younger than her seventy-two years. When she walks, she and her body are on excellent terms.

Lenny is exhausted — bad flight, delays, stormy weather. He begs off having a long conversation with his mother. Mrs. Goldberg understands. If sleep is what he needs, his old room is waiting. If only he were married and settled she wouldn't be so worried.

Of the three women she invited to the Seder, the one who canceled was the one Mrs. Goldberg was pinning her hopes on. A shame, since Donna Bass had taught in the city's school system, left to live on a commune, and then returned, a potential model for Lenny's return to teaching, starting a normal life instead of doing whatever it is he does — or doesn't do — in Berkeley.

First things first: she must finish cooking. Thick aluminum foil covers the counters where she cuts, dices, chops. Soon four huge pots are sending clouds of steam into the scrupulously koshered kitchen. Boiling water is sufficient to kosher most of the kitchen, but the iron parts of the oven require a blowtorch. Guzman, the Cuban super, cooperates with the building's Orthodox Jewish tenants, relying on the flames inside the sub-basement furnace to turn the removable metal parts red-hot, and kosher for Passover. By noon, when she will wake Lenny, there will be nothing left to prepare except the *maror*, the bitter root she will grind by hand, and the chopped mixture of walnuts, dates, cinnamon, ginger, and sweet wine for the *charoset*, adding bananas and apples right before the Seder just as her husband did when he was alive.

At the other end of the apartment, Lenny prays that the pressure he feels above his eyes is not a migraine. In the semi-darkness of the small bedroom, he dresses quickly, pulling up his pants and buttoning his shirt. Hair still uncombed and face unwashed, he walks barefoot into the kitchen, his step so quiet that when he cries out, "Any coffee?" he startles his mother and the egg she's holding slips from her hand, cracking on the black and white linoleum. Lenny, still struggling with sleep, is unaware of the yellow mess on the floor. He retreats into the living room, lowering himself into one of the old deep chairs. Even though Broadway is only a stone's throw away, by the time the noise of street traffic reaches the fifth floor, it's transformed into a universal hum muffled by the windows and the thick curtains. The room is too dark to make out the paintings on the wall, but Lenny knows them by heart, tedious abstract landscapes of the Galilee and the desert hills of Judea. But their presence, like old friends, comforts him.

A few minutes pass before Lenny's mother pushes open the swinging door and enters with a tray carrying a bowl of steaming mashed potatoes and a glass of borscht.

"Hey, I'm still on Pacific Coast time. Can't handle much beyond coffee, lots of sugar, and cream if you got it."

Mrs. Goldberg leaves the room, only to return several minutes later with the tray now bearing a pot of hot water, a jar of coffee, sugar in individual packets, and a small pitcher of milk.

She would like to criticize her son's discourtesy, no manners to speak of, and his grooming is practically primitive, those dirty feet and horrible uncut nails — disgusting. Doesn't he have any sense of where he is? But she does not want to charge the atmosphere with criticism. After Lenny finishes his first cigarette, Mrs. Goldberg remarks that he looks a little thin. Ordinarily defensive about any aspect of his appearance, Lenny chooses a benign response. "It's a special diet I'm on. I may even package it."

"That would be nice," Mrs. Goldberg does not actually smile, but her cheekbones rise a fraction of an inch. A second cigarette brings on a shrill, harsh cough, practically lifting Lenny off the ground.

"Do you want some water?"

Lenny waves away the offer. Mrs. Goldberg asks how he's feeling, and he mutters that everything is just fine.

The coffee is strong and sweet, a rush of adrenaline. Maybe his mother is right, maybe it's time to move back home, come clean, confess his miserable life to her, that he's nothing but a pothead.

"Are you coming to the synagogue tonight?" Mrs. Goldberg is buying time.

"Am I expected to?"

"Only if you want to."

"Then don't count on it."

If he moved back to New York, would his mother encourage him to live the life of an Orthodox Jew? Could he ever go back to the old ways?

"Listen, I'm going down." Lenny grabs his jacket and slips into his sneakers. "There are some people I want to see." What he has in mind is Riverside Park, the place to be when blessed with a surplus of time — volley a ball, jog a mile, or chew two pages of Plato under a sun-dappled tree, all solid investments in a healthy, worry-free future.

"You really don't have to come to synagogue if you don't want to."

Lenny is gone, leaving Mrs. Goldberg alone with a cloud of cigarette smoke. Curious, she reaches for a cigarette butt that her son left behind. Holding it between her lips and experimenting in front of the mirror, she wonders why men think a cigarette in a woman's mouth is sexy. What would happen if she started using lipstick, started smoking — stranger things have been known to happen. Her husband smoked, but he claimed that a cigarette in a woman's mouth was unbecoming. He said he smoked for health reasons, to calm his nerves, and the ridiculous thing was she actually believed him.

Inhaling, a feeling of nausea seizes her. She cannot believe that Lenny breathes this into his lungs every day. Or can one grow so accustomed to poison that the mind translates a noxious gas into a delightful sea breeze?

She waits ten minutes before entering his bedroom. First she makes the bed, airing the blanket and straightening the sheets.

She takes a deep breath, mouths a silent apology to her son, and then gets down on her knees to open Lenny's cheap plastic suitcase, the handle practically coming apart. What she finds when she unzips the suitcase repulses her. There is not one clean white shirt in the suitcase. A pile of unsorted socks. Two ties, both stained. Dirty pants, none folded properly. She doesn't understand how anyone could pack such a suitcase. And where are his personal care items? Doesn't he use aftershave or underarm deodorant? But her objective now is not inventory. She is looking for any sort of illegal substance. She's been hearing more and more about such substances, and she is inclined to believe this is Lenny's problem. She does not know what marijuana looks like, but she's been told it has a sharp smell. Since her son is not a botanist, she will assume any plant she finds must be marijuana.

From one of his shirt pockets, she extracts an open packet of sugar. She has seen enough late-night movies to know that cocaine is white. She has seen the characters in these movies smell the powder, and taste a tiny amount before lifting it to their noses to snort it. What she spills into the palm of her hand doesn't feel like a powder, its tiny crystals an exact duplication of real sugar. But she is afraid to taste it. She has heard that LSD can be put into anything: cola, chewing gum, dried raisins, so why not sugar? She has been suspicious of Leonard for years, but she has never had the guts to confront him. This year she will bring it up. It can't go on any longer. He needs help.

Mrs. Goldberg begins turning pockets inside out and sure enough, inside a dark blue suit jacket — no matching pants as far as she can tell — she finds half a hamburger roll. Mrs. Goldberg wants to wring Leonard's neck. *Chametz*? In her house! Up until now she always felt nothing but pity for her son, but this is intolerable. She is about to shut the suitcase when she realizes that she must examine every pocket.

By the time she is finished, she has a collection of candy wrappers, a piece of black licorice, raisins, a half-eaten piece of taffy as hard as a rock, dry potato chips and cookies so old they crumble in her hand like aged plaster.

All this forbidden food makes her feel stained. Just possession of chametz is a major, major sin. At this very moment, a little Oreo cookie turns her into a violator of the very foundation of Judaism, the laws of Passover. She doesn't understand why exactly, but this is how she has always lived her life. The laws are so strict that any derivative of the five basic grains, in any form whatsoever, no matter how minuscule the amount, must be removed from the house. That's why weeks before Passover Jews start scraping and cleaning. How many years has Leonard had this habit of thrusting pieces of food into his pockets, turning her home, all that meticulous care of uncovering every last bit of chametz, into a place of sin?

Does she really have any idea what she's getting into by inviting Leonard to move back into her home? He'll have to do his own laundry. She'll cook for him, but not laundry.

Avoiding the elevator, Lenny slips into the stairwell, pulls out his traveling pipe, fills it, and before you can see the flame die, he has two fat hits deep into his lungs, taking extra long breaths to guarantee that none of the distinctive sweet odor of the weed slips through the doorway's crack, a suspicious neighbor putting two and two and you-know-who together.

He flies down the five flights, three steps at a time, gliding past the doorman, flying in his Adidas out into the street, true to his own high.

Bouncing as he waits for the light to change at Eighty-eighth and Broadway, Lenny's gaze rises to the massive rooftops, noticing the angle created by Broadway's flow and it's obvious why Broadway is Broadway and not Thinway or Sliceway or Newway because she alone, among all her famous brothers and sisters, defies the authority of the grid, turning rectangular blocks into unique shapes, the geometry of possibility.

Wow! He liked his head in the Apple. Hey, maybe New York City was his kind of town, to get off on the new all the time, even if it's just new rooms to eat in, purple awnings, black interiors, secret mirrors, lots of Lucite. What if he can pull it off, and actually move back with his mother?

For a cloudy, somewhat wet day, Broadway is crowded, and Lenny has to sidestep mothers and baby carriages, not easy while feasting on foxes, and oh, the multitude of races and yellow cabs eating dust, the bookstores with food in the window, and the food shops with book displays, a thrill to be alive.

A right-hand turn on a side street and he's slow-trotting the long blocks to the park, so that by the time he gets there he's out of breath and welcomes the opportunity to rest on the huge cobalt gray boulder just beyond the fringe of trees hedging the folks and the buildings on the Drive.

But the wind is too strong to light up. He needs a protected nook, trees, branches. Who's he trying to kid! Living with his mother would mean he'd end up using the street to get high, and New York City highs are overwhelming. How can you feel real when the long skinny island you're standing on has no guts left, its insides torn up with miles and miles of subways, a system of steel braced to support these iron boxes screeching maniacally, feverishly, insane speeds for humans, the ancient granite rock riddled with a billion volts of electricity?

Fall through the wrong grating and the underground tunnels will make sure you're never heard from again. Even part of the park's belly was hollow — railroad tracks underneath Riverside Park.

He has to find something hard, solid, a bench, no, a tree, a grove of shady trees where he can light up, to erase, to undo. Just be you, brother. Be true. To thine own self.

In spots the path is muddy, recent rain, while above, the sky is virtually cloudless, but it's a cold blue, without soul or heat.

He finds his trees, not a grove, but lined up like soldiers guarding New Jersey, somewhat off the main path. There's reason to fear if he strays too far, but he won't give in to fear just yet.

Out of the blue, he hears someone call his name. He makes an about-face, but the park is stubbornly empty except for a flock of pigeons above. When they get closer, the formation takes a sudden dive, low enough for him to hear a chorus of transcendent altos sing his name at the top of their pigeon lungs.

Slow down, Lenny. Pigeons do not know a person's name, pigeons do not sing, though carrier pigeons could be exceptions. There were two mysteries: their song, and his name.

He turns to the nearest tree, reaching out to shake hands. Do you know my name? Lenny can't believe it when he hears a yes. "Say that again." Again a yes.

Could this be it, Lenny stumbling into an unannounced meeting with the Tree of Knowledge — Riverside Park the Garden of Eden? And it turns out that trees, alive with feelings and memory, possess a phenomenal existence of their environment even though they don't have cigarettes with their coffee, or nervous breakdowns. Or read the *Times* every day. Wait a second, Lenny thinks, this tree doesn't have to read the *Times* — it is the *Times*. Maybe every tree in existence has some kind of phenomenal knowledge of every word that has ever been written on the skin of its brothers and sisters.

Lenny steps back; he doesn't even know his tree's species. A sycamore? An elm? Maybe there are civilizations, other planets, other dimensions, where trees walk around and the humans grow in the ground, amassing nothing but thoughts while the trees trim our toenails.

Lenny realizes that if he shares his thoughts, they'd think he was nuts. So what! If being nuts means that you understand the thoughts of trees, it's worth it. In fact, maybe nuts were called nuts because they hung out with trees. Contemplating the lower half of the tree, Lenny translates trunk and bark into flesh and curves, and he comes up with a one-thighed woman, short thick horns of branches jutting forth that look like a bridge between cut-off penises and mounds of vulvish flesh. Lenny affectionately brushes a troop of ants from its bark, then checks to see if his arms are wide enough to embrace the tree's vast girth. Immediately a message from the tree warns Lenny to keep his filthy hands to himself. He turns red, the heat of shame rising to his brain, and promises the tree he'll keep his distance.

Whoosh! Lenny is out of there, as quick as a blush, but a twisted branch trips him and before he can put his brakes on, he is diving head first into second base. Luckily a carpet of winter's fallen leaves cushions his fall, but not completely. When he picks himself up to assess the damage, his hands are bloody, knees scraped, dirt everywhere. A piece of skin on the inside of his right palm hangs loose and when he pulls at it, a cry of pain escapes from his teeth, clenched tight to kill the scream.

"The guests are here. Dress quickly," Mrs. Goldberg instructs Lenny as he walks through the door, hair askew, shirttails sticking out of his pants.

"What about a shower?" he asks.

"No time. I need to know one thing — while you were out, did you eat any bread?"

He has no idea what she's talking about.

"Do you have any chametz in your pockets, any crumbs?"

Lenny shakes his head. "No, of course not." He's about to prove it by pulling his pants pockets inside out when he realizes that he'd have to explain the funny bag of oregano he was carrying, and the pipe. Did he smoke oregano, his mother might wonder.

Mrs. Goldberg decides not to press the issue. "Guests are waiting."

Heaving aside socks and t-shirts and a couple of pair of pants, Lenny can't find one clean white shirt. Was he stoned when he packed? Don't answer. He can't even find a toothbrush, not even a comb.

But there on the bedspread is a fresh shirt his mother has laid out for him. His bloated fingers, however, find it hard to get all of the buttons into the buttonholes, and when the top button flies off, Lenny, unable to see where it's fallen, bends down with some difficulty and uses the palm of his hand like a rag, moving back and forth across the wooden parquet floor. Lenny doesn't know if he's still stoned or not, but his preoccupation with the geometric shapes of the inlaid wood when he should be handing out the Haggadahs makes him question his decision to toke up one more time in a phone booth on Seventy-ninth Street, his back against the glass doors.

"Leonard?"

"I'll be right there," he calls out.

"Is everything all right?"

"Two and a half seconds."

Lenny examines himself in the mirror, another whacked-out drummer in an aging rock 'n' roll band, hair everywhere, eyes partially closed and lips partially opened as if waiting for someone to stick something there: a joint, a Life Saver, a rosy nipple. His major flaw is his teeth, stained a greenish yellow, the gums weak and prone to bleeding. He must remember not to smile.

He counts to ten, takes a deep breath, and begins his walk toward the dining room, an actor who knows all his lines but each performance includes a cast of players he's never met, let alone rehearsed with. As he makes his grand entrance, the hum of voices around the table, aglow with his mother's finest, stops. Lenny sees sentences hovering above the room, never to be finished.

His mother introduces everyone. "To my right is Ariella from Israel, Ella Saunderson from Chicago, Rabbi Noah Belinsky from New Jersey, and now may I present my son Leonard, a poet from Berkeley, who has just arrived for the festival."

Ordinarily his mother's female guests, people she meets at the synagogue, were long past their first flush of youth, the mascara, the eyeliner, and a virgin-looking strand of pearls, critical. Ariella should probably consider dieting, though a fine jaw line holds back the march of time, at least from the neck up. Her hair is thick, dark, a Mediterranean lushness, while Ella's pale, gaunt features only dramatize the effect of her shorn hair, an African-looking skull-cap crowning her head. If he didn't remember from the capsule descriptions his mother sends him a week before his arrival that she was a Buddhist re-acquainting herself with her Jewish roots, he would suspect chemotherapy.

"So you're the last guest." Noah the rabbi greets Leonard with a curious expression, enthusiastic but distant, cautious. "And a poet, too. That's wonderful. I remember a Seder where Allen Ginsberg's work was interspersed with the suffering in Egypt. Now that was exciting."

Lenny glares at his mother. And he's supposed to be on his best behavior. How many times has he asked her not to mention his poetry? Nothing penetrates. He does not want to be thought of as a poetic specimen preserved in formaldehyde, a West Coast exhibit. But he knows she means well, the introduction intended to serve as an ice-breaker for the women who invariably have demonstrated an interest in the written word.

Noah questions how Berkeley is these days. "I haven't been there in more than ten years."

The rabbi's voice grates against Lenny's ears, more Massachusetts than New Jersey, maybe even Harvard. Probably no more than fifty, his defiant glory a majestic Isro with specks of early gray. Actually, he looks more like a poet than Lenny does, tenure too.

"I think I will love Berkeley," Ariella says. "I always wanted to visit there. They say Israel is like California."

"Really?"

In an attempt to shift the Berkeley focus, he engages Ella, "May I ask what it is that a Buddhist does?"

Ella hesitates, as if pondering the correct way for a Buddhist to address strangers. "I do nothing."

"So what's the difference between a Buddhist who does nothing and a regular guy who does nothing?"

"Nothing."

Lenny was enjoying this; Ella was a godsend. "You don't worry about things? You don't worry about where your next meal is coming from?"

"It's already waiting for me. All the meals of my life are waiting for me. My death is waiting for me. There is no reason to hurry toward it, or to run from it." Her voice is like evening rain, steady, comforting, hypnotic.

Mrs. Goldberg appears confused. "Does a Buddhist believe in God?"

"No."

"I don't understand," Ariella says. "Isn't that an atheist?"

"Not at all," the rabbi leaps into the fray. "To believe in nothing is a form of belief. The idea of nothingness is perhaps the most difficult idea in the universe to grasp. A subtle difference between not to believe in anything, an atheist, and to believe in nothing, a Buddhist."

"That's too complicated for me," Ella confesses. "All I know is that the universe is perfect. Life is perfect, death is perfect, health is perfect, disease is perfect. Buddhism is about the perfection of nothing and everything simultaneously."

A moment ago her voice resembled rain, steady and comforting, but the gentle downpour has become stormy, a gray fog permeating the room, as if all the oxygen is being sucked up. In an effort to break the silence, Mrs. Goldberg says, "I think it's time to start the Seder. Please open the Haggadah."

With the Haggadah open — an abridged history of the Jewish people — the Seder is off and running. Usually Lenny officiates, but he finds it hard to focus on the page. What he'd really like to do is get high, but he can't do that because he's high already.

They chant kiddush over the wine, then they wash without a blessing, dip radishes in salt water, break the middle matzoh, ask the Four Questions, dip their little fingers into the wine each time one of the ten plagues is mentioned, sing the famous songs with Mrs. Goldberg taking the lead, a strong rousing voice, and finally wash the hands again but with a blessing this time, and the first bite into the matzoh, everybody famished because explanations take time, especially if they're considerate, and since Lenny is not providing answers, Rabbi Belinsky takes over — or at least he doesn't defer to Lenny when the questions come his way.

After the bitter herb sandwich named for Hillel the Elder, shockingly strong horseradish without the sweet beet component, it's time for the meal itself. Rabbi Belinsky *oohs* and *ahhs* with the arrival of each course, fish so delicate it leaves the tongue enthralled, and the soup, how could soup be so loving, and what kind of noodles were these?

Lenny can't take it anymore. Fish so delicate ... and the soup ... gimme a break. Sharing the "secret" ingredient of the meal, not some kosher exotic ingredients but the unusual fact that these pots and pans feel the heat of flame only one week each year, is usually one of Lenny's glorious moments, but the rabbi has beaten him to the punch, stealing the words right out of Lenny's mouth. Since when do guests steal the show? Did he travel across the entire continent to watch this yo-yo, busily helping himself to a second portion of roast chicken, manipulate these two women to eat out of his hand, the Buddhist half-brain, and the Israeli who pretended to be interested in Berkeley, which he now knows was just an act.

Unexpectedly, Lenny throws a question at Rabbi Belinsky. "By the way, exactly what does a non-practicing rabbi do?"

"Actually, I also have a degree in law. My specialty is real-estate law."

"I don't believe it."

"Rabbi Belinsky was kind enough to estimate the value of my lease," Mrs. Goldberg adds. "You cannot imagine how much it's worth. Leonard, you look pale, are you all right?"

No, he is not all right! If he were skeptical about the ex-rabbi earlier now he is convinced that there is treachery in the wings — filling old ladies with stories about their gold-plated leases!

Unable to keep his fury locked inside, Lenny turns to Ariella. "Do you remember where you were last year for the Seder?" This was the question he always saved for the end of the Seder, allowing all the wandering guests to provide eye-opening accounts of their past, tracing the chain of events leading up to this very moment, like the woman who shocked everyone when she revealed that she used to be a Carmelite nun, converted to Judaism, married, but her Jewish daughter became a Catholic and eventually took on the vows of a Carmelite nun.

"Well, it's really not very interesting. I'm ashamed to say I went to the movies. But Noah, I mean Rabbi Belinsky, had a very interesting Seder. He was in Tokyo where I understand many Jewish people make their homes."

Lenny bites down on his lips so hard that he tastes blood. What the hell is going on here, a conspiracy? "Forget Tokyo, it's time to open the door for Elijah."

Flipping through the pages of the Haggadah, the rabbi points out that it's much too early for the fifth cup. Lenny ignores him, pouring wine into the silver goblet designated for Elijah. He explains to Ella that tradition has Elijah the Prophet visiting every single Seder, a feat that can only be accomplished because he's invisible, one of the highlights of the Seder for children who wait patiently to see if they can discern the slightest change in the goblet of wine. Lenny feels rather proud of his explanation until Rabbi Belinsky questions the accuracy of this so-called tradition. "It's a little more complicated, don't you think?"

Ella is not aware of the minor altercation taking place between the two men. Confused more than surprised, she says, "Well, doesn't Elijah sound a little bit like Santa? One comes through the door and the other down the chimney?"

"This may not be my business," Ariella offers, "but why do you bring up Santa Claus at the Seder! It is not right."

"Wrong," the rabbi says. "She can ask whatever she wants. We're not afraid of questions here."

Lenny cannot believe what he's hearing. Was he asleep when Noah Belinsky became this evening's host? Or was Rabbi Noah raised to believe that wherever he sat was the head of the table? Actually, Ella's question was right up Lenny's alley. All he has to do is sort out a few thoughts and allow his tongue to flow freely. But apparently the sweet Malaga wine he's been drinking like apple juice has thickened his tongue, slowing him down.

Noah's voice reverberates like a judge instructing a jury. "My dear Ella. You've come to the right address ..." And he doesn't stop, on and on, stressing differences, how Santa, an old man riding a sleigh, may be a wonderful expression of the importance of sharing, the warmth around the hearth, the innocence of children, but one shouldn't forget that Elijah is a raging prophet, fiery chariot and fiery horses disappearing in the sky with a message of fire and brimstone. Second, Elijah's invisibility at the Seder means that he can be anybody, the drunk in the subway car, the beggar with his fingers missing, even the fat white-bearded gentleman in front of Macy's.

And fourth ... and then fifth ... and yadda, yadda, yadda. Whatever answer has been taking shaping in Lenny's mind cannot keep up with Noah. With one roll of the dice, Noah is being declared the winner, the whole pot going to the rabbi. What did he know about raging prophets of Israel? Just because he wore a yellow tie. At last year's Seder, a guest named Weisman or Weisberg began to spout psychological theories about Freud and his sister-in-law. Couldn't shut him up. Where does his mother dig up these creeps! Maybe the rabbi knows how to talk the talk and walk the walk but he's still an idiot, vain and selfish to boot. Finally his mother has brought home a dodo. Maybe it was not a foregone conclusion that his mother's guests always fall for the other male, anyone but Lenny.

Ella thanks Noah for his analysis.

"If you're through with Santa Claus," Ariella says to Noah, "I would like very much to see a picture of a Seder in Japan. Did you have the matzoh shipped in? Or do they sell it in the supermarket? In fact, what are Japanese supermarkets like?"

"One thing at a time," Lenny demands. "I think our friend Santa needs a little defense. Ho, ho, ho!"

His mother whispers to Lenny that they're finished with Santa for now.

"But it's not fair. The great rabbi can speak and I can't?" Lenny won't take no for an answer. "It's not just about red suits and bellies and white beards. I, for one, would like to say something positive about Mr. Claus. I mean, this is a democracy, right? Innocent until proven guilty."

Embarrassed by Lenny's incoherence, the guests stare at each other, afraid to contradict him. Mrs. Goldberg does not want to confront her son, but she knows it's her duty to come to Ariella's defense. "Please listen to me, Leonard. Let the conversation take its own course. It moves from here to there. And back. There is no reason why we cannot hear about the rabbi in Tokyo. Furthermore," she adds in a low voice, almost a whisper, "not everything ought to be discussed at all times. Forget Santa Claus."

Mrs. Goldberg is adamant. "Rabbi, I am very curious to hear about your Seder last year. It's not every day we have this kind of guest."

Noah clears his throat — twice. "To be frank, I was never inside any Tokyo supermarkets. My hosts took care of such matters. But what really amazed me was how many of these Jewish men had learned Japanese, and as I translated the Hebrew into English, they translated my words back into Japanese for their wives. If they knew Hebrew as well as they knew Japanese, I would be gratified."

Lenny is disgusted. He has no clue why his mother allows the spotlight to remain focused on the rabbi. "That sounds so pathetic, 'If they knew Hebrew as well as they knew Japanese …' Who appointed you Commissioner of Hebrew for Wayward Jews?"

"Excuse me?" The rabbi looks aghast.

Unable to restrain herself, Mrs. Goldberg raises her voice high enough to send a chill through the room, "Leonard stop right now!"

Ariella steps in to recover what can be rescued. "Your mother showed me a poem, and I think it was good. Very good."

"The Nostrand Avenue Merchants Award," Mrs. Goldberg adds.

As if stunned into silence, Lenny slowly turns red, then white. "Ma, that was ages ago. Now you're really embarrassing me."

"It was really better than very good," Ariella insists.

Lenny's eyes are unable to focus, everything a blur, a collage of noses and teeth and sneers. The last thing Lenny wants is to talk about that poem. Why is she bringing it up? He does not want to talk about poetry, he does not want to face the fact that he feels as if he's been writing his entire life on a glass surface with a broken pencil stub. What he needs is closure, finito, the damn thing packed away — because the damned thing took over his life, kept growing as he fiddled with it day in and day out, stoned or not stoned, broke or not broke, whether in New York or California, in parks, in libraries, at cafeteria tables, never without his trusted notebook, and never able to honor his manuscript with a simple two-word farewell, *The End*, loose-leaf after loose-leaf absorbing more and more characters, incidents, sonnet variations, grocery lists, travel guides, lists of foreign words, names from the telephone directory, weather reports, an eight-hundred-page tome that will either be acknowledged as a work of genius authored by a genuine American underground man, or his ticket to the cemetery where finally he will instruct his survivors to carve on his gravestone the rather ominous, but exceedingly appropriate, summation, "The End." What he couldn't do in life, he would do in death. If he really wanted to be cryptic he would exclude his name and age, leaving nothing behind except two last words.

"You know Leonard, I think you might be right," the rabbi acknowledges, nodding his head ever so slightly. "Nobody appointed me a commissioner of anything. But one thing I do know is that a Seder should be open for little innovations. Why don't we include a little poetry at the Seder. Anyone you'd like to recommend?"

Lenny's eyes, now fixed on the reflection of the burning candles, notice that even Ariella's turquoise necklace hides a tingling flame as it grazes the rise of her breasts. Maybe he should have flirted with her earlier instead of obsessing about the real estate rabbi. There is something vibrant about her passion for jewelry. He stares at the silver bracelets dangling around her wrists, attempts to count the gold rings on her right hand and the silver rings on the left...and then finds himself staring into the depths of her brown eyes, a burning flame caressing the black of her pupil.

"Have you published anything lately?" Ariella's eyes are expectant, almost pleading. "I would love to hear you read."

Ariella's insistence excites him, but what can he do—he has published nothing, lately or not lately, just the Nostrand Avenue poem.

"Where is the street whose award you won?" she asks. "I do not know Brooklyn. Except the parkway where there is a big museum."

Lenny explains it's a major avenue, running almost the entire length of the borough. "We lived there before my father died, and then we decided to move to Manhattan, that is what my mother decided. I was already in California."

"Is Nostrand Avenue beautiful? Your poem is."

Ariella's voice, the musical cadence of a continental accent, lures him deeper into her cave, giving him the feeling that she will be the perfect address to share the history of his secret writings. Before he knows what he's doing he finds himself admitting that yes, he had a couple of poems in a West Coast journal called *XYZ*. "I'm sure you never heard of it."

Noah claps his hands. "What a coincidence. My nephew Richard just had a poem accepted there. You're being too modest Leonard. *XYZ* is a prominent journal. I'll ask him to look it up."

Blood rushes to Lenny's face. "For personal reasons, which I prefer not to divulge, I used a pseudonym."

"Leonard," his mother says. "I'm very proud of you. Why didn't you tell me?"

"Leonard Goldberg is a fine name," Noah advises, "and the next time you publish, don't be shy about who you really are."

"I'm not shy. I said it's for personal reasons."

"What is the poem called?" Ariella says. "We all want to know."

"I prefer not to talk about it now."

"Can you say what the subject is?"

"I said not now."

"Then what issue is it in?" Noah asks. "I'd love to see it."

"For crying out loud, forget I said anything!" Lenny's voice is loud, almost a snarl. Pounding the table, he discovers that he has just reduced a perfect unbroken matzoh into a sea of crumbs. "I lied. There is no issue. No poem. No pseudonym. Nothing. Okay?"

Lenny gnashes his teeth, nervously grating them. For some reason he cannot locate his tongue inside his mouth. It's there somewhere, but seems to be playing hide and seek. Pushing his chair back, Lenny excuses himself. His mother, several steps behind him, asks where he is going.

"I think it's called a john. With your permission."

In the dark, Lenny pulls out his mini-pipe. Lighting up, the only sound in the room is the hiss of the burning match as it hits the toilet bowl. One hit isn't enough. He lights up again, takes a deep suck of smoke as his eyes adjust to the dark. He feels like a boxer, light on his toes, sizzling, ready to ravage. His brain, virtually on fire, cooks up the different names he knows for marijuana into one magic spice: pot, weed, grass, smoke, herb, cheeba — but dope is his favorite. Which is interesting, and strange, given that under the influence he usually thinks of himself as rather brilliant, sharp, insightful … Wait a second, it's a game right? It's a way to fool the forces, let them think you've become a dope when in reality … when in reality … yeah, tell me about it Ms. Buddhist, there is no reality … Lenny can't think straight, his mind inching into a space as thin as a postage stamp. It was dumb to get high. High, he needs to fade into the twilight zone slowly, he needs the weather just so, not too cold or hot, no heavy rains but a warm drizzle is fine, and close to food, an all-night place if he wants to dream over coffee, or some park if he wants to be near a tree.

The fact is that he doesn't want to return to the Seder table — feels stupid after his outburst, a fool. He should tell them he was pulling their leg, a bit of April Fools on Passover, just joking.

But when he returns, the rabbi again clears the frog from his throat. "This may not be my business, but it's all right to exaggerate a little. We all do it. You should not feel bad about pretending. We understand."

"What the hell are you talking about?"

"Your mother explained that you're a fine poet who moved to the West Coast a good number of years ago, and you shouldn't let the rejections hurt you."

"Is that what you all think, that I was lying? I wasn't lying! I was pretending that I was lying … And I don't think it's your business telling me that you understand that I was lying. That's patronizing me, okay? With a capital 'P.' So 'P' off, rabbi."

Horrified by Lenny's rant, Ariella looks as if she's about to fall from her chair.

"Please listen to me, Leonard," his mother pleads, but Lenny ignores her, his anger aimed at Belinsky. "Why are you getting involved in things that aren't your business?"

"Maybe you're right. I'm sorry. I guess a big part of being a rabbi is trying to help."

"Help who? You or me?"

"Whatever you say Leonard."

"Whatever you say Leonard, just like a parrot. What are you, a parrot, rabbi? *Cluck, cluck, cluck.* Hey, what makes you a rabbi, a piece of paper, some certificate? I bet you don't even believe in God. You probably believe in the federal government."

"That's it," Mrs. Goldberg says sharply. "Do not talk this way. If you can't control yourself, please leave the table right now."

"It's my fault," the rabbi says. "Please, if anybody is going, it should be me."

"If you go anywhere rabbi, I will not forgive you."

Lenny is bewildered — why is his mother siding with the enemy? For years he's wanted to tell the single male guest what he thinks of them, how he can't stand their little grins, their know-it-all attitudes. Why has he never met a humble male guest?

"Rabbi, do you believe in God?"

"Do you?"

"Absolutely not. But the strange thing is that God believes in me. We have these conversations you see."

"And when the God that you don't believe in speaks to you what language does He speak in?"

"I don't know. It doesn't matter. A private language. But the point is that as long as you wear that yellow tie, Mister Rabbi, the only thing you can get in touch with is the yellow tie god inside you.

"Really?"

"Absolutely. God hates yellow ties."

"Did God also tell you this in the toilet, or the last time you took dope?"

Lenny has to control himself from pummeling his mother's guest. In a low trembling voice he says, "How dare you talk to me this way."

"Mr. Goldberg, what are you on right now?"

"I don't have to listen to this crap. How dare you embarrass me at my own Seder."

Lenny turns to his mother. "Why do you let a guest insult me?"

Mrs. Goldberg, afraid of her son's rage, looks away.

"Say something, damn it."

"I can't take this anymore," she confesses. "God tells you this, God tells you that. Enough. Enough with the God talk."

Lenny can't believe his ears. Who are these people? Total strangers; they could be anyone. He pushes his chair back, but his movements are clumsy, and in the process he knocks over a full bottle of Malaga, creating a stain as large as the Red Sea.

"Screw you, you bastard. Look what you made me do."

Rabbi Belinsky smiles but with lips shut tight. "Thank you very much Mrs. Goldberg, but I must be going. I'm sorry for everything."

A dark, eerie silence descends, brooding, thick. If Lenny starts crying now, he'll take that bottle and swipe it across Noah's ugly puss. What's the sound of one hand clapping? A slap across your face, Rabbi! Lenny needs to be alone, shut the door of his room, get into … no, bed is not a good idea. Bed is very, very bad!

Lenny's mother feels violated. In one evening she has aged twenty years, her face transformed into a map of shadowed caves. This has never happened before. Mrs. Goldberg turns away from the table, the sight of this ugly stranger — her own son — repulses her. How long will he sit there? Doesn't he understand that he has destroyed her Seder? Doesn't he appreciate everything she's done for him, all her sacrifices?

Rising awkwardly, Lenny plods out of the room, slamming the door behind him. But the sound of shattering glass stops him in his tracks — apparently a loose pane in the dining room door. Bending down, Lenny feels a wave of hot air engulf him. Either he's on fire or the building's heating system has misread the thermometer — Lenny is boiling. If he doesn't get some air in this room, he'll suffocate. He moves efficiently to the living room window and opens it.

"Leonard, don't."

Was that Ariella or his mother? Grabbing, touching, lunging hands.

Are they crazy, did they think he was going to jump? He hadn't thought of it, but wouldn't mind taking that Noah with him.

"Hey, Rabbi, where are you? Show your face."

Noah moves closer, placing a hand on Lenny's shoulder. "Don't worry, everything will be okay."

"Nothing will be okay. You brainwashed my mother. You're evil." Without thinking, he grabs Noah's neck, knowing instantly that he doesn't have the strength or the will to grapple him to the ground, but before he manages to release him, Ella, faster than a speeding prayer wheel, unleashes a jab to the back of Lenny's neck. The pain, a palpable message to the center of his brain, brings him to his knees.

"I didn't mean anything." Lenny has never felt so frightened in all his life. "Just let me go back to California."

"Please let yourself be treated," his mother says. "Rabbi Belinsky has many connections. He will get you into a wonderful facility."

"What are you talking about? I took a little speed. A diet pill. Is there a law against losing weight?"

He was beginning to feel sleepy, but these people didn't know Lenny G. As good as you or...He would shut his eyes, feign sleep, and then when no one was looking, bolt like a cat, so fast their eyeballs would pop. Fly down the staircase, seven steps at a time. Find a way to get to the airport, the return ticket in his pocket, good-bye New York forever. Good-bye, Mom, he was never coming back. He could stay up for seventy-two hours straight if he needed to, he was live wire, electricity, steel — hell, his body had smoked so much dope he was used to anything. But before he manages to stand up, their hands are on his body — strangling octopuses. Around him, the clatter of a brigade of feet. Stumbling to his knees, he feels a trailer truck ram into his chest followed by a powerful vacuum cleaner trying to suck his soul right out of his body. No, he won't let these bastards take him alive. He has to fight off their clawing, pawing fingers. He needs a lawyer. They're violating his constitutional rights.

Lifting himself to his full height, and with the last ounce of strength he possesses, he flings himself toward the couch, trips, and finds himself diving toward the window's billowing white curtains, his body as light as a cellophane wrapper. To his absolute amazement nobody blocks his path, no one pulls him back into the room that, astonishingly enough, looks like a child's drawing, violent primal colors afloat in a two-dimensional world. Confused where the floor ends and his feet begin, there is a sudden roar of a thunderstorm exploding in his heart, and ten thousand tiny razor blades frantically giving him one last dry shave across his entire body. High above him, inside an apartment where a Seder has just taken place, he hears a scream, a shattering, haunting scream, and he knows that it's too late for him, all over, the sad end of a sad life. But all isn't wasted because for one split second, just before his brains turn into scrambled eggs for good, Lenny understands with a mind-shattering clarity the original meaning of getting stoned. But just then a second thought, faster than the speed of light, sneaks in with a strange and startling request: will the last guest please remember to shut the lights…

Lights out!

acknowledgements

Without clear-headed readers, I'd be lost.

Thank you for being there to read, to listen, to challenge: Shelly Swirsky, Jeanette Goldsmith, Hank Beck, Ellen R. Topol, Roy Getzel, Shalom Goldman, Joel Zabor, Gabi Trunck, and Shelly Gewirtz, my long-time script collaborator.

To New Rivers Press, and particularly John Dufresne, for turning a wandering collection into a book with an address from the heartland. My heartfelt thanks to the editorial team of Al Davis, Suzzanne Kelley, Nicole Davis, Elizabeth Zirbel, Sarah Bauman, Nikkole Martin, as well as to the design team of Amber Nelson and Alyssa Nelson for their dramatic cover.

To Thomas H. Hackett, extraordinary teacher at Rabbi Jacob Joseph School, who first pointed the way to Bernard Malamud; my writing teachers at Brooklyn College, Randy Goodman, of blessed memory, and to Peter Spielberg; my devoted writing teachers at San Francisco State, Arthur Foff and Wallace Markfield, of blessed memory.

To the memory of my friends Hesh Hoenig, Abe Malowicki, Walter Fish, and Irv Zarkower, with whom I shared the love of writing fiction, poetry, and music.

To the people on this planet whose lives are interwoven with mine in ways that only the practice of fiction can take apart and put together again. My father Lazar Lampart; my mother Ruth Lampart, of blessed memory, whose strength of character pushed me in a certain direction; my sister Evelyn Lampart, a published writer and poet whose critical eye has taught me the significance of the right word at the right time; my brother Steve Lampart; my son Yonatan Lampart. And to Oriana Zweig Lampart who, for better or worse, put up with the travail of a struggling writer.

The following stories appeared in somewhat different form in the following publications:

"The Muse of Ocean Parkway," *Commentary*, April 1975

"Still Life with Scar," *Commentary*, April 1983

"Joanna Loves Jesus," *Commentary*, August 1987

"Miss Finkelstein," *Greensboro Review*, Spring 2008

"Happy," *Green Mountains Review*, Vol. 23, No. 1, 2010

author
biography

Jacob Lampart was born in Legnica, Poland, in 1946. After a few short years in France, he came through Ellis Island in 1950 to Brooklyn, New York, where he attended Orthodox Jewish yeshivas. After earning a BA at Brooklyn College and an MA at San Francisco State, Lampart worked a variety of jobs: caseworker, college instructor, technical assistant at the New York Public Library, editor, and translator. His short stories have been published in *Commentary*, *Greensboro Review*, and *Green Mountains Review*. Since the mid 1980s he has been living and writing in Jerusalem.

"Jacob Lampart's debut story collection, *The Muse of Ocean Parkway*, is an authentic literary event. These are enduring stories of enormous verve and invention, of great range, wit, and compassion. The characters, both brave and misbegotten, navigate the mythical neighborhoods of Brooklyn with a reckless momentum, dragging with them a tragicomic burden of history and tradition; and they earn their redemption the old-fashioned way, through suffering. Lampart is a genuine original and his book, irresistibly rich, made this reader feel more giddily alive."

— **Steve Stern, author of *The Frozen Rabbi***

"Jacob Lampart's stories beautifully set up parameters of real/unreal discourse between the sexes, as well as the unending problems of the artist. The protagonists undergo one sort of extreme tribulation after another, dramatic tension wonderfully sustained throughout.

The record of NYC a few decades ago, the realism of the environments, and the driven inner lives are real, central subjects. The capturing of cultural nuances and voices in the context of (often) religious/spiritual self-questioning, with a healthy dose of carnality thrown in ... For example, there is the satire of sex-driven Russian-American literati and the disputation between them in the title story, one I can compare emotionally to Malamud.

A main theme is a person alone, wrestling with his inner and outer worlds in privacy or obscurity. Kafkaesque at one extreme, but more of a quotidian life of lonely apartments in NY buildings, a world approaching Dostoyevsky from another direction in the passionate drive of rushing roller coasters of interior monologues, exciting in their unpredictability and freaked-out emotional action. These are great 'unreliable' narrations, surreal and yet psychologically logical throughout, building to wonderful reversals, denouements ... The control of voice and character and most of all the antic humor, central in just about all the often appalling and excruciating circumstances in these stories, is the glue that holds everything together."

— **David Schloss, author of *Group Portrait from Hell***